Galene Angelica

Saviour Angel

~ Reborn ~

Title: Galene Angelica, Saviour Angel, Reborn

Author book: Lee Martin-John

Published by: Lee Martin-John

© 2015, Lee Martin-John / Amazon

Paperback, ISBN: 978-0-9934847-0-4

Kindle version, ISBN: 978-0-9934847-1-1

Chapters

Galene is shown in our earth's history, merely as a stone of harmony, which creates a balance in both the physical, and of the spiritual world.

In a time before time existed….
The almighty Graumus disagreed with Gaia, (mother of the Earth), of her view on how the earth should be, so she cast him aside. The son of the almighty Pontus- that being Nereus fathered Galene (Galaneia) who befriended and obeyed Graumus relentlessly. Their union would have severe consequences upon the Crystaluradom Empire, would eventually lead to the Crystarlisis Aura.

They were all Pre-Gods, to our new world.

It is only now in this Tic Toc
-created by the Guardians,
-That in this time!
-Upon this earth,
- All has just begun to turn

- Tic Toc 1943!
-The year 1943!

Earth time revolving the sun: Unknown

...

They fell-

Thousands of shimmering crystals that gleamed radiantly

in the morning sun,

They- sent the rain down to quench the raging fire of

destruction from an Aurora Sky,

Scattered across this world, they- waited... Patiently...

ever so patiently!

......

Then the Tic toc was created for the 'Saviour Angel'

Tic Toc – Tic Toc

The final countdown,

And so it finally begins....the Tic Toc

...

Prologue

Aurora

It was early September, 1941 on the outskirts of *Minsk, Belarus.* Another ordinary day as one might think…

… Two hands waved high up in the air. They swirled around, before a glistening dust fell from her fingertips…

"Bi zozoak, bi bele, waft dirdira hau uzten ditugu aurrean" –
"Two blackbirds, two crows, waft my face to cease this glow"

It was only once those words were spoken, that two large black birds accompanied by two large crows flew in from the West. Like mechanical toys in sequence, they rested upon the flat tar-painted caravan roof, which overshadowed a burly woman sat below.

She was sat reciting spells from her *historic* memory, humming to herself amidst her huffing and puffing from the extreme heat of the day. She had teased ringlets of auburn hair. Her skin was a healthy, flustered glow.

Slapping the harness reins upon the rear of a single horse in front of her, the cart wheels of the wooden caravan, threw up a *tornado* of dust.

The woman's name was, of course, *Syeira Angelica, Superior of the earths- Aurora Borealis Gateway.* She monitored the sky, waiting patiently for the sign of the next return.

The birds began swishing their wings much faster above *Syeira,* to create a breeze upon her head. Their eyes focussed upon each other, being enemies of the sky. *Syeira* wiped beads of sweat from her brow using a stained cloth from her apron pocket, before using it again to dry her moist, rather sweaty armpits. She was humming *Ring a Ring O' Roses* to herself, whilst fidgeting to adjust her posterior on the hard seat plank, on which she sat.

"Mmmm... the birds are frighteningly quiet today," she thought to herself. Grinning from ear to ear, as she was travelling along the desolate dirt covered track. Even the birds that flew above her head never squawked or squabbled like they would normally do.

It was then, a complete silence fell upon the surrounding land. A silence that would signify something wondrous was about to happen- even the clicking crickets stopped grinding their legs in the fields of military wheat.

Syeira interrupted the silence with her own *aged* voice...

"She must be here! I cannot see her, though... Wonder where she is?"

Syeira eyes were averted upwards to see, something moving in the sky. The clouded heavens had a misty, crystal glow about them. Multi colours began to shimmer above... *Syeira* stopped the cart suddenly,

"Whoa!" she cried. The horse halted at the side on an uneven, ochre grass verge. Syeira watched the dancing lights move across the dusky skyline. Bright turquoise blues, tidal reds, vibrant yellows were but a few of the colours that she saw.

Her thoughts were drawn to remembering a beautiful, far off land that she knew, and hoped to return to very soon as this could be the final *Tic Toc*. A domed city with an *Aurora sky*, all that remained visible was the earths *Aurora Borealis*. She contently smiled at the thought and hoped that this would finally be the *Tic Toc* to freedom, the return from imprisonment.

"It is time; I can feel that it is finally... the earth time. A beautiful Aurora created yet again by the wonderful crystals, the Tic Toc is upon us once more!" she said to her horse, as it wagged its tail rapidly in agreement.

"Can you feel it too?"

A cold chill travelled through her spine, the birds above her head departed, flying off towards the East, Squawking angrily at one another.

Syeira stepped backwards down the wooden steps to the parched soil beneath her feet. She placed her hand to shade her eyes, only to witness at last, a girl falling from the clouds, spinning, and falling violently fast towards her.

Syeira clasped her hands to her mouth, before shouting,

"STOP...Over here, bring her here... I know what to do!"

The girl was dropped at Syeira's feet by a mass of shining shape changing crystals. Syeira stroked a crystal before it departed. A bright rainbow shone high above, despite the lack of rain.

The girl was wearing a black robe. Underneath she wore a ripped, green velvet suit. Syeira quickly removed, the girl's clothing that she was wearing, covering her with a patchwork quilted horse blanket. She removed a handful of etched stones from the outer pocket of the velvet suit. They jangled as she rolled them around in her palm.

"This will not do! You will have to create them yet again, my dearest!" Syeira smiled, as she tossed them into the crisp dry grass. Syeira tilted the girls head onto one side, whilst she examined her ear. "There you are," she said, gripping a fine strand with her small finger and thumb. She pulled a small object out of her ear.

"Now my angel, sleep a little longer, whilst I sort this bag of yours..."

Syeira emptied the bag upon the ground to search for a *small book.* She kissed a clasp, which held the pages tightly closed. The lock was released. She ripped the centre page out of its binding. She watched the page enlarge, all the words scattered from view. A small trinket box with *S.A* initials engraved opened, releasing fine strands of hair onto the dusty ground.

'Wonder whose hair this is?' Syeira questioned out loud.

Climbing on-board the trailer, she opened a tin box with a key hanging from an old boot lace around her neck. Inside, she placed the page *once more.* The tin box was decorated with a rainbow; the label was addressed for a date in the past.

It undoubtedly stated,

~Tic Toc -1897- *Send to Mr Baum, the Wizard man, America~ the separated continent.*

Syeira stroked a *small lace tattoo* across Galene's shoulder,

"I see you know nothing once more!" she said with a smile, before dressing her in a new pretty floral dress with a red russet ribbon, which was fastened around the waist. She had retrieved the new dress from a leather case filled with dozens, upon dozens of the same style and same colour. The two items of clothing that she had removed from the girl, she now wrapped in brown paper, separately, so that she could deal with later.

Syeira stroked the young girl on her forehead. The girl had beautiful, strawberry-blond hair, gingerly –red to be more precise, which fell into Syeira's lap as she supported her head.

The bright lights in the sky began to fade as the night's moon forced the sun off the edge of the world.

Syeira clicked her fingers, before reciting the mystic *Basque language* once more,

"Gaueko izaki horregatik da distiratsua"

"Creatures of night make it bright", she said, waving her hands rhythmically in the air, to call upon the fireflies to light the darkness. Hundreds of small flying insects with glowing bodies began to hover in circles above her, creating a string of light, as she began to gently sway the girl, which lay fast asleep upon the ground…

"Wake up my dear! It is me -Syeira Angelica. I have been expecting you - as always! From now on I want you to call me Ma!" she said, gently stroking on her cheek.

"Call me Ma!"

Chapter 1

The Meeting

02 August 1943

The fading sunlight was strewn across the rotten wooden floor from various narrow gaps in the panelled wall. The light shone upon numerous faces within the darkness. Some were small children within the confined space. They cowered as they clung close to their mother's bodies. Many cries of fear could be heard from the disparate voices, crushed together in the cramped, locked hot swaying room.

A whistle screamed repeatedly, annoyingly so. A scraping of metal upon metal drowned out the wails, as the brakes 'slammed on' hard bringing the rocking motion to a standstill. On the outside, a few dogs could be heard, barking incessantly.

BANG!

There was a deathly silence, but not for long....

"ACTUNG! ACTUNG!"- *Attention, attention*! A German voice could be heard shouting on the outside the rotten box.

A boy called *Jeremiah* pressed his face against the splintering wood, to peer through a very small opening.

Jeremiah was a fourteen year old boy. He had dark soft curly hair. A deep defined chiselled chin. The dimple on his chin softened his harsh features. His eyes, a bright

Forget me not blue. He rubbed his left eye before looking again through the opening. The daylight was blinding him so. Lying on the floor lay a body- still- totally lifeless. A dog was sniffing at the pockets of the body in an attempt to find some tasty treat. The soldier had his foot resting on the chest of the corpse. He threw a biscuit onto the body for the dog to eat. He adjusted his tie, before brushing his jacket with his leather wrapped hand. His *swastika logo* with its gold embroidered stitching had fresh blood splattered across the cloth. There was a powerful flash from a camera.

The Swastika logo is remembered more for the Nazi Party (War of 1939-1945) than any of its former meaning of peace, or religion. The symbol is over 12,000 years old. The clockwise, turning legs are a positive symbol- meaning life.

"Actung!" the camera man stated, as the flash sparked yet again.

The intense light forced Jeremiah to rub his eye, once more, to induce some tears, in some feeble attempt to moisten them. At the same time, a hand pulled hard on his torn jacket from behind. He stumbled backwards onto some suitcases, which had been thrown in the corner of the carriage. He wore an armband with a yellow star stitched upon it. The word *JUIF- Jew* emblazoned in the centre of the star. The armband came loose, falling down onto his wrist. He quickly manoeuvred it back into position.

"What the hell?" he remarked as a soft hand hushed his mouth.

"Shhh! Our meeting was destined to be... I'm *Galene Angelica*. I am from Romania"

Jeremiah sat against a large scuffed brown suitcase. "AND! Do you want a reward for that?" he said angrily,

"Listen to me... My mother was a traveller, and she told me almost six weeks ago that we would meet here- today. *(Breathe Galene's mind said to her, trying to calm her rapid speech)* My future is with you now, please do what I say and follow my instruction quickly!"

Jeremiah tried to move, but Galene pushed him backwards.

"... Our future together has all been foretold. We must stick to the plan, if we are to succeed in getting out of here! I am..."

Jeremiah turned his head away. Galene grasped his cheek to manoeuvre him into looking at her.

"I will be your... *guardian*." She said, with a ghost like, whispering voice.

"What are you on about?", "What do you want from me?" Jeremiah said, pushing himself into an upright position.

"I am looking for my father and mother. That's all! I am not looking for someone who is working for the German Nazi's"

The girls face flickered in and out of a stream of light from the broken panel. He saw her pale skin. Her eyes were a hypnotic green. They gleamed in the flicker of light. Her strawberry red hair that flowed down her neck was tied with a shredded pink ribbon. She was wearing a dark green velvet trouser suit, which would have aged her at about nineteen, but in fact she was only fifteen years old. The suit was torn in many places, it had various odd coloured patches covering the ripped areas, and even the *Jewish star, yellow* with a brown triangle was placed strategically to cover a ripped piece of cloth beneath. A painted black *Nazi swastika logo mark* was hand painted across the lapel collar. Galene saw Jeremiah focussing on the German logo.

"I am not a Nazi, I may have helped create the logo many thousands of years ago, but *(Galene stopped what she was saying, as she became confused with her Deja-Vu moment… which she then forgot entirely!)* Please, we can't stay here any longer, time is running out. This way!" she grabbed Jeremiah's arm, pulling him to the corner of the carriage, which was hidden behind a stack of suitcases.

"Help me move these wooden trunks!" Galene began to push the heavy boxes from the corner to reveal a broken floorboard within the carriage.

Jeremiah saw the outside world through the gap, before he commented on the opening,

"We can't fit through that. It's such a small opening" Galene pushed him backwards. She swung a large, heavy trunk, which had metal corners onto the small hole in the floor. The surrounding boards creaked, before cracking. The carriage was filled with voices,

"What's going on?" What are you doing over there?" What are you doing?"

"Erm… Nothing…"

The carriage door was flung to one side. It slammed heavy on to the frail shell of the boarded walls. The daylight was escaping. A red glow from the sun setting was cast over the visible buildings through the open doors. Spotlights lit the interior as well as what seemed to be a makeshift platform.

"Quick, we must hurry" Galene pulled on the broken floorboard within the carriage, allowing just enough room to squeeze through. The German Soldiers began shouting at the carriage occupants, waving their guns very freely at them!

"Follow me," she exclaimed lowering herself through the small gap. Her feet kicked upwards on the dry soil beneath, creating a flurry of dust. Jeremiah grabbed his ten year old brother's hands. He lowered him through the hole in the floor. His brother, Asher remained quiet, very much scared by the events unfolding. His lower lip trembled as he was passed through the hole to Galene. Jeremiah forced his bulkier body through the gaping hole onto the hard ground. In the process, he ripped the pocket on his jacket up on a piece of jagged wood. It pierced a hole through the silk lining. Jeremiah cracked the shard of wood off his body and clothing. He angrily threw it to the ground. He felt the hole with his finger, only to realise, that there was paper, an envelope within the lining.

"Who is this? He was not in the vision given to me by my *sphere*? I see that you have received the mark from '*them*' upon your face" Galene firmly stated with a frown, as she touched a *nonagon* shape on Jeremiahs cheek, but then she just couldn't remember why or what she had just said.

"This is my younger brother-*Asher*! Where I go - he goes. I am not leaving him alone- with those monsters".

Asher was ten years old, very small for his age. His mousy straw hair was always unkempt. He was a nervous child. Yet, he had a caring nature. His dirty unwashed legs were visible from his short, grey trousers that were held up with a black leather belt.

Galene placed her hand over Jeremiah's mouth, indicating the "Shhh!" sound on her lips with her finger. German voices began to scream at one of the women in the carriage. Dogs barked once more. Legs began to appear on the platform above them. Another gunshot was fired. A body fell onto the platform edge. The doll like face stared at all three of them under the carriage. Asher gasped as blood trickled from the side of the mouth, dripping onto the stones below.

"Don't look! This way, follow me... Keep your head down and move quickly!" Galene almost mimed as she crawled along underneath the steel chassis of each carriage, followed by Jeremiah and Asher until they reached the last carriage. They could hear German instructions being shouted to the prisoners above them.

"Get ready to run with me, don't speak, just keep up with me, and keep your head down. I will tell you more when we have got away. The guard towers are busy watching the platform" Galene whispered to Jeremiah. She then nudged him on his leg with the palm of her hand, before sprinting across the long grassed field. Her body, slouching, was snaking side to side, to avoid detection from one of the watch towers. All three of them ran towards a twenty foot barbed wire fence, which surrounded the camp. Jeremiah held on to Asher's hand, nearly pulling his arm out of its socket as he ran, Asher remained silent. Upon reaching the fence, they hid in the long grass, waiting for the remainder of the daylight to completely disappear. A spotlight shone above them from one of four tower structures that surrounded the fence. Jeremiah looked back towards the train. Thick black smoke billowed out from the engine. The platform was lit by metal shaded lights that flickered on and off, as the power wavered from the generator. Jeremiah read the sign out to himself, which was nailed to the wooden building on the platform,

"Treblinka"

...Treblinka 'was' an extermination war camp for Jews in the German occupied Poland. It was near the village of Malkinia Gorna - which was two and a half kilometres away. It was one hundred kilometres from Warsaw. The camp was opened in July 1942 and remained open until October 1943. The estimated death toll for the camp was near 870,000 to one million.

They watched as the people were forced off the train, along the platform to an open space. Their luggage from the trains was being sorted into valuable items, clothing, and shoes by another Jew inmate who was kept as servants by the German soldiers.

"What is that dreadful smell?" Jeremiah pinched his nose tightly. Galene removed his arm band by untying the knot. She sat behind Jeremiah, who placed it over his nose and mouth to breathe through. She did the same for Asher, who still sat silently. Galene commented briefly,

"It's burning flesh... My *Ma* told me what they do here. She told me that *Salvation* would be here soon afterwards"

All three of them, sat staring at the white smoke wafting through the flickering lights.

"The rain will be here on time as predicted, and then we can leave!" Galene threw some stones out of her pocket onto the hard ground. The stones had symbols etched by hand upon them. Jeremiah focused intently on Galene's peculiar demeanour, as she held her hand above the small stones chanting quietly. She suddenly stopped!

"We are still on schedule," she said, picking up the five stones from the soil, she blew on them again, before placing them back in her pocket.

"How do you know all this?" asked a somewhat, bewildered Jeremiah. "We cannot discuss this now, you will have to wait", was the reply.

The train whistles screamed once more, breaking the deathly silence. The night sky was ablaze with fire. Jeremiah nudged Galene to look back at the camp, only to see flames licking the night stars.

"It has begun!" Galene quietly whispered, "The people have revolted against the German guards, this will be our chance to escape. My *Ma* was right yet again!" All three watched as the fires spread in the buildings. Gunshots were fired, followed by screams. The constant whistling, which could be heard throughout the camp was deafening. The night was filled with lost voices. The train was reversed back from the platform through the open gates. Its numerous wheels slipped up on the track as they rotated too quickly.

"Sound the sirens! The prisoners they are escaping!" A German guard shouted, as prisoners began to run through the open gates of the departing train.

The noise was unbearable for Asher, who had now placed his hands over his ears to block it out. The silent night, had been awakened by a battle for freedom.

Complete darkness finally crept over the field where they were all sitting. Galene glanced up to the sky, waiting patiently for the rain. In the distance, thunderbolts lashed at the earth.

"God Zeus is angry" Galene stated, as the dark clouds came closer. "Be gentle with us, please! I was always good to you!" she said, but then was left feeling bewildered by her own comment. The thunder rumbled in time with Asher's hungry, empty stomach.

Rain fell softly on the small grass plain, upon which they lay. The thunder began to get louder with each moment that passed by. Without warning, a huge cracking noise, hit the nearest tower structure. Thunder exploded loudly around them. Asher moved closer to Jeremiah, who placed his arm around him. The rain began to bounce off the hard soil. Galene's hair stuck to her face as the water ran down her forehead onto her cheeks. The electric fire, struck the high barbed wire fence once more, creating a firework display of brightly coloured sparks.

 BOOM!

The thunder raged, making the ground shake. The Shockwave travelled along the fence to the towers, momentarily knocking the spot lights out of action, creating a complete darkness. Only the moon lit the night sky, but this was being sliced repeatedly with the heavy rain.

"We must go now, come on!" Galene shouted, running towards an opening at the base of the fence that the rain had created. Galene pawed at the soft mud with her hands. The gap was just big enough for them to crawl through. The mud clung to their clothing as they squeezed under the razor sharp barbed wire fencing. When they reached the outside of the camp, the tower lights came back on. Their movements were highlighted by a beam from high above. Pea whistles blew alerting the guards and dogs to come running through the gates- which were only a mere seven hundred feet away. The beam of light from the tower suddenly tilted upwards towards the night sky as one of the watch tower operators was shot. Prisoners were still running through the open gates to freedom. Some were killed instantly. The soldiers were overpowered by the volume running. Many were escaping on this very night.

"KEEP RUNNING, Hold my hand" Galene screamed back at both Jeremiah and Asher.

Asher stumbled as his feet slipped upon the wet earth. "GET UP! Quickly" Jeremiah pulled Asher to his feet. The barking dogs were getting closer. Without warning, the ground fell away from under them. A large hole had opened up in the grassy soil, sending all three of them falling. Galene hit something solid with a thud, her grip on Jeremiah tightened. The rain water was streaming down her arm, making her hand feel numb. A shooting pain from her shoulder kicked her chest. Jeremiah began to slip from her hand. With all her might, she pulled him onto a plank of wood that had wedged itself across the gaping hole about twenty feet down. Jeremiah pulled Asher up as he dangled in the vast space below. Asher was crying. The tears were lost within the mud, and rain that ran down his cheeks. The wood began to judder ever so slightly. It slid a few feet more into the hole. Asher shrieked with the fall. "Slide this way, Galene shouted, down the wood that was now tilting. She could see lights appearing above her. The wood was wedged in a small opening, which led to a tunnel. Just as Asher was pulled into the opening by Jeremiah, gunshots whizzed passed them into the emptiness below. Numerous guns were fired, hitting the wood, which fell deeper into the never ending pit. The dogs barked above echoing into the shaft, as an aggressive German voice spoke,

"You must be dead! If you fall into the deep pit! "He laughed, another voice croaked,

"That's one less JEW to worry about!"

The thunder echoed further in the distance, it was just rumbling now. The rain slithered down the tunnel entrance highlighted by the torches from the guards above. Asher clung onto Jeremiah, his lips quivered from being cold. His clothing was totally drenched from the heavy downpour. Galene moved closer to try and keep him warm. The pain from her shoulder grew stronger. They huddled near to the edge of the tunnel, only to witness a flashlight fall from above.

"Fritz, don't stand so close to the edge of the pit!

The flashlight - still lit, wedged itself on the edge of the tunnel entrance, interrogating Galene. She gasped, before chanting some unknown peculiar words. She spoke the words in a language unknown to him.

"Beheko astindu, mugitu alde batera utzita. Rumble; Rumble batera ride zion eramango vueltas bat egin. "
Translated she said...

"Ground shake, move aside. Rumble; rumble make a tumble that takes him along for the ride"

Jeremiah placed his hand over her mouth to silence her... Galene pointed her fingers at the earth surrounding the pit. She then clawed downwards in a pulling motion. The tips of her fingers glowed red. Asher's jaw dropped open as he watched her fingers move. At the exact same time the guard who commented on *"one less Jew"*, tumbled, falling passed the tunnel opening into the emptiness below. The damp earth had given way around the edge of the chasm causing a landslide. There was a cry from another German soldier,

"Fritz, FRITZ!"

Jeremiah whispered to Galene, "Was that you?" he paused, waiting for a response, but none came back.

"We must move further into the tunnel, we need to find somewhere dry- so we can rest"

Galene listened carefully, to hear if the guards had gone from above. No voices could be heard, so she reached out her hand, grabbing the torch from the mud. She lit the tunnel ahead. The tunnel sloped downwards. As they lowered themselves further into the passageway, the earth became drier. Eventually they could stand upright and walk. The roof of the tunnel had tree stumps supporting planks of wood which were holding the soil above their heads. Warm air began to flow passed them as they progressed further into the passageway.

Galene could not hide her shoulder pain any longer, she collapsed onto the floor. Her face turned a shade of grey as she passed out.

"What is this place?" Jeremiah asked out loud, even though he knew for himself that he would never get a reply. He was walking further into the man-made cave

Asher shouted,

"Jeremiah, stop, look Galene has fainted"

Jeremiah turned around very sheepishly, not knowing what to expect. Asher was already at her side standing above her, not knowing what to do. Jeremiah began slapping her face gently. Galene woke up, but shrieked in pain as she lay on the cold soil. Asher bent down towards her. He grabbed her hand to comfort her,

"Please don't cry Galene" he stated in such a panic. Asher's hand began to light up with an orange glow. He jumped backwards, letting go of Galene. Jeremiah also moved backwards as the orange light travelled up Galene's arm to her shoulder. Galene sat upright.

"How did you do that?" She said to Asher smiling. "I feel no pain now. My shoulder... it has been healed,"

Asher began panicking, "Honestly... it was not me!"

Jeremiah helped Galene onto her feet as Asher was now pacing around the area mumbling to oneself.

"You Okay? You had me worried."

"I am fine, we need to move on, and I need to talk to both of you later about the special powers that you both have been given. *Ma* told me all about you and many others with powers. I think it was my *Ma* that told me... I cannot really remember much" Galene grabbed her bag. She pulled Asher towards herself before landing him a huge kiss on the cheek. Asher blushed.

After walking for thirty minutes or so they arrived at a steel door. Galene placed her ear against the panel to see if she could hear anything on the other side. The only sound that she heard was a dripping faucet. She gave the torch to Asher.

"Help me," she stated, as she began to pull the door open onto herself by leaning backwards. Jeremiah released his grip from Asher's hand before he also pulled on the handle. The door slowly creaked open. Rust fell from the hinges onto the hard ground. It was a dark room. Galene shone the torch around to see whether it was safe to enter.

All of them entered cautiously. The room had a few metal tubular framed tables and a chair's stacked upon each other, against one of the walls was a large box filled with old blankets and newspapers. Shelving ran the across the middle of the room indicating some kind of partition, that divided it into two separate areas. Layers of dust, debris and cobwebs covered every surface. The shelves held sealed jars of food substances. The room was warm. A vent was letting heat come from somewhere else. Asher was no longer with both of them. He had found a light switch on the wall by another door. He switched it on, it clunked loudly. Two bulbs sparked into action, the room became dimly lit from the flickering bulbs.

"Sorry!" he stuttered.

"Quickly, close that door, lock it so the light does not escape into the tunnel" Galene exclaimed in a panic. Jeremiah ran to the open door, and yanked it into a closed position. He took off his wet jacket, throwing it at the gap at the base of the door. Jeremiah's finger caught in the hole made from the broken splinter in the jacket, so he ripped the lining more to reveal a wet envelope with his name on it.

"We need to get out of these wet clothes, see what we can wear from that trunk?" Asher had already begun pulling numerous items from it, placing them in a neat pile on the floor. Galene had the first choice. Jeremiah and Asher had to turn avert their eyes whilst she removed her wet muddy velvet suit. She indicated this to them, with a finger gesture which they understood immediately. Jeremiah glanced to see Galene's body with a strange tattoo across her shoulders, it was alive! It was moving. It resembled a lace shawl. He turned away so she did not see him looking.

"Ok, I am undressed, and am now covered up" She said pulling a cover over herself.

Jeremiah commented on the floral table cloth sheet that Galene had encased herself in, "It looks better than that suit you had on" he said, before smiling. Galene grinned back.

"My suit needs washing and drying before we can move on out of here, where ever here is?" Galene glanced around the room. Both Asher and Jeremiah had already removed their clothing and began covering themselves in the two grey ripped blankets that lay on the floor. Asher tucked a large gold locket hanging on a chain into the blanket. Galene grabbed all the wet, muddy clothing. She dumped all of it into a large stone sink in the corner of the room.

"Asher, get me my bag, now look at the bottom of the outside pocket- there is a large block of soap". Asher removed what appeared to be a chunk of *carbolic soap* wrapped neatly in a piece of brown waxed paper. Galene began to rub the clothing vigorously with the soap to remove the mud. She grabbed the *Romani gypsy* star patch that was sewn onto her outfit. With her fingers, she proceeded to rip the emblem of her suit.

"Won't need this anymore," she said, throwing it on the floor. "Our time together starts here, as predicted by my *Ma and the clear water!* We have a lot to do. The future will be our making…Whatever that may be?" Galene stopped herself from saying any more by biting on her lip. Her finger quickly moved to her mouth to seal the words within. She gripped her lips with her fingers before making a growling noise whilst shaking her head.

"As I am still unsure what is going to take place in the future Ma!" She said, gulping.

When all the clothing had been washed, she hung it on the shelving near to the warm air vent. Water dripped musically onto the floor from the sleeves of the jackets. Jeremiah had removed some of the dusty, dirty jars from the shelf. He opened one jar by popping the spring loaded seal. The jar contained apple's in the juice. He gave the jar to Asher with an old newspaper to rest the jar on. Asher popped the spring loaded lid, the liquid spilled upon the newspaper that he had spread across the floor.

"That's quite alright. At least you did not spill it on the article about *Oz and the wizard*. I want to read that! I have always been interested in his fantasy stories. Father used to read them to me at bedtime. I imagined the faraway place *over the rainbow...*"

Asher sat on the floor with his legs crossed, eating the contents. Some of the jars had fermented. Asher was beginning to feel tipsy from the alcohol. He began to laugh at absolutely nothing!

"I think you have had enough of that jar, Asher!" Jeremiah removed the jar from Asher's wobbly hands.

Galene was washing her hair in the sink with the soap. When she had finished, she tied another dusty table sheet around her head. Jeremiah opened more jars of which they feasted upon. He managed to find jars that had not fermented for Asher to eat.

"We must rest before we leave this room." Galene said, expanding more blankets on the floor for them to lie on. All three of them huddled together on the floor, covering themselves with an abundance of blankets. Asher was still giggling, before falling asleep. Jeremiah listened to the water faucet dripping in time with Galene snoring. In one hand he held a penknife, in the other was an unopened letter addressed to him, which he had retrieved from the lining of the jacket.

Eventually, Jeremiah fell asleep.

....

Knock, Knock, Knock!

Knock, Knock, Knock!

Asher woke up suddenly to the sound of banging upon the metal door got louder. He nudged Jeremiah to wake him up. Jeremiah woke up rapidly, feeling dazed. "What, What is it?" His head was banging from the alcohol. He felt dizzy.

"What is all that noise?" Galene asked, as she heard the knocking too.

Knock, Knock, Knock!

Tap, tap, tap!

"It's coming from the cave" Asher said warily.

"But how, no one followed us" Jeremiah replied.

Galene's hair was flat on one side, but ruffled on the other from sleeping on the hard floor.

"Who is going to answer it?" Jeremiah said, trembling.

Asher rose to his feet, no longer scared, he approached the door,

"Who is it? What do you want?" he said sharply.

Knock, Knock, Knock!

                         Knock, Knock, Knock!

Asher looked back towards Galene and Jeremiah; they both just shrugged their shoulders. Asher undid the bolt slowly.

He pushed outwards on the heavy metal door.

The door became slightly ajar….

……………… Whoosh!

….Then it came in!

"What the… Arrrh" Jeremiah screeched.

Chapter 2

The Evil let loose (*Once again*)...

18 months earlier....

"Berlin's Radziwill Palace, Reichskanzlei, Wilhelmstraße 77"
the palace, was built in 1738 by Schinkel. It was bought by the
Reich to accommodate the Chancellery in 1875. The New Third
Reich took over the building in 1939, where the main operations
in World War II took place. In 1945 the building was destroyed.

... 20th January 1942.

SS-Sturmhauptführer (*Captain*) Heinz Bieg-Brauchitsch
entered a rather austere building, dressed in his full Grey
military SS uniform. He had been summoned by the
secretary of the *'Führerwohnung'* Führer's Apartment to
retrieve a letter, which he needed to take immediately to
the *Convention in Wannsee.*

Heinz walked by numerous doors along a corridor, until
he arrived at the *"Ladies room"* or reception as it was now
known. Being a former Palace, each of the rooms still
retained their original status. Inside the room, a few of the
desks were occupied by Steno typists. The sound of
clicking from the type writer's kept perfect rhythm to the
clock mounted on the far wall by the window. Heinz
approached the nearest desk to the door,

"I am here to retrieve an important message from Lieutenant-
General Schmidt. My name is Captain Heinz Bieg-Brauchitsch.

He is expecting me!" he said, in his softly spoken German Voice.

The secretary stared sternly at the Captain, her cold eyes pierced through Heinz uniform to his very soul. Heinz was a tall man with jet black hair combed neatly into a side parting. A scar from being burnt, adorned the right side of his neck. At the age of seven years old, he was pushed on to a fire in a fight with another boy from his school. A piece of hot coal left the burn mark.

"Have you got your Identification papers?" The secretary asked scrunching her face at being disturbed from her busy schedule. Heinz undid the silver button to his jacket pocket to retrieve a folded card. The card held all his personal information. Attached to the document was a photo of himself that had been stamped through with an embossed *"Reich Symbol"* of an eagle. Heinz placed the papers in the secretary's hand, so that she could scrutinize them with precision. She kept looking at the black and white photo, and then intensely at Heinz who stood staring at her. Once finished, the secretary handed the Identification back to Heinz.

"This Way... Follow me." she said, rising from a stiff leather burgundy swivel chair. Heinz marched directly behind the secretary along another corridor, passing through the dining room until they reached the Winter Garden. Her perfume of lilies caressed his nostrils on the way.

The Winter Garden was a peaceful retreat, benches, tables and chairs surrounded by large shrubs, flowers and trees in ceramic, porcelain pots. A lonely figure was sitting reading official paperwork whilst eating breakfast.

"I shall wait for you here" the secretary stated very abruptly, she remained stationary in the doorway entrance.

Heinz carried on walking until he came face to face with a man sat reading a *Berliner* newspaper. The secretary watched as Heinz was given a sealed envelope, along with a small black box.

"This resolves, eradicates one situation! German SS-Obergruppenführer Schmidt remarked, whilst folding the newspaper neatly on to the table.

"The leaders would also like "this girl" to be found" Lieutenant Schmidt handed a brief description of the girl. The main text was about the book. Lieutenant Schmidt, then passed over a photo of the book, the photo had been partly burned in a fire.

" If she is in possession of the book, then bring her here-forthwith to be questioned...You must also see it as part of your mission to burn all the unnecessary literature, that does not teach the "Reich" way of life! Heinz was wiping the blackened edges of the photo, Lieutenant Schmidt commented, *"Fear not about the book that she possesses, as it cannot be destroyed. It would rather save itself from the flames or any other matter of injury- than be destroyed"*

Heinz saluted the Lieutenant-General Schmidt by raising his arm fully extended, forward in the air. His boot heels clicked together

"Heil" he said, as he turned to walk back to the secretary waiting impatiently in the doorway. Heinz placed the

sealed envelope in the waist pocket of the jacket before re-joining the secretary by the doorway. The secretary never spoke a word. Heinz was escorted once more down the corridor, down a stairway to the *Staircase room* or *'Treppenzimmer'* which was a small, Darkroom. The windows had been blacked out with sticky tape to prevent glass exploding inwards from a bomb. Despite her harshness, the secretary offered Heinz a coffee before he was to depart the building. Heinz declined with such sincerity, before stepping out the building. Heinz placed his hand in his pocket to ensure that he still had the envelope. He then removed a small handkerchief from his trouser pocket to wipe the sweat from his brow. Wet patches had appeared under the arms through his Grey suit material, from the sheer panic of the meeting.

Heinz carried on walking on the footpath of the deserted street. A car followed slowly behind him. He removed the envelope from his pocket. He took a deep breath before viewing the contents. Heinz read the message before summoning his car to come forward from behind him.

20. Januar 1942

*Die jüdischen Infektion von unsere Nation
unerträglich werden. Das ist nicht mehr nur
eine Heiden Problem, sondernein weltweites
problem. Sie sind aber eine Krankheit,
müssen gezwungen werden aus der Gesellschaft.
wir müssen in der Lage sein, atmen Sie die Luft
ohne bacillus infiziert den Leben unserer Menschen.
der Prozess um eine " Endgültige Lösung" für*

34

das Problem ist bei uns. Kolleginnen und Kollegen,
ich wende mich an die Dringlichkeit für den
prozesszu beginnen mit sofortiger Wirkung.
Obergruppenführer *Schmidt*
20 January 1942
The Jewish infection of our nation has become
intolerable. This is no longer a nation's problem
but a world problem. They are but a disease that
must be forced out of society. We must be able
to breathe the air without bacillus infecting the
life's of our people. The process to bring about
A "Final Solution" to the problem is upon us.
Fellow colleagues, I address the urgency for
the process to begin with immediate effect.
Lieutenant General Schmidt

Frederick, the driver pulled the car over to the stone curb side, the engine annoyingly grumbled as it came to a halt. Two shiny calf boots appeared on the large stone pathway to open the door of the car. Heinz stepped inside, sliding himself along the crisp black leather.

Frederick was a skinny man. He wore a pair of small gold framed, highly magnified spectacles for his failing eyesight. He was confident, decisive and somewhat arrogant. He had a tattoo on his right hand of an eagle, its talons piercing the flesh of a small mouse.

As Frederick entered the car, he glanced up at the rear view mirror to see that Heinz had opened a small black box. Although Frederick could not see the contents, Heinz' fearful expression had said enough to him. Frederick sat waiting for instruction from Heinz on where to drive to. He glanced up again at the mirror to see that Heinz hair had begun to fall out onto his lap. The car was becoming super charged with electricity. Sparks began to jump from the bonnet to the cast iron lamppost nearby. Heinz had not moved from the same position from when Frederick first saw him. His statuesque position scared Frederick. So he leant over towards the back seat as an instant gut reaction. He grabbed the box, slamming it shut. The box dropped onto the seat, scorching the leather. A pungent smell of burning hide, reminded him of the war camp in *Treblinka*. Heinz began to talk very abruptly and without any feeling. *"Take me to Wannsee immediately; it is of the utmost urgency that I get to the meeting before the end of today"* He remarked. His breath was cold as he spoke. Ice crystals had formed on his eyelashes. Heinz sat back in the seat. He grabbed the box, placing it in his pocket. As Fredrick acknowledged with his hand, he felt the coldness emanating from behind him. He dared not look again. Instead, he placed his foot hard on the accelerator pedal. The seat creaked as the car sped off in the direction of Wannsee *for the Convention.*

The Wannsee Convention was a meeting of the top official Reich Leaders on the 20 January 1942. They discussed the outcome of the imprisoned Jewish people, and those that still remained free. The convention was well remembered for the "Final Solution" that was agreed upon that day by all the officials who attended. The execution of the Jewish people who were held captive would begin in all the war camps that held them.

36

Captain Heinz arrived at the convention meeting with the letter. Frederick noticed something bizarrely strange about his manner as he stepped from his car. His eyes had also changed from a passionate green to a total blackness. All his emotion had gone. Heinz sternly walked in the direction of the meeting. As he was not on the official list to attend the meeting, he left the letter to the secretary of the SS-*Obergruppenführer* saying that he must receive this letter with immediate effect. The visit was brief before Captain Heinz sped off in his car to find the girl.

It was not long before, he received news that she was travelling with gypsies. The last sighting of her was heading from Minsk to Warsaw on 19 January 1942. Heinz instructed his driver Frederick to travel to Minsk, where they would question locals if they had seen the girl.

....

Heinz eventually arrived in Minsk somewhat three days later after staying over in (*Jewish*) now German residences. He arrived on the 24th January 1942. The search for *Galene Angelica* known only to him as *"the girl"* began almost immediately. His search was suddenly halted as he was requested to assist with the celebration of the *Red Army* of the Soviet Union – it was to be marked by a mass killing of Jewish people.

On February 23rd, 1942, 18,000 Jews were taken to a Jewish cemetery in Minsk to be executed. Bombs were used to create mass grave pits. The humans were thrown into the pits, then shot. The killing never ceased. On March 08th, 1942, another 8000 were taken in trucks to be slaughtered. On April 29th,

preceding the May Day Holiday, another 11,000 Minsk Jew's
was massacred by the same Nazi methods.

Heinz assistance was to oversee the operation. His efforts did not go unrecognised by his highest ranking officer, Lieutenant Schmidt, who messaged him by telegram…

"Thank you for your contribution to the War. Any updates on the whereabouts of the girl?" he asked, in his brief, heartless message. Heinz did not receive recognition of his efforts with any greatness. It was all in his days' work. It seemed the girl was more important to the *Reich Command* than Heinz ever imagined. So Heinz made it his mission to find the girl above everything else.

He finally left Minsk on the 18th May 1942 to continue his search for the *girl and the book*. As they left Minsk, they walked through a layer of *green crystal dust* that covered all the unmarked mass graves. The dust dissipated under their feet, whispering gently away!

Both he and Frederick travelled to numerous cities, villages with the hope of eventually finding the girl - *Galene*.

Months passed by.

Heinz appearance was changing day by day.

The endless search continued….

Chapter 3

Jeremiah Dershowitz

16 months earlier…..

Gora Kalwaria on 15th March 1942.

The small town of Gora was steeped in history dating back to the 13th Century. Prior to the 19th century the Polish officials had banned any Jewish settlement within the town. The town eventually became a hub to Hasidic Judaism. The Jewish people created their own community with its Gur Dynasty. Jeremiah's parents were somewhat more modern. They established a lucrative business by creating dinner silverware for all of Europe. They lived in a 19th Century house by the River Vistula (Wisla).

Jeremiah stood patiently by the open door waiting for his younger brother Asher to come from the upstairs bedroom with his leather football. Asher began bouncing the ball down the wooden staircase step by step.

Gita the maid shouted,

"You had better stop that this instant, young man. This is not a playground"

Asher grabbed the ball tightly, before running to the Jeremiah, who was standing in the doorway. "What are you doing?" Asher asked. Jeremiah's pointed across the street to numerous flags being dropped out of the top windows of the house. The red flags had a strange cross emblem in the centre.

"Wonder what it is?" Asher enquired to Jeremiah whilst thumping the ball against the wall.

"Mother said it's the German flag, something to do with the *Nazi Army*" Asher shivered. "I don't know where Mr and Mrs Bunim have gone? Mother has not said anything to me about it. When I asked, she just sat there with tears in her eyes" Jeremiah grabbed the ball in mid-flight. "Let's go, we shall pick up *Isaac* on the way"

As they both walked to the end of the street, two dark grey tanks roared around the corner. Dense Smoke billowed from the exhaust.

Asher made noises that resembled the engine "GrrrRRRR!", whilst pointing at the symbol on the metal plating,

 "Look, it's that army you were talking about"

Jeremiah's eyes were averted to Isaacs's house just further along the street. Furniture was being removed from the building. It was being piled up high upon the pavement.

"Quick, let's investigate!" Jeremiah indicated as he walked faster towards the house, Asher hopped and skipped to keep up with Jeremiah. When they arrived at the house, there was no sign of Isaac. They ran into the house to see workmen in beige overalls moving all the furniture. As they reached the top of the stairs to Isaacs's bedroom, they saw all his wooden toys being thrown into wooden crates. Asher stopped to ask the workman,

"Do you know where our friend Isaac has gone?"

"I cannot talk as I will be in trouble... "He whispered, "They have taken them away. That's all I can say", He carried on with removing items of clothing from a large mahogany chest of drawers.

"Let's ask mother where they have gone" Jeremiah grabbed Asher's shoulder. He pushed him towards the stairway.

....

At home, Mrs Dershowitz was reading the newspaper in the front lounge. A photo of the *Reich Army* marching through *Berlin* was on the front page. Mr Dershowitz was using a magnifying glass on a scroll that was made from papyrus. It was written in Hebrew. He placed the scroll in the bureau cabinet as Gita entered the room.

Both Mr and Mrs Dershowitz were of the same height. Mrs Dershowitz always wore tight fitted bodice dress with petticoat ruffled drape tail piece. My Dershowitz always dressed such fineness in his three piece tweed suit with watch hanging from a gold chain in his waist jacket pocket. Both seemed rather old-fashioned for this century, they were more in keeping with the Victorian era.

Gita, the maid, brought a silver tray with tea in a silver caddy into the room. She placed it on the large dresser by the window.

"Thanks Gita, we shall both being have tea today"

Gita poured the *colour changing tea* into, two small porcelain cups patterned with a floral design. She pulled the milk jug forward on the silver tray just before leaving the room.

"It's getting very near to the *tic toc* dearest, very soon we will have no choice but to leave!" Mrs Dershowitz awkwardly remarked.

"I know *Syeira* has made it all very clear! We must make sure that we tie up the few loose ends before we move on. If you deal with the *'room'* I will write the letter." Mr Dershowitz remarked, whilst pouring milk into the two tea cups. The milk changed colour to blue, then pink, yellow then green...

"It is all destined to be this way, as foretold by our ancestors in the scroll." Mr Dershowitz began tapping his finger on the papyrus paper.

"I certainly hope Jeremiah and Asher will be able to cope with the task that is laid out before them. I am just so upset that we cannot tell them anything about it. It will be painful to leave them in this cruel world... *their* world!"

Mrs Dershowitz sipped on the edge of the teacup as Mr Dershowitz paced up and down in front of the large lace, window dressing. Mrs Dershowitz picked up a brown paper package that contained a black robe from the office chair. There was a blinding flash of light as Mrs Dershowitz disappeared for what could only be a few seconds, before reappearing again to sip on the hot scalding tea.

"The *Aurora room* is prepared as you requested dear! I was instructed to install another *Ticker* from a note I found placed with the robe. Syeira was quite specific! She said in the note, "The *final Tic Toc* is here" very confidently this time... I have hidden the *Ticker* on a bookshelf. Instructions were also given to the *tubular* creature with the extra ticker of where to find it, when all the *Tic Toc's* are in alignment"

Mr Dershowitz nodded in agreement, as he began contemplating on what to write in the letter to Jeremiah. On occasion he would pull on the lace curtain dressing, to see the flags billowing in the wind. He stirred the cup of tea in his hand needlessly as he pondered on his own thoughts. Mrs Dershowitz pulled the drawer open; she undid the clasp on a gold locket, to view a photo of a young girl.

"It has been painful, to lose her so many times on this earth. This dearest child is our Saviour. If only she knew it!' Mrs Dershowitz eventually stood beside her Superior in the window, Mr Dershowitz.

"We cannot change destiny, my dear. Nor can we predict or interfere with *their* timeline. It could result in repercussions for *all* the children and the reformation of the *Crystarlauradom Gateway*. All we can do is just hope that *she* will look after them..." Mrs Dershowitz said, before stopping Mr Dershowitz stirring his tea.

"Look my dearest... it's raining..." he said, the spoon carried on stirring as he released his fingers.

"So it is! Can you see a rainbow over the river? Look how it glistens; the crystals are working harder than normal..."

The rainbow was more vivid than normal. It was sparkled brightly, as very fine crystal particles fell from the sky. They were being refracted in the sun's rays. White shards of luminescence were sent across the sky, piercing the dark clouds. The bilious cloud was being cut to pieces.

"Yes, I can see it, very clearly... It is so beautiful, maybe it is a sign of good fortune?"

Mr Dershowitz quickly retrieved the scroll from the bureau. He unrolled the top part, revealing the *Hebrew* text once more. He coughed before translating the scripture near the end of the rolled up parchment. His finger tapped on the paper...

"It is here in the text. It is a sign– it's not fortune dear, it's the *Tic Toc*. A multi coloured waterfall that stabs your very soul, shall start the journey on the fifteenth *tic*, third *toc*... That must be today, it is the 15th March in earth's timing. The scripture foretold this day. At last my dear, it is true, *Superior Syeira* was correct. We will eventually all be set free. This is the very sign we have waited an eternity for ... the *Tic Toc* has definitely begun! Our eternal damnation will finally be over"

Mrs Dershowitz, kissed Mr Dershowitz hands, with her cheek, before remarking,

"The *Tic -toc* is finally upon us all, it is now the countdown!"

Mrs Dershowitz dropped the gold locket back into the drawer.

A blinding flash of light followed... They were gone!

....

Jeremiah suddenly halted... two German military trucks rumbled by him. Asher managed to catch up whilst Jeremiah was standing still, observing them as they passed by. When they finally arrived home, they found that the front door was wide open, just as in Isaac's house.

Jeremiah began to call for mother repeatedly, whilst Asher called out loud for "father". There was no response. As they entered the house, Jeremiah saw his favourite jacket lay neatly on the hall chair.

I wonder what this is doing here?" he thought, as he put it on. Asher ran upstairs to search, but arrived back looking rather disappointed.

"They have gone!" Asher groaned, rather out of breath, "Even Gita, is nowhere to be seen"

"This is very bizarre! We only left the house not that long ago" Jeremiah walked into the drawing room to find two cups of steaming hot tea on the bureau desk. The desk was open. All of the paperwork had been removed. The only item that remained was a fountain pen with the cap placed neatly to one side. Jeremiah's feet crunched on a pile of green crystal that lay by the bureau.

"How very strange, look at my feet! Have you seen this Asher?" he pointed to a crystalline powder glowing around the soles of his boots.

"What are we going to do Jeremiah? I'm scared" Asher cried, whilst standing in the same spot as his mother, by the window. His feet were also surrounded by green crystal dust. He stared at the flags across the road as they flapped in the wind.

"There must be a reason for all this? Mother and father would not just have left without saying anything!" Jeremiah finally concluded with Asher. "We must search the house in case they have left some kind of message to both of us!"

45

Asher disappeared hastily into the dining room, whilst Jeremiah began to search the *drawing room* for any clues. One hour later they returned from searching. They met again in the hall.

"I cannot find anything Jeremiah. Nothing has been taken. Mother and father's clothing still hang in the wardrobe upstairs. There is more of that powdered crystal in the Kitchen by the stove!" Asher garbled out amongst a tear flurry.

"I found nothing, except father's wallet" Jeremiah opened the wallet up. It still contained money, addresses and two silver toothpicks. "This is so strange, why would they leave without telling us?"

"Maybe they have been taken as well? Just like Isaac! What are we going to do Jeremiah?" Asher mumbled, with his hands tucked neatly in his pockets. Jeremiah remained in a deep thought for a few moments. He paced up and down the polished floorboards. The front door was still open, more trucks passed by the house. Jeremiah, closed the door, "I cannot think with all that noise"

Asher sat on the second step of the stairway, waiting for an answer.

"That's it! We need to find mothers address book! Maybe they have gone to our *Warsaw* home" Jeremiah ran back into the drawing room to find the address book in the bureau drawer. From the drawer he removed numerous items. A penknife that father had confiscated when he was caught etching out his name on the balustrade. He also removed a gold locket with the photo of the girl.

"Wonder who she is?" he said, showing Asher the photo. At the back of the drawer was the address book. It contained numerous addresses of Father's business contacts, relatives, but most of all it had the Warsaw address wrote clearly on the front page. Jeremiah slipped the small book into his jacket pocket. Asher picked up the locket. He placed it around his neck, tucking it neatly inside his shirt. He also picked the pocket knife up, but Jeremiah took it off him,

"That's mine," he stated as he opened the blade out to its full potential. He then flipped it back before placing it in his inside pocket.

"How are we going to get to Warsaw?" Asher quizzed Jeremiah. "Do you think we should leave a note in case mother and father return?"

"Great idea Asher" Jeremiah removed some of the writing paper from the drawer. He scribbled a few words,

Gone to Warsaw, We will see you there. I have father's wallet. We will be cycling all the way from Gora Kalwaria to Warsaw. Jeremiah x

Jeremiah placed the note on the open bureau writing top. He weighed it down with a cup of tea.

"I wonder why they chose red in the flag." Asher inquired, waiting for Jeremiah to answer. Jeremiah was preoccupied rummaging for the outbuilding key which contained the bicycles. The key had a paper tag attached with string that read "אופניים" *in Hebrew.*

"Found it... Come on Asher let's go!" Jeremiah said, running towards the kitchen door.

The green crystals on the lounge floor began to pulse a bright blinding light, before they disappeared.

Chapter 4

Warsaw beyond Freedom

15th March 1942

Jeremiah fell off his bicycle rather awkwardly, as he crash landed in a very deep ditch at the roadside. His knee hit the solid ground extremely hard. He heard a loud cracking noise from his right knee socket. Asher followed him over the bank edge. He was thrown over the top of the handlebars, onto some long grass. He came face to face with a hare. It turned around kicking him on the cheek departing rapidly into the long growth. Jeremiah wanted to scream out in pain, but he was too scared to even do so. Above on the roadside, were marching uniformed men heading in their direction towards the village of *Gora Kalwaria.*

"Why are there so many soldiers, Jeremiah?" Asher whispered, whilst brushing his jumper with his hands to remove the dead grass. He then stumbled forward onto Jeremiah's knee; he had lost his footing on the uneven soil. His hand grasped tightly onto the bruised, swollen part. Instead of Jeremiah yelling out with pain, he was silent! Jeremiah watched his knee glow bright orange as Asher's hand gripped on tightly, trying to support his body. Asher was staring at Jeremiah's face. It now began to glow with an orange light.

"What's happening?" Asher was dumb founded. He removed his hand rapidly, falling backwards. Jeremiah continued to glow. Light from all of his body shot towards his injury. As the light faded, Jeremiah was amazed to see that there was no injury. The pain from the joint had gone completely.

"I don't understand. How is this possible? What did you do Asher?" Jeremiah said, in a low, quiet voice as a car had ground to a halt above them by the ditch. Asher, who was mortified, began to comment in a high pitched voice,

"I didn't do anything!?"

"Shh! Listen" was the reply from Jeremiah.

Jeremiah listened to the Commanding officer sat in a car. The Officer gave instruction to the Main Leaders,

"You will search the town of Gora Kalwaria. Be on the lookout for a girl carrying a large book. All other books are to be burned as normal". A photo of *Galene,* when she was a mere ten years old, was given to the men to view.

Jeremiah tried to peer at the photo, but feared that standing up would attract attention.

"A substantial amount of money will be paid to the one who can find her first. The priority is, Clean up the Town. Send all captured to the Ghetto Warschau (Warsaw Ghetto)" the commanding Officer, stated, as he raised his arm in salute.

The Warsaw Ghetto was the largest of all the prisoner of war camps during World War II. It covered an area of Warsaw by 3.4 km² .The area held over four thousand Jewish people, an estimated 30% of the population of Warsaw at the time. A wall

approximately three metres high with barbed wire on top prevented movement beyond the perimeter. Any Jew trying to escape was shot.

"What is *"this Ghetto"*?" Asher quizzed very quietly to Jeremiah.

Jeremiah placed his finger to his mouth, "hush!" He continued to stare at his knee in disbelief.

The soldiers marched on. Cries of *"Heil"* sent a shiver through Asher's body. The troops moved further away into the distance. The car also pulled away at a very high speed, sending dust over the edge of the ravine. Asher coughed as a layer of dust entered his mouth and nostrils.

Jeremiah pulled on Asher's arm to make him rise to his feet.

"I still don't understand how you fixed my knee!"

Asher was just as bewildered.

"Anyways grab your bike. We need to get to the house to see if mother and father are there." Jeremiah had already pulled up his handlebars off the floor whilst talking.

As the dust began to settle from the departing soldiers, both Jeremiah and Asher continued for Warsaw.

....

On arriving at the city, they saw that most of the streets were deserted. "Do you think we should hide?" Asher commented. "It is rather strange that there is no one in sight. Maybe we should move around like we are playing *Hide "n" Seek"*

They ditched their bicycles in what was mother's favourite haberdashery shop, *Nunnelee*. The door was open, the windows had been smashed. Writing across the name plaque in paint spelled out the word *"Juif"*. Asher grabbed a handful of bright red buttons from an open drawer. He threw them in the air as he ran towards Jeremiah.

Jeremiah was staring at the buttons…

Asher commented,

"What are you looking at Jeremiah?"

"Turn around and see!"

Asher's head flipped around before his body in a quick pirouette style. He gulped as he saw the buttons floating in mid-air.

"Wow, How amazing! How are you doing that Jeremiah?"

"I am not doing anything, I thought it was you!"

The buttons began to form shapes.

"Isn't that the shape of a girl?" Asher enquired as he grabbed a pencil from the counter, drawing the shape on a piece of brown wrapping paper.

"I think so… Look a star! And a planet…"

"Don't know what that is?" Asher said whilst drawing it.

Asher drew the shape of a Nonagon (nine sided shape).

All the buttons began to merge with it on the paper. Asher dropped the paper. Jeremiah held on to his shoulders whilst they both watched the buttons pile together on the drawn out shape, that Asher had just finished on the paper.

"What the…...." Jeremiah said out loud.

The last button strategically placed itself on the top of the pile balancing on its edge. It began tapping on to the others. One click, two clicks… the sequence went on. Just like a clock it was ticking in constant rhythm. Asher began to count. At nine clicks, the buttons began to shake. Without warning the pile, exploded outwards scattering all the buttons. Jeremiah was hit repeatedly in the face. His flinches indicated how powerful the buttons were flying at him. Asher dived under the counter worktop. Jeremiah dropped on the floor. Buttons covered him. The final one hit the counter bell, making it ping.

Both of them rose to their feet.

"Your face is bleeding Jeremiah" Asher indicated. Asher grabbed a piece of cloth from the floor. He wiped Jeremiahs face to see that a *Nonagon shape* had now appeared from the cut marks on his face.

"You need to see this" Asher held up a reflective tin lid that held safety pins, towards Jeremiahs face.

"I don't believe it.!" What is happening? What does all this mean?" Jeremiah and Asher stood up from behind the counter, when an almighty crash occurred from the far corner of the shop, beneath a pile of storage tins and material. Asher hid behind Jeremiah as he moved forward to see what the commotion was about. On removing a few of the tins, an arm of a young girl appeared.

"Hello," she said, "I'm Isabella"

Asher stood by the side of Jeremiah to view her. She sat upright against the dull grey painted wall. A mouse trap snapped shut as her dress fell sideways into the mechanism.

"What you doing here? Where are your parents?" Jeremiah enquired.

"They disappeared two nights ago. I have waited here for their return. I had to hide when some German soldiers ransacked the shop. "

"I'm Jeremiah, and this is my younger brother Asher. I didn't know the shop owner had a daughter!" Jeremiah quizzed as he pulled the girl to her feet by her arm.

"They don't, I'm her niece. She is my aunt... We were visiting on our way to Italy" Isabella said in a soft spoken voice. Isabella stood facing Jeremiah. Her blonde hair flowed down upon her shoulders. Her skin was pale, smooth, but her cheeks glowed radiantly. She was wearing a pinafore dress with white stockings. Jeremiah's eyes gleamed with excitement and puppy love. A smile beamed across his face as his hand fell into hers. Asher stepped forward,

"Our mother and father have disappeared also! We are going to our house not far away to see if they are there, in Warsaw to be precise" Asher spoke so fast, he was stumbling over the words. He just couldn't help being nervous around strangers. Jeremiah still had hold of Isabella's hand. His cheeks flushed with embarrassment. Isabella pulled her hand away. Isabella brushed her pinafore dress down to remove the fluff gained from sitting on the floor. The mousetrap fell onto the open tin filled with ribbon.

"Do you want to come with us?" Asher asked.

Jeremiah was just stood staring intently at her!

"I can't.... What if my parents return? I need to be here for them!"

"Shh! Listen" Jeremiah stated, German voices could be heard approaching on the outside of the shop.

"This way, climb through here, into the side alley. Don't worry about me, I shall hide yet again." Isabella lifted a door curtain which hid an old disused coal chute. Asher climbed through first, Jeremiah grabbed onto Isabella's hand, and he kissed her on the cheek before he too disappeared into the small space. Both Jeremiah and Asher arrived onto the cobbled side alley. Both of them hid behind a few garbage bins. Jeremiah had a huge grin on his face. The two soldiers stopped at the shop, one lit a cigarette. They spoke onside the shattered windows of the shop, the safety pin tin that was perched precariously on the edge of the counter fell onto the floor. Both soldiers removed their guns from the holsters. They entered the shop. One soldier spotted the dress of Isabella amidst the stacked up boxes. He pulled hard on the material. The boxes, tins fell, as Isabella was dragged from deep within.

"What have we here then," said the German soldier. *"It appears to me that we may have a very pretty runt."*

Isabella tried to run, but the soldier held on tight to her dress at the neckline.

"Wonder if it's the girl that they are looking for? If not, she will make a nice servant girl for the Captain", Remarked the second soldier as both of them dragged her out of the shop into the quiet street.

Jeremiah's heart sank to the floor as he witnessed the harshness of the soldiers on Isabella. He wanted to shout out, but it was more important to find his own parents. Instead, he watched as they held onto Isabella's arms, as they took her towards a truck parked at the end of the street.

"I can't see what's happening Jeremiah?" Asher said. He was bending over in his fifth attempt to tie his shoe laces.

"Nothing much, once the truck as gone, we shall continue to our house" Jeremiah sighed. Both of them waited, the truck remained at the end of the street, for quite some time. Jeremiah sneakily saw Isabella sat on the bench in the rear of the truck. She glanced over at the alleyway. Jeremiah tried to wave, but feared being spotted by the guard sat next to her.

"Your face is still bleeding" Asher commented.

Jeremiah wiped his cheek with his dirty coal dust covered hand. He then gave another sigh, in disbelief, as the truck disappeared around the corner. Asher saw how Jeremiah had changed upon meeting Isabella,

"I am sure that we will see her again, Jeremiah!" he kindly remarked.

"Hopefully... Wonder if we can find out where they are taking her" Jeremiah sighed once more. "We need to get to the house before it gets dark," he said, glancing up at the sky.

The sun began to make its departure. Jeremiah rambled off in the direction of the truck. Asher began fidgeting, somewhat loitering behind him.

....

Jeremiah and Asher finally arrived at their second home near to the *Vistula River*. He remembered it was not far from the *Tragutta Park*. He thought back to all the times that he rode his bicycle along the many pathways. The house with its many floors had a never ending staircase. Although he had not been at the house for quite some time, he knew his mother and father frequently visited whilst on business meetings in *Warsaw*.

Jeremiah knocked on the door, hoping that Housekeeper *Klara* might answer it. Asher also knocked on the door. There was complete silence. Asher peered through the front window by standing on the stone balustrade leading up to the house,

"There is no one here Jeremiah. The white dust sheets are still covering all the furniture"

"We need to get inside for we need some food and rest, besides which it is getting dark out here" Jeremiah practically stated. Asher was already keen to his suggestion. He had found that the cellar window was open slightly. He could quite easily climb through if Jeremiah was to help him. Jeremiah grabbed Asher by the waist, pushing upwards on the wall towards the window. Asher flicked the catch inside, so that he could fully open the window. As Asher squeezed through the opening he knocked numerous tinned food items onto the slab stone floor. Jeremiah waited by the front door. It opened with Asher stood there with a grin across his face.

"Okay… you did well!" Jeremiah quickly responded.

Once inside Jeremiah stared upwards to the grand dark wood staircase, it seemed to be an eternity away to the skylight window at the top.

"Your leg it is bleeding" Jeremiah told Asher.

Asher looked downwards at the trickle of blood running from his leg into his sock. Asher touched the cut, his hand glowed orange once more, and the wound was instantly healed.

"How do you keep doing that? It is freaking me out"

Jeremiah stated. Asher's smile dropped from his face as he shrugged his shoulders.

"It's ok; I just wish I had an ability to do something wonderful like that"

Asher smiled again.

"Let's go to the kitchen for some food." Jeremiah held Asher by the collar, pushing him towards the cellar door leading towards the kitchen.

Chapter 5

Galene Angelica – I'm Not a Witch!

Six Weeks before *"The Meeting"*…

On the outskirts of the village of *Malkinia Gorna* on the 04th July 1943, a small campsite had been set up by a small group of Romani Travelling Gypsies. The final addition to the camp on one of the hottest days was a woman and her child.

Malkinia Gorna is a small village, with the main rail connection to Treblinka Extermination Camp. Its population in 1943 was only a few thousand. It was the connecting point between Malkinia Gorna and the Treblinka camp. From this point all the trains switched tracks, transporting Jew's, Romani Gypsies and women in the camp.

50 miles away in Warsaw was a Ghetto, where all the prisoners were forced to live in a barricaded, segregated area of Warsaw that covers 1.3 square miles. As this area became too overcrowded, with an approximate 400,000 occupants, the German Soldiers were instructed to send them for extermination to Treblinka.

Syeira Angelica began to remove an array of Pots and pans from the back of her curved Top trailer caravan. The trailer was made entirely of wood. A rusted metal chimney protruded from the canvas covered roof. She was greeted by her regular traveller's with sniping, swear words.

"Be off with you!" she retorted, "Don't treat me like some novelty monkey on a travelling fairground" she waved a pan at her fellow travellers.

"Galene! Get that sweet, little ass of yours, out of that bed and set up camp. Do you hear me? This very minute! NOW..."

Galene never had time to respond, for a pan hurtled through the air hitting her on the head.

"Clunk..."

"Uh-uh! Ma that hurt" Galene squealed.

She climbed out of the bed, fully clothed, wearing a cotton floral dress with a deep russet coloured ribbon tied around her waist. Syeira pulled her dirty beige apron from a wooden peg by the door. She placed it over her head, and then wrapped the cord around her buxom frame twice, before tying it at the front. Syeira was a rotund woman, loved her food very much. Her hair was auburn, rolled up on the top of her head in a neat bun. Her pale complexion was interrupted by numerous freckles.

"Don't unpack everything, as *you* shall not be staying here for too long, *you* will have to keep moving during this War, Galene!" Syeira commented. Galene was preoccupied singing to herself. "One day you will listen to what I am saying to you... GALENE!" Syeira shouted.

"Yes MA?" Galene glanced over at Syeira's stern face. "Sorry!"

"You will learn all too soon what your responsibility is. The time is approaching fast. *You will....*" Galene interrupted by miming the remainder of the sentence."...

You will endure adventure, excitement, more pain and turmoil than any human would have to endure?"

Syeira began to throw pieces of wood from the surrounding ground, along with dry grass to make a fire.

"Put the horse in the field, Galene" Syeira instructed, whilst bending over striking a flint stone with a hard rock. One strike, two strikes to make a spark to ignite the golden strands of dry grass. Eventually, after three or four tries, smoke began to appear. Syeira blew gently to create a flame, before placing some small kindle wood at first to create a campfire. Galene had released the horse from the trailer. She had attached a long rope to the harness. In the field, she forced a stake pin into the hard solid ground. Syeira never saw how she forced the pin into the ground. Using just her index finger accompanied with an incantation, Galene began to push downwards,

"Finger indartsu , boterea eta bultzada - gidatzeko iltze hautsa sartu"

"Finger strong, power and thrust – drive the nail into the dust"

A constant spark jumped from her finger to the nail head. When Galene returned, Syeira had begun to boil a sheep's liver for dinner. She threw some wild mushrooms that they had picked from a wooded area, only a few hours earlier. On retrieving a large bolster cushion from the interior of the caravan, Galene placed it on a large boulder, where she sat watching her *Ma* cook.

Syeira was interrupted by a groping hand on her backside. Galene laughed, as Syeira turned around to slap the person doing it! A man stopped her so.

"It's me! My sweet Syeira" a smile forced its way onto the wrinkled, tanned cheeks of *Hanzi*. "I couldn't leave without saying hello to my favourite woman in the world," he tugged Syeira towards his body, landing her a kiss on the lips. Syeira pushed his arms downwards,

"Get off me, you randy old devil!" but smiled in the process.

Galene removed the cushion from under her backside; she then hurled it at *Hanzi*, "Leave *Ma* alone!"

"That's no way to talk to your father" *Hanzi* began laughing to himself.

"I have told you before, you aren't the father of Galene, she is a miracle from *heaven*" Syeira kicked *Hanzi* in the ankle who eventually released his grip from her waist.

"Quite a few of us will be heading to *Pustelnik* to hide in the forest, from being taken by soldiers for questioning. Will you join us?" Syeira was shrugging her shoulders at the remark, looking towards Galene for a reaction. Galene just smiled back at both of them, she was preoccupied, wiping a chalky dust from her hands, which she had gained from the rock surface.

"Wish this war was over! We are running out of places to travel to... I have been stopped four times today by German Soldiers wanting to see my paperwork." Syeira remarked, as Hanzi whistled the others to start the journey. "Anyway, my lovely, if you do change your mind, then we shall be heading for *Pustelnik*, a step closer to Russia." Hanzi indicated with a sly wink. Hanzi grabbed the handle, and then jumped up onto the trailer, which was being pulled by two horses.

"Wait!" Syeira yelled as she ran to the trailer. "Would you be a dear and drop this parcel off to the address on the label for me... It is very important that it arrives at the address written on the package"

Syeira handed Hanzi a brown paper parcel tied up with string.

"Who do you know that lives in this cottage? Last I heard it was taken over by a German military family!" Hanzi said, squeezing the paper wrapping, "let me see... it feels like material. What are you up to?"

"Never you mind, just deliver it! Promise me that you will? I hand delivered the other package quite some time ago. It is vital that this gets there before..."

Hanzi interrupted Syeira before she finished the sentence, "Anything for my lovely"

Hanzi nodded before blowing a kiss towards Syeira.

Sitting beside two other younger males, Syeira watched as the dust created from the hooves and wheels subsided, they cart disappeared out of sight.

"Galene, make sure that you watch the pan whilst I get some sleep, this heat is killing me!"

Syeira climbed upon the creaking steps, to climb inside the trailer. She disappeared through the doorway, pulling a ripped, drab blue curtain across the opening.

Galene began to stir an oversized, hand carved wooden spoon in the pan mixture. The aroma of mushroom with liver filled her nostrils.

....

Two hours later, Syeira poked her head out of the doorway by pulling the curtain aside. The air was still hot and humid. She removed a large floral handkerchief from her pocket to wipe the cleavage. Galene had removed the pan from the fire, placing it on a few rocks just to the side. Checking the contents of the pan, Syeira lifted the tea-towel that was draped over the rim. She wanted to see that the contents were fully cooked. Galene was nowhere to be seen. Syeira called out numerous times to attract her attention.

In the wood nearby, Galene was gathering some small stones from the edge of a small stream. She had already begun to carve symbols upon each one of them with a knife, before dropping each of them into her front pocket of the floral dress. Upon a tree Galene had pinned a drawing of a German soldier, which she had ripped from a poster in the previous village. She began to throw some of the stones at the drawing. Each stone thrown was followed by an incantation. The words somehow, seemed to reverberate against the trees. The trees responded with a leaf rustling sound. The stones never hit the target. They fell to the ground forming a circle around the tree. She pulled out the final stone. It was much larger. It filled her palm with just enough room for her fingers to grip the edge. The stone had two symbols etched deeply within the rock face. Galene began muttering,

*"Lurraren -Rocks bilduz. Bat egin mine eskuaz nire plazer egin.
Boterean Hartu hire argitik - kentzeko me itzalak , nire egoera
latza egin!"*

 *-Rocks of the earth come together. Join with mine hand- to do
my pleasure. Take in power from thy light – rid me of the
shadows, do my plight!*

She hurled the large stone towards the tree. The rock
slowed down in flight. The sunlight in between the trees
was being drawn, stolen by the rock. Eventually the rock
hit the tree. The tree groaned its leaves shook rapidly, the
rock fell to the ground with a thud. Syeira saw the trees
shivering, upon what was a calm day as she stroked the
horse in the field. Galene swirled her hands high in the air,
a fine mist appeared from her fingertips which were now
glowing red.

The smaller stones moved closer to the tree, forming a
semi-circle. The large stone in the middle rose off the
ground to the height of the drawing. A piercing beam from
the stone ignited the bottom right hand corner of the
poster. The drawing attached to the tree caught fire; it
burned slowly upwards engulfing the picture gradually.
The soldier in the picture writhed in pain. The drawing
came to life. He tried to climb out of the paper. He was
clawing at the restrictive box, which he was trapped
within. The stones glowed brightly on the ground as
Galene held her palms outstretched towards the sky.

"Galene, STOP that this instant!"

Galene spun around to see her Ma, standing behind her.
The rocks ceased to glow. The large rock fell to the ground

with a thud. Steam hissed from the rock as it hit the cold earthy ground. Galene lowered her arms.

"Sorry Ma, but you told me to practice."

"Not here Galene, it's too dangerous!" Syeira firmly stated, pulling Galene towards her body. She glanced around to make sure that no one was watching. The drawing of the soldier had finished burning. The black charred paper floated off high into the treetops.

"Collect your stones, it's time to eat"

Galene collected the small stones from the earthy soil. She blew on them, before placing them in the floral pocket on her dress. Picking up the large stone, she hurled it into the stream. Steam bubbles popped on the surface where the rock had been thrown.

Ma arrived to camp first to witness that a car was parked linear to the trailer. The car was matte black. It was covered in a fine layer of dust. The chromed wheel hubs were tarnished. A small *Swastika flag* was pinned to the grill at the front of the car.

A German soldier, in full military attire was sitting in the rear seat, wafting himself with a document folder. The driver had already got out of the car to clean the half sized windscreen with a cloth.

"*May I help you?* Syeira said in very fluent German.

"*Where is your Paperwork? The SS-Captain Heinz Bieg-Brauchitsch needs to see your papers,* the driver responded.

Galene stopped at the rear of the trailer to avoid being detected, she ran to hide in the long grass. Syeira rummaged through a wooden box on the trailer step.

Galene hid close by in the field, but listened intently as the conversation took place. Syeira returned to the car with a small booklet. She handed it over to the driver who passed it to the occupant in the rear seat. He scanned it thoroughly. Every so often he would glance upwards at Syeira through the open window. His eyes like glistening crystals on a chandelier each time the sunlight hit them. Syeira thought it bizarre that he sat with his hat and gloves on, on what could only described as one of the hottest days so far.

"Seems to be in order, State what you are doing here?"

"I am here tonight. Tomorrow I am going to move to Russia to stay with the family" Syeira replied.

"Are you alone? I am searching for a young girl aged about fifteen. She is wanted for questioning. This is a photograph of her when she was approximately ten years old?

Syeira tried to hide any reaction from her face, as the photo of her daughter Galene, was given to her by Frederick, the driver. She looked intently before shaking her head side to side.

"NO! I have never seen her before in my life..." Syeira replied, in a confident German voice, but felt very uneasy with her answer.

The Captain stared at her for a few seconds, before he slapped the small booklet on the side of the door.

"Driver that will be all we need from her..., SS- Captain Heinz Bieg-Brauchitsch stated.

The driver then returned the paperwork back to Syeira. He wiped his spectacles with a cleaning cloth before starting the engine of the car. Dust blew upwards from the exhaust fumes. *"Heil..."* Frederick said, raising his arm towards the sky. The car moved away at speed.

Syeira slumped on to the step of the trailer to catch her breath. She wiped her brow with her apron. Galene crept in from the field of gold,

"Are you ok Ma? Why do I have to keep hiding when the German soldiers appear?" she said inquisitively.

"Galene, we need to have that talk, which I have been promising you. The day is getting so, so much closer. I need to tell you things about your father." she paused, and then sighed as it was exhausting, "Grab the dinner plates, we shall eat! Syeira jumped to her feet. Galene climbed the wooden steps into the trailer retrieving two plates, knife and forks. Syeira stirred the pan. She prodded the liver with a knife until pieces of meat fell into the mushroom liquid. Galene removed two chipped glasses from the box attached to the trailer.

In the distance above the woodland, smoke billowed upwards into the approaching night skyline.

"It never stops. There is always constant burning within that *Treblinka camp!*" Syeira muttered to herself.

Galene poured red wine from a corked bottle, filling the glass half full. Syeira gave Galene a plate with the stew on it. She ripped large pieces from the loaf of bread, placing some on Galene's lap.

They both ate until their stomach's ached.

"I think I am going to pop Ma!"

The sky was clear of any cloud. Galene was counting the visible stars, as the daylight departed across the field. Syeira placed both plates in a tin bucket which was swinging freely from a hook attached to the underside of the trailer. Flies swarmed to feast upon the remains that had dried to the plate's surface. Galene grabbed a multi-coloured padded blanket from the trailer to sit upon in the field with her glass of wine.

Syeira joined her. The night was calm; it was swelteringly hot making Syeira waft herself.

"Soon I will be leaving you. I want you to promise me that you will not be afraid!"

"Where are you going MA?" Galene asked whilst pulling a few strands of long grass from the ground. Galene was not paying too much attention to *Ma* talking; instead she began to plait the grass with her delicate fingers.

"I am going somewhere where you cannot come for a long time Galene" Syeira paused for moment whilst she scanned the surrounding fields for spies.

"Listen closely Galene to what I am telling you and remember what you can of it"

Syeira moved closer to Galene,

"You will be taken on a train journey, where you *MUST* escape into the darkness of night. This time...you will meet a boy by the name of *Jeremiah*. Take him with you to Warsaw. Take the book with you on your journey. I have left you more instructions in hidden text. Also, *View the Clear Water* Galene as it will guide you with the necessary steps that you must take...."

Syeira coughed, "You will know what to do when the time is right. You must remember why the *Tic Toc* was created" Ma said, as a tear rolled down her cheek, "We simply cannot keep repeating it!"

"It's all way too vague *Ma*. Why won't you tell me where you are going?"

"I cannot tell you as you are *NOT* to intervene with any event that happens. If you know the outcome, then you might stop it, or alter it in some way! This could be catastrophic for the repeat sequence" a fly suddenly lodged itself in the back of Syeira's throat, she coughed violently to expel it, but without avail, so instead, Syeira took a huge gulp of her wine to wash it down. Galene began to tie both ends of the braid together to make a bangle for her wrist. She was playing with the braid by pulling it up and down her arm.

"Galene, I need to tell you who your father was – is!" Syeira coughed, her eyes rolled as she began to speak, "It's important you know as its one of the reasons I have kept you hidden from the German soldiers" Syeira was lying, but Galene did not know

Galene sat up abruptly to listen at every word that Ma was telling her. In the process, she knocked her glass of wine over which soaked into the dry parched ground.

"Your father is a fellow *Superior*" Syeira waited for a response, nothing was returned.

"Erm...He is at present a fine man, a wealthy businessman in Berlin. We met by chance. *Superiors* should never meet upon this earth. It could have been dangerous for both of us. The meeting was brief. I never saw him again from that day. He never knew about you. I began travelling from that day on. I bought this trailer, caravan that you see, to take you places that no other child would ever go. No one ever knew about you, until one day, you performed magic in front of a young Austrian boy from *Hafeld* near *Lambach*. He had somehow obtained a photo of you. He has never forgotten about the book or you… He too searches, relentlessly for the power that you possess. Enough of this, all I know until you stop *Tic Toc* then it will always happen"

Galene, laid on her back on the blanket on the ground, "Ma, why did you not want me to know who he was?"

"*Tic Toc* is difficult to control Galene. Your father was living in a pretend marriage to another woman. It would have been dangerous for both of us to stay together. He carried on with his married life when I left. I had you to think about from that day forward. Being the Superior of…"

"Ma, is he still alive? What was his name?" Galene interrupted.

"With the war on, I would not know if he is still alive. His name was Leopold Z Goldstein" Galene smiled at the thought that she had a father somewhere in Berlin.

"Ma, why are you telling me all this now?"

"Listen to me Galene… You need to know as he will be a new part of the future that you create, he will help with…"

Syeira stopped her sentence by grabbing Galene around the shoulders and pulling her towards her body. She placed a kiss on her forehead. She refrained from saying any more, as the information that she knew was dangerous.

"One day you will understand why! Enough for now! We had better start to clear away these items" Syeira paused for a brief moment to contemplate her next sentence; she choked slightly at the start of the phrase. ".....YOU... will be ready to move on in the morning"

Syeira eventually rolled onto her side, to aid herself in a kneeling position, to stand up from the blanket on the ground. The darkness became even darker as the moon hid behind clouds that crossed the sky. Galene jumped to her feet before pulling the blanket from the baked grass. She shook it vigorously to expel the dust and seeds trapped within the thread. Both of them moved in the direction of the trailer, which was fifty yards or so. Galene held on to Ma's arm for support in case she tripped on the uneven ground. The moon made an appearance again highlighting the trailers tin covered roof.

"Leave all the items from the trailer, you can clear them away tomorrow" Syeira said as she broke in to a yawn, "I am so tired of time; tonight I could possibly sleep forever!"
"Yes Ma"
"Tonight Galene, as it's a lovely evening I would like you to sleep in the field, watch the stars, to snatch some wishes for both of us. I don't want you to be in the way of what will be!" She pulled Galene towards her bosom, kissing her on the head again.

"You know how much I love you! Don't ever forget it!"

"Ma, I know" Galene replied, whilst thinking about the stars.

Syeira climbed up the steps onto the platform ledge of the trailer. She pulled on the curtain to open it back against the frame.

"Goodnight Galene, tomorrow the journey begins"

"I won't Ma" Galene had begun to make her way to the field ten yards away. She turned as Syeira popped her head from behind the curtain.

"I will be here forever Galene" Syeira shouted. Her voice quivered, tears streamed over her rosy cheeks.

"I love you Ma!" Galene replied, she stretched the blanket out, flattening the long grass with her feet to make a mattress. Galene lay on the blanket, pulling a grass strand from the hard soil. She placed it in her mouth. She chewed away at the long stem, until it all was in her mouth. Using her finger, she rubbed the gooey mess across her teeth to clean them. When she was satisfied with the laborious chewing, she spat the remainder on the ground. Syeira, sat on the stool just inside the door of the trailer, waiting!

The silence of the night never really was that silent, as an owl cooed and crickets rubbed their feet together creating a humming noise.

It was very late.

Syeira's heart had begun to beat faster than normal as headlights from an approaching vehicle headed in the direction of her trailer. Syeira climbed down the step onto the ground, waiting patiently for the vehicle. She opened the wooden box by the door to remove a carving knife. She placed the knife within the apron pocket. Her fingers ran down the edge of the blade to see if it was sharp.

The car stopped, blinding Syeira with its headlights. She held her hand up to shelter the glare.

"Who is it? What do you want at this time of night?" Syeira shouted, in a perfect German accent. The door of the vehicle opened, two shiny calf boots stepped onto the dusty ground. The figure slammed the door closed on the car.

Syeira caught a glimpse of the flag on the bonnet.

"I see that it's you again, are you alone? Where is the Captain? There was no reply as he moved closer.

Syeira could see a gun in the gloved hand. It was aimed directly at her.

What do you want? Syeira said again, trying to disguise her voice as a German woman.

"You will remove all your clothing for me! The driver said, as he undid the buttons of his trousers.

I will do nothing of the sort. Go home to your wife! Syeira replied, whilst laughing at him.

"You will not laugh at me Whore... in anger the guard fired the gun at the feet of Syeira who jumped backwards,

"Take off your clothes NOW!

Syeira's hand, grabbed onto the blade in her pocket, blood seeped through the apron as she gripped the knife with such ferocity.

Galene had heard the gunshot. She had bolted upright, into a seated position to see what was happening. She also knew whatever happened, that she was not to interfere as her Ma had told her not to. She watched as her Ma removed the knife from her pocket, gripping the handle tightly.

Syeira ran at the driver screaming.

BANG...!

Thud...

The noise deafened Galene, her hands covered her ears at first, but then they were forced into her mouth to stop the pain escaping, as she watched her mother fall to the feet of the driver.

"Wer ist da? Zeige dich?"- *Who is there? Show yourself?* The driver shouted. His head turned back and forth to see if he could see someone. He stepped around Syeira on the floor to the car to reach into the glove box compartment to remove a torch. The beam of light scanned the area to where Galene sat upright. She had understood the German spoken language, but could not speak it. The driver could only see the long grass swaying, as he manoeuvred the torch back and forth.

Galene ignored all of her Ma's instructions of never to use an *Invisibility spell* in front of others.

" Mysterious iluntasuna hire argia ahuldu egingo dela . Itzali txinparta distiratsuena . Egin hire gorputz desagertzen kanpoan , ezereza egun honen gainean . Egin ikus nire forma bidez horiek argi egiten horiek glare blinding batera begiradak berean. Behin nire buruari behin ere ikusten dut, me ikusiko dute besteak beste, hori ikusgai ziur da. "

- *"Mysterious darkness that dims thy light. Switch off the brightest spark. Make thy body fade away, in to nothingness upon this day. Make them see through my shape at a stare with*

75

blinding light that makes them glare. Once I see myself once more, they will see me visible that- is for sure."

She had reacted quickly out of instinct to the driver's outburst by becoming invisible. She could only sustain the invisibility for the duration of the verse. Once the whispered verse had ended, then so would her invisibility. Galene had to concentrate on the swaying grass to become part of it. It was one of the spells she had memorised from her Ma's book to help her steal fruit from the many orchards on her journey. Syeira never knew.

Syeira reached her bloody hand outwards to grab the driver's boot. She drew three circles entwined, and then she dotted the inside circle four times with her finger, that was covered in blood. Her hand became limp. She became very still. The driver wiped his boot on her apron. Bending over her body, he stripped her of all the gold jewellery. A locket on the gold chain contained the current photo of Galene. He opened the clasp to view it before dropping it in his jacket pocket. Her rings were unusual. Each ring had a different coloured crystal. There were seven rings in total. The red crystal was the largest. He dropped each ring in his pocket, after he had inspected it under the light of the torch. Switching off the torch he threw it onto the passenger seat of the car before starting the engine.

The engine rumbled into life, as Syeira lay lifeless. Galene watched the red glow of the rear lights disappear into what was left of the remaining night time. The car headlights faded into the distance.

As the night silence was restored, Galene ran to her Ma. She threw herself to the ground, grabbing her hand. Her tears were drained from the parched soil. Galene's knees felt a sharp pain from a pale clear crystal powder substance that surrounded Ma's body. The crystals resembled broken ice. She ignored the pain…

"Why did you have to do this Ma? Why?" Galene repeated over and over. She wailed for an hour or so swaying her body, whilst she watched the sunrise over the distant forest. She sat singing a lullaby to her.

Galene suddenly snapped out of her daze, to see that her Ma was still beside her. She rose to her feet to obtain a blanket from the trailer. Galene brushed the crystals from her knees with her hands; coldness tingled through her fingers. *"What is this substance?"* she thought looking down at the shimmer, emanating from the remains that lay on her palms.

Galene covered her Ma with the blanket. Before pulling it over her head, she kissed her cold cheek.

Galene knew what she had to do. Galene began to remove items from the boxes attached to the trailer. She filled a large handmade material bag with numerous items. At the rear of the trailer was the bed, Galene pushed two of the metal studs on the side of the panel, which released a hidden door. Inside the panel under the bed was a piece of black cloth. The cloth was wrapped around a small object. She placed the object in her bag. Numerous items were dropped into the bag from shelving above before Galene stepped back onto the dusty ground outside. She removed the lantern attached to a hook by one of the wheels. She unscrewed the seal that held petroleum oil. Walking around the circumference of the trailer, she poured the oil. She threw the lantern inside the trailer and stood watching as oil trickled from the opening covering the wooden floor. Walking over to the boulder upon which she had sat, she pulled out of the bag the black cloth which held a book. She peeled the cloth back slowly to reveal a small book, which she removed from the cloth; she placed it carefully in the long grass.

"Book, liburu , liburu hain txikia, eta hazten benetako big, koipe eta altuera. "

-*"Book, book, book so small, and grow real big, fat and tall."*

Galene said whilst pointing at the book with her glowing hand.

The book began to grow bigger, its pages, its leather binding all enlarged. Galene watched, but constantly jolted her head side to side to ensure that nobody was watching. Eventually the book stopped increasing. Galene rubbed her hand over the silver grey, tanned leather embossed cover with its mysterious symbols. No pages could be turned due to the strange lock, which had *kiss* mark emblazoned deep into a metal clasp. An amulet made of crystal which would have been held in place by the binding in top right hand corner which would have resembled a face, (*as indicated within the book by a drawing*), this was also missing. The two binding clips had been removed, but left an impression that was still imprinted deep in the outer cover. Galene knelt on the ground, her shoes kicked up dust as she did so. Bending over the book, she stroked the spine gently with her fingers before kissing the metal clasp. The clasp clicked open. Galene opened the book to the first page. A loose piece of paper in the book which listed her favourite spells. She ran her finger down the list of spells, until she found what she was looking for. Galene understood the strange text within the pages of the book.

"That's the one I need," she said, flicking the pages over. Galene began to read the spell out loud.

"Objektu Distant lurretik igotzen , bildu momentu thee gidatuko dut inguruan ".

-"Distant object rise from the ground, gather momentum as I guide thee around".

Galene pointed her glowing red fingers at her MA"s lifeless body. The body began to rise from the ground. She guided the levitating body towards the trailer. Eventually her MA was placed upon the bed inside. Galene climbed aboard the trailer avoiding touching the lantern oil stained areas.

"Goodbye MA, I will try to make you proud of me," she said, pausing for a moment, as she pulled the cover back over her MA on the bed with her trembling fingers. Taking a small pair of scissors from the hook by the bed, Galene snipped a piece of her mother's hair. She placed the strands in a small trinket box. The silver trinket box had her mother's initials engraved upon the lid. She dropped the box into her bag. She kissed her mother's forehead, before climbing down the steps of the trailer for one last time. Standing by the rock on which she had sat earlier, Galene closed her eyes tightly.

"Flames beraz goi zerua salto."

- *"Flames so high- jump to the sky."* She said, rubbing her palms together. Flames sprang up from the oil on the ground.

The heat was so intense, that Galene had to quickly step backwards. Plumes of black smoke rose from the burning trailer. *"I must leave before someone see's the smoke!"* she said to herself. Galene shrunk the book with another spell. A billowing white smoke paused in mid-air, above the trailer. The wisp of smoke headed in the direction of Galene, who was crouched over the shrinking book. The smoke circled above Galene before dissipating extremely fast into the open pages of the small book. Galene fell backwards, falling on to the hard soil.

"What was that?!" she said out loud, before she placed the small book back into the black cloth, and then dropping it in her bag.

As Galene walked across the long grassed field to untie the horse, she kept glancing around to see the burning trailer. *"Rest in Peace Ma, I did listen to what you told me"* Galene said, whilst removing the horse harness. She then slapped its rear to make it run.

The blazing sun was shining down, making her squint; as she made the final head turn towards what was the remainder of the burning trailer. Tears began to stream down her rosy cheeks.

Galene carried on walking towards the dense growth of the woodland, with many thoughts of her Ma. Her thoughts seemed to surface as many expressions across her face.

She eventually disappeared into the shade of the trees.

Chapter 5

Clear Water

08th July 1943

Galene was running out of food, her stomach was telling her so, whilst she hid deep in the woodland. She was finding much amusement in practicing simple magic spells from the book. Her deepest thoughts of her *Ma*, seemed to aid her into forgetting that she was hungry. But the pangs and cries from her stomach, could not be forgotten anymore. Not far from the wood, she knew of a row of small houses that had numerous outbuildings, with maturing onions tied with string, potatoes in dirty hessian sacks. Even fat juicy, red ripened tomatoes in a glass house in one of the long gardens. Not wasting a moment longer, she threw all of her items back inside her bag, to set off in the direction of what would be a fulfilment to her whining stomach.

It was getting dark, *"a perfect time to sneak into the buildings without being seen,"* she said to herself, as she swung the bag in her hand. The yellow dusty road wafted upwards into the air from the motion created. A trail of swirling, yellow haze seemed to camouflage her body as she walked.

Arriving at the first house, she threw her bag over the wall before clambering over herself. Her dress caught on a rusty nail, which held up a trellis for a climbing clematis plant.

"Damn! Sorry Ma for ruining my dress!" she said, under her breath whilst trying to inspect the damage. Galene scanned the area for people, before walking across the dry uneven soil. Her shoes sank into the dirt. Scary as the dark night seemed, her heart was beating normal, that was until she walked into a figure just a few feet in front of her,

"You frightened the life out of me" she whispered, to a scarecrow, dressed in German military uniform. From that moment on, the beats of her heart deafened her.

Galene finally reached the greenhouse. The wooden door creaked, as she tried to open it slowly. Inside, she could smell tomato plants. Her hands reached out to grab the largest, ripest one, that she could see hanging from the stem. It snapped of the bush so easily. Galene took a large bite of the succulent fruit; it exploded with delight in her mouth.

"Mmmmmm!" she said out loud, before collecting a few more for her bag. On leaving the glass house, she opened the rickety wooden shed to see sacks of potatoes in the corner. Hanging from the shed roof was drying wheat sheaves. They brushed against her face. In the corner stacked up against the panel, in a large plant pot stood numerous bamboo canes. She grabbed a few potatoes for these were what she was looking for. Her bag was heavy, the straps dug deep into her shoulder from the weight. It was a small sacrifice to pay for satisfying the aching hunger pangs.

Galene stood on a box by the wall to climb back over. Just as she lowered herself down over the wall, the door of the house opened. A German officer stepped outside in full military uniform. She ran along the dusty path back towards the wood to avoid being detected by the soldier.

Deep in the wood Galene removed the items from her bag onto a blanket that she had left upon the ground.

" Hain beroa Hands", -"Hands so hot"
She slapped them together in a clapping motion

" Eskuak estututa , egin elementua sua honen barruan "
-"Hands so tight, make this item fire inside"

Galene grabbed a huge potato in the palms of her hands. The top of the potato opened outwards with a popping sound, steam began to appear from the opening. Galene placed the hot potato onto a handkerchief with her mother's initials embroidered neatly on one of the corners. She removed the small book from her bag whilst the potato cooled down a little. Galene had now learned how to enlarge the book without speaking. She placed her palm on the centre of the book, her other hand she placed above. She began swirling her top hand above the book hidden under her palm. The book began to swirl underneath in time with her hand. The centrifugal motion enlarged the book. She stroked the spine before kissing the clasp. Galene summoned *fireflies with a spell* to light the pages. She opened the book half way through by flicking numerous pages all at once. She passed Images of dragons, potions, before she reached the centre. The jagged edge of the centre still revealed a missing page. Reading the page before to see if she could figure out what the missing text was about.

ortografia 3 tic 8 toc 9 tic 2 toc

"Kristal zeruak ezohiko denbora zabaltzen den dirdira bat bidaia bat hasiko da , eta nirea nahi zer da aurretik dugu azkenerako free izan daiteke bete dira A piezak aurkitzeko. Let bidaia honekin hasten"

... *A crystal glow in the heavens unusual to the pull of time shall start a journey to find the pieces that belong to mine, fulfil what is, before we at last can be free. Let the journey begin with this...*

Galene viewed the following word on the next page.

Galene- giltza - *"... Galene- key."*

..She began flicking the pages to see if the other page was lodged somewhere loose in the book.

"...Nothing!" Galene remarked to herself,

"I wonder where it might be and why it was removed."

"And...Why on this earth is my name in the book?"

The potato had cooled enough for Galene to eat. She ate whilst reading a few more spells in the book. Some spells just seemed to lodge so easily within her mind. She could recall spells, without seeing them written on the page.

With her stomach full, Galene's eyelids became heavy, so she clambered across the blanket that lay on the ground. Using her hands, she made a *crumpling of paper motion*. The book began to shrink to a small size.

"Go away now, I need to sleep," she told the fireflies.

The flies dissipated into the darkened wood.

Galene repeated the process every night. She had read the book in full. Certain spells did not make sense to her.

Some were far too easy to use, especially *the Invisibility spell, Mouse, Small spell,* or even the *Walk on Air spell.*

....

31st July 1943

Memories of her Ma came into Galene's thoughts, as she prepared herself for her main adventure of the night time once again, to obtain more food. Butterflies filled her stomach, as she crossed the garden towards the glasshouse to make her selection of the ripened tomatoes. Galene opened the door slowly, as she knew the old wooden glazed door creaked once more upon its rusty hinges. She hooked the bag straps over her shoulder, to free her hands for picking the ripest fruit on the branches.

Galene took a bite out of one. The juices ran down her face, small seeds from within formed freckles on her chin. Her hand, grabbed another and then another. Her bag was half full before she made her way towards the old rickety shed near to the house. Removing the latch that secured the door shut, she pulled the door open, slowly at first, but it was caught on something inside. Galene yanked it with one almighty tug. It was then that she realised that this was a trap. The German woman had tied a piece of string to the shed door. A combination of loops allowed string to be hooked up to a large brass bell hanging by the window of the house.

Ding dong, ding dong!

The bell rang loudly, the German woman came running out of the house, towards the shed. She pushed Galene inside, *placing* the outside lock firmly in place.

"Got you now, you little thief! My husband will deal with you when he gets home tomorrow." She said, in a snarling voice. Galene understood key words that the German woman spoke, but not all. She slumped upon a potato sack. Her heart was racing so fast, that she could feel it on the outside of her torn dress. Emptying her bag onto the floor to find her book, she knew that inside the book, was a spell that would help her get out. All the tomatoes ran free to the corners of the uneven floor. But then an inner voice took over, her Ma seemed to tell her in her mind to *"let this course run as it should be, it is as -clear as water Galene, Clear as water!"*

"Clear Water.... There is a spell that uses clear water!" Galene excitedly said, as she began to enlarge the book. She stopped, when she realised she wouldn't be able to see the text clearly, nor the fact that she had any water to perform the spell. *"Damn...I was so close- yet is now so far away from doing".* Memorising spells were so easy; however, this one did not stay lodged in her mind. The only light within the confined space was through the broken pieces of wood in the door. Galene decided to sleep instead. The best she could find to sleep under was an old cover, which she found in a box. She would wait until daybreak, when more light would pierce the gaps for her to be able to see the text.

....

Slicing through the gaps in the wood of the shed, light hit Galene, waking her from her sleep. A spider had spun a web across two crates, directly in front of her face overnight. The air inside the shed was becoming stagnant, as the temperature began to rise externally. She could only hazard a guess as to what time it was. *"Must be about seven thirty"* she thought. Galene sat up on a crate, the door swung open, the German woman who was tall, skinny with a broken, crooked nose spoke very harshly,

"Breakfast, Eat. Here is some clothing for you to put on to replace that ripped dress. She said, throwing a paper wrapped package tied with string, in the direction of Galene.

She placed the small plate on the floor, which contained a boiled egg with one slice of bread. Galene stood up. At the same time the woman slammed the door shut. Galene removed the floral dress given to her by her Ma. She opened the brown paper package, which contained a green velvet suit. Fumbling her way into the clothing, she felt a few patches stitched onto the garments. There was a large patch on the arm.

"Even this one has been repaired, she thought to herself" not actually knowing what the patch was. Galene grabbed the plate, the egg rolled off onto the floor under a small wooden box. *"Damn"* She cried out, placing her hand underneath to search for it.

Snap!

"Ouch, my finger" Galene shouted, pulling her hand from underneath rapidly. A mouse trap was hanging from her index finger. Galene released the spring mechanism to loosen the trap. It fell to the floor. She had what appeared to be two bruised marks across her knuckles. In annoyance

she kicked the trap into the corner of the shed, before crouching on the floor to search again.

The door of the shed opened just as she grasped the egg, *"There you are...come here!"* Galene remarked to herself.

"What on earth are you doing? Never mind... Here you are" the German Woman said in bewilderment, as she placed the glass of water on top of one of the crates.

"I see that the disgusting green dress suit, which was left on the doorstep by someone some time ago, fits you!"

Galene stood up from the floor with the egg in her hand. It was then she saw that the patch on her arm was a yellow star with brown triangle stitched onto the clothing.

The German woman slammed the door once more. Galene's eyes took a few moments to adjust to the darkened shed yet again. In the meantime, she had begun to peel the shell off the hard-boiled egg. Her hands were covered in cobwebs. A spider was crawling over her fingers.

"Here you go!" Galene said, as she placed her hand on a crate, for the spider to crawl off her skin.

As Galene took a bite into the egg, the water shimmered from the light streaming through the many openings in the wood.

"At last... *Clear water*," she said, gulping down the last piece of egg. She then Burped...

Galene enlarged the book. She stroked the spine. She bent over to kiss the clasp, flicking through the many pages until she reached,

ortografia 2 tic 6 toc 3 tic 5 toc .

Ur garbia dago, beraz, oraindik zutik ur garbi,
Altxa, swish eta biraka.
Bildu momentu , jartzailea zerua.
Jarrai hire begi bihurtu swirling .
Etorkizunean zer ekartzen ikusteko me.
Gida betiereko eraztunak bidez neuk
Sua, lurra eta ura ring A
Batzen
Utzi To tic toc aukeratzeko ,
`Egin Betirako da eta betirako.`
Spell 2 tic 6 toc 3 tic 5 toc.

Clear water, clear water- standing so still,

Rise up, swish and swirl.

Gather momentum, pierce the sky.

Keep swirling to become thy eye.

Let me see what the future brings.

Guide myself through the eternal rings

A ring of fire, earth and water

Come together

To let the tic toc choose,

Make it Eternal and forever.

Galene watched as the water rose from the glass. It began swirling around in a circle as she had said it too. The water formed a sphere, the soil from the shed floor was being pulled upwards into the centre, and sparks began emanating from the merging of the water and soil. Galene stared intensely at the ball perched upon a stem of dark composted soil, which had fallen from the hessian sacks of potatoes. Images began to appear inside the moving globe.

"*Jeremiah* I'm scared" Galene heard, followed by images of a train, a sign saying *Malkinia Gorna* merged with that of

Treblinka. A newspaper dated *02nd August 1943 became clearly visible.* She saw a storm ensue with a train whistling in the distance. A broken barbed wire fence flashed into view, with her and the boy climbing underneath. She saw herself fall onto the train at *Malkinia Gorna* Station.

The shed door was being opened. Galene crumpled the book rapidly. She threw it into her bag. The water sloshed onto the floor. It dissipated between the gaps of the wooden floor onto the soil below. Standing in the doorway was a young German man in his early twenties with golden hair.

- So this is what Mother was on about. You are quite pretty! He said, as he pulled the door closed upon him. He stood directly in front of Galene.

"-Shall we have a little fun, me and you? Come here...

The German boy grabbed Galene's hand, pulling her from the crate to a standing position. His hands began to grope her body. Galene slapped him hard across the face. He just laughed, pushing her up against the wall of the shed. Flower clay pots began to fall off the shelf, smashing upon the wooden floor. Galene screamed out loud in a hope that someone would come to her rescue. The man began to rip her clothing with his hands in an attempt to get to her body. The cloth ripped easily showing her lower neck line. Galene became angry. In a temper, she kicked him in the shin. She then slapped him yet again extremely hard across the face. The door of the shed was flung open by the German Woman, the mother of the boy.

"*Bruno, get off her now! We do not touch this vile creature. She will be dealt with by your father when he comes back from his mission,* she shouted in disgust.

Bruno immediately let go of Galene by pushing her, she toppled over a wooden crate, tumbling backwards onto the dusty floor. Her hands had already formed into a fist shape ready to punch him.

- "*I was only teasing with her - mother. I was not going to hurt her.*" Bruno replied. His mother pushed him towards the house, slapping him around the head numerous times.

Galene could hear her shouting at him, as she stood behind the door of the shed.

The water was all gone from the glass. Galene found herself cursing, since she knew for sure that there would have been more information about her meeting about the boy on the train. Her hope was that the woman would bring her some more water soon. She now only had one and half days left before the dated journey as predetermined by the *Clear Water Spell*. The German woman did bring her another glass of water later on in the day, with some more food, but the glass was only a quarter full. Not enough water to make a big enough sphere for her to see into. She enlarged the book looking for a spell that would light the pages of the book clearly. She flicked the pages rapidly,

"Found it. This will do nicely," she said, whilst she rehearsed the spell in her head.

"Hitza hain tristea orriaren gainean, dirdira eta iluntasunean distira. Garbitu eta lodia beraz, ikusi ahal izango dut , orria starlight batzuk " gainean ekarri"
- *"Word so dull upon the page, glow and shine in the darkness. Clear and bold, so I can see, bring upon the page some starlight"*

Galene swished her hands above the page, twinkling dust fell upon the book, and each letter on the page attracted the shining dust particles. The words began to glow.

"I need to know what to do next" Galene said out loud to herself. *"There must be a spell in here that can help me…"*

Galene began flicking the pages over, one after the other.

"Found it, this will be perfect" Galene muttered to herself, *"I know Ma said I should not use spell magic in front of people as they won't understand…but I have no choice!"*

From the corner of the shed she grabbed *eight* bamboo canes. She grabbed the garden twine from the shed floor to tie the sticks together. From the shed roof, she pulled a hanging, tied wheat sheaf down from its fixing. She began to fix the wheat sheaf to the end of the canes using a few strands of the wheat as a secure tie. The heat in the shed was becoming intolerable. Galene needed desperately to get out.

I'm ready! Galene thought to herself. Galene sat holding the bamboo canes firmly in her hand. She began to read the spell. *Spell 1 tic 5 toc 2 tic 7 toc.* Over and over again to memorise it! She had but one chance of this spell. She knew that the vision in the *clear water* only showed what the future could be! Galene crumpled the book, and then threw the bag over her shoulder.

Galene began to feel tired, her eyes kept momentarily closing. On hearing the rattle of the lock on the shed door, she perked up.

"Yes at last...." Galene smiled.

" Makila eta adarrak , bilduta , beraz, estu , egin nire bidaia hegaldi batekin hasi. Bota zidan haize gainean, me goi hartu. Ondoren ikusmena. "

– "Stick and twigs, wrapped so tight, make my journey start with flight. Throw me upon the wind, take me high. Then out of sight."

The door opened fully, a male in a German military Uniform, was standing in the doorway.

Galene had finished saying the spell. The combined sticks began to shake violently. The German male spoke,

"If you are the girl that the Captain has been looking for... I will be handsomely rewarded for this" he said, rubbing the palms of his hands, *"let me look at you!"*

His flashlight shone upon Galene's face. It was too late the bamboo sticks began to move forward, pulling on Galene's hand. Galene straddled over the top of them, and held on tight. She jolted forward, the sticks rammed hard into the soldier's stomach.

"Oomph" he exhaled as he fell flat on his back.

Galene was moving. Galene's feet left the ground, she was flying high into the night sky, upon the moving canes with its wheat sheaf tail. She took to the sky so fast, a trail of dust whooshed upwards from the shed floor. The moon highlighted her movement across the clear night, as she flew off into the distance.

The German woman cried out from the doorway of the house, *"She's getting away. Shoot her Hermann. Shoot her!"*

Hermann jumped to his feet, he began firing at Galene as she disappeared out of sight across the clear moonlit sky.

....

The following day, a car pulled up outside the front of the house. Its mini flags lay still upon the chrome of the bonnet of the car. The driver jumped out of to open the door for the rear passenger. Two shiny black boots stepped out, onto the yellow dusty road.

"Sturmhauptführer Heinz Bieg-Brauchitsch is here to retrieve the girl" the German woman exclaimed, peering through the window. Heinz marched up the garden path to the front door, to be greeted by Bruno.

"Heil" he said, saluting, -*"My father as been expecting you after I contacted you about the girl!"* Bruno was staring at Heinz, whose face was blistering. Heinz never removed the dark sunglasses from his face. His hat hid the hair that remained on top of his head. Clumps of hair adorned his shoulders on his Jacket as it fell out. Heinz never replied, he continued to barge his way into the house where he was met with the German woman.

"Pleased to meet you, Sir," she said, whilst curtseying.

Heinz progressed further, pushing her aside to reach the rear garden. The door was still open on the shed. He was followed by the German woman and her son Bruno. Heinz began sniffing hard inside the building, like a wolf hunting its prey. *"That smell is so distinctive, so where is the girl?"* Heinz sternly asked. Hermann arrived tucking his shirt into his trousers. He began fastening his buttons on his military jacket.

"Captain... Sir! The girl she has escaped."

"Why did you let her go, you incompetent fool?" Heinz reaction was abrupt. He removed his hat to brush his hand over his head, more strands came loose falling onto his boots.

"You will not believe it! She flew off on a broomstick"

Bruno laughed, as he stood directly behind his father. Hermann turned around quickly to summon silence from him. *"So you let the girl escape!"* Heinz reached deep into his jacket pocket. He turned around to speak to Hermann. He pulled his gun out of his pocket.

... BANG! Thud

... BANG! Thud

... BANG! Thud

Heinz stepped over the three lifeless bodies as he walked back towards the kitchen door. He did not show any emotion. He just brushed more clumps of hair off his shoulder onto the three corpse bodies, as he stepped over them. *"Frederick, clean up this mess... Burn them!"* he said as he sat back in the car.

Chapter 6

Jeremiah's Voice

08th July 1943

Jeremiah and Asher were abruptly awaken by a German soldier, prodding them with the butt of a gun,

"Bis auf die Füße!" - *"Up on your feet!"*

Asher was startled to see this tall man, with a gun pointing at his face, looking down on him. The soldier appeared to Asher as a toy soldier, for the sunlight from the window was blinding his eyes, and he thought he was dreaming. He soon realised that this was not a dream of his play fighting, when the soldier prodded him once again with the gun,

"Up on your feet!" the German soldier repeated.

Asher stood up quickly, but began kicking Jeremiah to get up also from his deep sleep.

Jeremiah awoke somewhat annoyed,

"Asher, stop kicking me, otherwise you will be in for trouble"

Jeremiah soon realised that this was not Asher, when the butt of the rifle hit him on the thigh bone.

"What the... Yes... sir!" Jeremiah responded, jumping to his feet.

"Where is your paperwork?"

Asher was miffed; he began to search his pockets in an attempt to find something. He pulled out a small chewed pencil, a pebble, along with some dried corn kernels. Jeremiah knew that they did not have any paperwork, as they had left it at the other house in the bureau drawer.

"It's at home; we don't have it on us!"

"*Move it!*" The German soldier pushed Jeremiah with the gun towards the door, Asher followed, before grabbing tightly onto Jeremiah's hand. They were taken out of the building, to a truck parked on the street. Both of them were placed on the truck by the soldier, to sit upon the bench with other people from the surrounding areas.

The engine spluttered, it groaned before moving away. Asher fell off the bench onto the floor as it veered around the corner towards the bridge over the river. Jeremiah pulled him back up onto the bench. All the other occupants remained silent. They all looked at the floor of the vehicle. Jeremiah found it uncomfortable to see people react this way. The truck turned onto *Dluga Street*, Asher nudged Jeremiah's arm to look out of the rear of the truck. Jeremiah glanced out to see a large wall that had been built directly across the street, across the road, across the gardens of houses. The wall never ended.

The German Soldier in the truck remarked,

"*The wall of hell*", followed by a cackle of laughter.

Asher gripped Jeremiahs hand, even harder.

"What is this wall? It was not there when we were here last?"

"This must be the Ghetto" Jeremiah said out loud.

The truck remained silent, only the soldier commented,

"Ihr neues Zuhause "- "your new home," he laughed. Two
Jewish males began talking. *"Silence"* The German soldier
shouted, hitting one of them with the gun in the stomach.

The truck arrived at a large gateway, to what appeared to
be a walled city. All the passengers on-board the truck
were taken off, then herded though numerous checkpoints
until being released within. Most were greeted by other
waiting family members. Some just dissipated into the
crowds. Jeremiah and Asher did just that. They were both,
giving up hope of ever finding Mother and father. The
walled city was over crowded with people, the area was
dirty, people were filthy, some walked around bare footed.
Asher cried onto Jeremiah's arm as he did not want to be
there.

"It will be ok Asher, I just know it!" Jeremiah commented,
whilst shaking Asher's shoulder.

Deep within the walled city of *Warsaw*, both Jeremiah and
Asher were eventually taken into a building by a
shoemaker and his wife. Food was scarce, so Jeremiah and
Asher had to help repair boots for the German soldiers, as
payment for the miniscule amount of food that they were
given in return.

....

29th July 1943...

Jeremiah awoke earlier than usual. He sensed that
something was not quite as normal today. He ventured
into the room that the shoe maker would normally sleep
with his wife to find the room empty. The bed had not
been slept in. He could hear shouting in the street outside,

so he pulled back the torn net curtain to see what the commotion was. A group of German soldiers had the shoemaker and his wife, along with at least fifty other people lined up on the far side of the buildings. A German soldier marched them all to the main entrance where they were loaded onto a three trucks. Jeremiah stepped out of the building to see if he could get the shoe makers' attention. He was spotted by a German soldier.

"Move it. Join the others now!" he said, whilst prodding him with the barrel of the rifle. Jeremiah instinctively grabbed the gun, pulling the German soldier off balance. The Soldier accidently pulled the trigger. The bullet was aimed directly towards Jeremiah.

Asher was awake. He was watching everything from the bedroom window.

"Jeremiah, NO!" he cried, but it was too late.

Asher just scrunched his eyes to witness Jeremiah as he placed his mouth over the gun barrel and blow deeply. The bullet stopped midway of the shaft. The force of Jeremiahs breath sent the bullet backwards, exploding outwards from the rear of the gun into the German soldier's stomach. The soldier fell to the ground, writhing in pain on his knees, before toppling over onto his back. Asher witnessed all, but felt helpless. He began running out of the building. Jeremiah just sat bewildered at what had just happened. He threw his hands up in the air in disbelief.

"That's just not possible! How did you…" Asher stuttered.

"I don't honestly know! I heard this voice in my head to just do it. So I did what the voice told me. I knew that I could trust the voice…the voice was fathers!!"

Asher began to pull Jeremiah to his feet,

"Quick, we must run before the other soldiers come back to look for him!"

Asher fell onto the hard cobbles, as they fled the area, Jeremiah ran back to pull him to his feet. Eventually they stopped running. Out of breath, both of them slumped against a tree, what was the remainder of a small park. There was very little of it left, as the wall sliced straight across the grass and footpaths. Even the fountain was smashed to make way for the fifteen foot wall. Jeremiah placed his arms around Asher, as they sat there in complete silence.

They heard the guards shouting in the distance as the dead soldier had been found. The noise of gunshots could be heard amidst the screams and wailing of the Jewish people. They were being punished for the death of the soldier. Asher placed his hands over his ears; he could no longer bear to hear the screams. The streets became silent as the night swept the daylight aside. Asher's stomach was rumbling from hunger.

"Come on! Let's see if we can find something for you to eat" Jeremiah stated, as he pulled Asher to his feet.

They arrived back at the Shoemakers house. The blood of the soldier had dried upon the stone cobbled street.

They searched numerous cupboards for food. There was so little of it to be found, Fresh food was extremely rare. They eventually managed to find a tin of beans. It had to last them numerous days. Both of them lost weight rapidly. Each day was a struggle as they searched the streets, begged other Jewish occupants for food.

....

31st July 1943

Jeremiah could not take any more of this torture.

"Asher, we need to get out of here. We must find a way!" he firmly stated. Asher just nodded in agreement.

They packed what they could into a small canvas bag. They closed the door on the way out of the building, despite that there was nothing inside that anybody would possibly want to steal. Asher skipped steps as he walked to keep up with Jeremiahs large strides.

"What now, Jeremiah? How are we going to get out of here?"

Jeremiah stood still; Asher overtook him, stopped and then turned around to see Jeremiah in a trance. He was frozen to the spot. Asher watched, as he began to speak to – nobody!

"Ok, we can do that. I repeat, I must go to the south wall, exhale and then..."

Asher approached Jeremiah with caution just as Jeremiah threw his hands in the air. Asher was knocked to the floor. Jeremiah began waving his hands like a conductor of music.

"One beats, tic toc, two beats, tic toc..." Jeremiah sounded like a clockwork toy. Asher sat on the hard cobbled stones just watching.

"Eight beats, tic toc, nine beats, tic toc…. Nine beats tic toc" Jeremiah began turning on the spot, his arm thrust upwards, with his palm turning outwards towards the sky. Jewish residents began appearing from doorways, they stood watching. A blue crystal substance began falling from the above, onto Jeremiah, his hands filled up with the substance. Jeremiah formed a ball with the blue powder. He kept the baseball size sphere within his hand.

"Why are you staring at me? Why is everybody staring at me?" Jeremiah blushed through embarrassment.

"You don't know… do you?" Asher jumped up onto his feet. "Look at your hand"

Jeremiah looked at the ball shape in his hand. He dropped it on the floor. The ball hit the floor, a thundering noise made everybody cover their ears. The noise continued until Jeremiah picked the ball up. All the people carried on as normal, it was as if they had forgotten what they had just seen. Asher stared at Jeremiah waiting for instruction.

"We have to go to the wall, by the broken fountain" Jeremiah stated with uncertainty.

…Upon arriving at the wall, by the fountain, both of them just stared at each other, to see if they knew what to do next.

After fifty minutes there was still nothing. Asher sat by the tree as he was getting bored. Jeremiah was throwing the crystalline ball up and down in the air.

Two hours later still nothing happened. Asher began to snooze against the small tree; his head flopped numerous times before he jolted into an upright position again. As the night-time crawled over the large wall, Jeremiah froze to the spot.

Asher sensed a change in Jeremiah once again. He watched as Jeremiah began to mumble unknown words from his mouth. Jeremiah began passing the ball from hand to hand. Asher knew it was time, so he jumped up onto his feet. Jeremiah cupped both hands around the ball. He then let go! The ball hovered in mid-air. Jeremiah took four steps backwards.

"Tic toc nine" He exhaled slowly. The air from his mouth began to move the ball. All of sudden Jeremiah blew hard, the ball was sent hurtling towards the wall. The impact shattered it into small crystals, which in turn pushed all the cement from the joints of the bricks onto the grass. The sound of a rumbling avalanche could be heard. A hole appeared, as all the bricks fell to the ground.

"Now, Asher, run, we do not have much time!" Jeremiah shouted, as he started sprinting towards the hole.

Asher began to run; he left the bag by the tree. He stopped to retrieve it.

"Leave it Asher"

Asher began to run yet again. Jeremiah dived through the hole, followed by Asher. An arm grabbed Asher's ankle. He was being pulled back through the hole by a German soldier. So he began to kick with his free leg. Jeremiah grabbed a loose brick. He hit the man's hand hard. The impact made a cracking sound. The soldier let go. Asher pulled his feet free. All the bricks floated in the air before being reformed in the wall. The German soldier's arm was encased in brick. The cement began to reset itself. Once again a solid wall stood in its place with one new addition, a soldier whose arm was firmly cemented in. Jeremiah and Asher began to run through the streets to find cover. Most buildings surrounding the wall were occupied by German military or businessmen. Eventually they found a hiding place by the river *Vistula*.

....

01st August 1943

The water sloshed against the side of the river wall. Jeremiah felt a chill from the breeze caused by the lashing of the waves. Eerily enough, despite this once being a busy, hectic, noisy city, it was now completely silent. The tranquillity stroked Jeremiah and Asher as they huddled close by the river wall together. Asher had fallen asleep on his shoulder. Jeremiah placed his arm around him, but was wide awake thinking about the day that they had just endured. He had to have a plan for tomorrow morning to keep Asher safe and alive. Jeremiah found himself drifting in and out of sleep before he finally fell fast asleep against Asher.

05.37A.M, Asher woke up suddenly as a bright light shone directly at him. He nudged Jeremiah to wake up. Jeremiah woke feeling dazed, but the glare of the bright light was blinding him. "Don't move Asher" he said, pulling him closer to his body.

The light scanned side to side against the river wall. The noise of an engine whirring could be heard against the rapping of the waves. Both Jeremiah and Asher remained still. The light moved forward highlighting the wall further down the bank side.

"We can't stay here much longer, we must keep moving as they will be looking of us" Jeremiah stood up, but was slouching over Asher, whispering.

"Come on, let's move... I think I got a plan; we need to get to the train station. We need to get out of here"

The Warsaw Train Station was one of the main links for the German soldiers to transport thousands of Jewish people to the Treblinka Prisoner of war camp. They began removing the people from the Ghetto on a daily basis to send them ultimately to their death at Treblinka.

Asher stood up, he yawned a few times. They both began their short journey to the railway.

Daybreak was in sight, as they arrived at the perimeter of the railway siding. They both watched as the German soldiers forced the Jewish people on-board the train. Carriage after carriage was loaded with people. Herded, crammed, forced into the cargo trucks. Asher gasped,

"Where are they taking these people, like cattle?"

"Where ever it is... we need to move with them. We have got to get on that train -out of here"

Jeremiah pulled on Asher's arm as an encouragement to run towards the train. They approached it from the rear. The soldiers were unaware of their approach. Both of them climbed under the train, and then pushed their way into the crowd. They became lost in the hundreds of Jewish people standing waiting to board the train. They brushed past an official figure who was giving instructions to the other soldiers. Asher touched the officer's trouser leg. His finger became so cold that it felt as though he had touched an ice cube. He looked back at the officer to see who this man was. The dark sunglasses and peaked cap made it difficult to see who he was. His greyed out face was rather strange.

Large wooden doors were flung open by the soldiers,

"Move, throw your luggage to the right, you will stand on the left of the carriage. MOVE NOW!" A German soldier shouted, firing his gun. He was pushing them with the butt of the gun.

Jeremiah and Asher were finally on the train, it began moving. Clanking, juddering as it did so. They had not got any idea where it was heading to. All they knew is that it would take them out of the now German Warsaw away from the tortuous ordeal of the *Ghetto.*

Chapter 7

Ashes to Ashes

31st July 1943

Heinz instructed his driver Frederick, to darken the windows of the *Mercedes –Benz 230 Lang W143* car. The brightness of the light from the sun was beginning to hurt his eyes. Frederick obtained black paint from the military stores. On painting the windows, he noticed a large amount of hair across the back seat. He brushed it out of the car onto the sidewalk. Frederick was getting rather nervous when Heinz was around; it was a strange sensation of tingling on the back of his neck that there was danger close by. Heinz was now walking under a black umbrella in broad daylight. Dark sunglasses adorned his face. His face was frighteningly pale. Frederick never looked at him directly when he approached the car, he always averted his eyes, only occasionally would he glimpse in the rear view mirror to see, Heinz sat in a frozen like state. The temperature always dropped on the journey to the next stopping point.

"Where would you like to be taken to Captain?" Frederick enquired as he started the engine.

"Warsaw" the answer was abrupt.

Frederick pushed his foot on the accelerator. The car sped off. When they arrived in Warsaw, there was a commotion from the soldiers at the gate of the *Ghetto*. Heinz gripped onto Frederick's shoulder to find out what was happening as leant over from the back seat. Frederick closed the door of the car as he stepped out to get more details. On his return He sat back in the car bewildered.

Frederick turned to face him, looking somewhat confused, *"Well, what is it?"*

"Captain, there is a soldier inside the Ghetto with his arm stuck inside the perimeter wall!"

"Take me to him" Heinz said, *"I need to question him"*. Frederick drove towards the large gateway. Frederick wound the window down to speak to the soldier guarding the gate. The gate opened, Frederick drove very slowly following hand signals from the other soldiers until they arrived at the broken fountain. The soldier lay with an arm outstretched through the wall. Frederick opened the door. Heinz stepped out of the car.

"Clear the area" Heinz instructed.

Within minutes all the soldiers had gone, all that remained was Frederick and Heinz.

Heinz stepped forward to the soldier lying on the ground. He was clearly in a lot of pain.

"Tell me, was this done by a girl?"

"No Captain" the German soldier winced.

"Let me see who did this to you…" Heinz removed the glove from his hand. He bent over to the soldier. Frederick saw that the hand of Heinz was burning, flames came from his fingertips. He placed his hand on the soldiers head. The soldier screamed out in pain, as his hair caught fire.

Frederick could not watch, so he turned to face the car. Heinz spoke,

"I see them, two boys… very interesting. They cannot have got far from here." Heinz removed his hand. The charcoaled body was all that remained. The soldier was burnt to a crisp.

"Dispose of the body" Heinz instructed Frederick, before he clambered back into the rear of the car.

As Frederick moved closer to the body, it exploded. Black dust rained down upon the trees and grass. There was nothing left for him to clean up. The black cloud of dust cleared, Frederick could see through the hole in the wall where the soldier's arm would have been. He walked back to the car brushing the dust off his clothing.

Frederick drove back to the soldier at the gate,

"All sorted out, the hole in the wall will need filling as it is now very much open" Frederick said, for his final acknowledgement on leaving.

"Take me to the Railway Station"

"Yes, Captain!"

....

Heinz stood on a large wooden box at the station, unaware of Jeremiah and Asher, who had already climbed under the carriage, through into the crowd and were mingling with all the other Jewish people. They brushed past Heinz, who was shouting instructions to the other soldiers.

"I am looking for two young boys all alone within this crowd, I will reward the first soldier who finds them" he demanded. It

was a needle in a haystack, there was just too many young boys being forced upon the train carriages.

Heinz watched as the train whistle sounded. Its wheels slipped on the worn metal track as it moved slowly away.

"Captain, there are reports of the young girl that you are looking for" A German soldier reported, whilst out of breath.

"That is good. Where was the sighting of this girl?"

"She was last seen in the village of Malkinia Gorna, by a farmer's wife. She reported that a young girl was stealing corn from her field. She also instructed the station commander for she wanted the girl stopped from stealing her produce."

"Good work, come with me! You will be rewarded for your efforts" Heinz instructed. The German soldier followed Heinz into an empty grain storage room.

Heinz exited the room by himself. Black charcoal dust followed behind him. He replaced his glove back onto his hand. Frederick was standing by the car. He opened the door as soon as he saw Heinz approach,

"We are going to Malkinia Gorna" he bluntly stated, as Frederick slammed the driver's door.

Chapter 7

Escape from Treblinka

01st August 1943

Galene waited patiently, whilst hiding in the corn field. She kept herself busy making corn dollies from the sheaves. Her book was doing strange things. Every time she opened it, another spell had appeared on a new page. It was getting more difficult trying to find all her favourite spells to use. She had memorised quite a few of them, but the book was creating spells faster than she could remember them. She found one spell that helped transform the *bamboo broom* that she had made, into a real broom. The real broom now clung to her side just like a faithful dog. She even had to tell it to *stay* on numerous occasions whilst she searched for food.

Sat patiently waiting for the day to arrive, she sang numerous nursery rhymes. Her favourite being *Ring a Ring o' Roses*, She couldn't stop singing it or humming it.

It was in her spell book written as a most peculiar spell, but the spell itself was different to the nursery rhyme that she knew. Every now and then she would read it to herself. It never made any sense. Galene lay on the field dreaming of food. It was then she saw herself gathering items from history in quick succession… books, clothing, tables, chairs… the items bombarded her brain!

"Stop...Enough she cried out shaking her head from side to side, "I cannot remember myself doing any of this"

Galene paused to think, *'or maybe I did do this at some point in my life, I am just not sure!' she thought.*

Galene stood up to view the setting sun over the distant field. It was time for a food hunt to ease her hunger pangs. She made her way toward the barn in a hope of finding some ripened corn. As she opened the barn door she was greeted by the farmer's wife and three men. Frederick and Heinz were stood glaring at her.

"Whoops, I think I shouldn't be here." She said closing the door again.

"Seize her" Heinz dictated.

The door of the barn flung open, knocking Galene to the floor as she began running back towards the corn field. Frederick dived towards her, but it was too late Galene had managed to scramble up onto her feet, she had started to run.

"Come here you Jew," he shouted. Heinz was standing by the door, watching. He removed his gun, he shot twice. Galene still carried on running. Her broom flew in from behind her, lifting her high into the sky. Frederick returned to Captain Heinz,

"It is true Captain, the girl has a broom, but how is that possible?" he said, whilst bowing.

"It seems very much so. We now know what we are up against. The book is more powerful than the Reich ever expected it to be!" Heinz firmly stated, *"I shall wait for you in the car,"* he said

with his strong aggressive German voice *"Set fire to the barn"*

Frederick thought that he had misheard, but then he glanced inside the barn to see two dead bodies of the farmer and his wife.

"Yes, Captain!" he replied, removing a petroleum lighter from his jacket pocket.

The flames from the barn danced into the night sky as they drove off towards the *Malkinia Gorna railway*.

....

02nd August 1943

Galene landed in a field by *the Malkinia Gorna Railway* in the early hours. She watched as a troop of German soldiers met every train. Placing her hand deep within the bag to remove a handful of small stones with etchings upon them, she began shaking them in her hand before releasing them onto the hard dry soil. The pattern formed a clock face, the hands of the clock showed four o'clock.

"So this will be the time -Four O'clock" she said collecting the stones again. She was unsure of the time at present; Galene needed to know the time, so she crawled on her hands and knees through the field towards the railway. Two soldiers were smoking behind some large wooden storage crates,

"Denbora tic toc denbora"- *"Time tic toc time"* Galene said, pointing at one of the soldiers. The soldier replied instantly,

"It's three-fifteen"

"I know its three-fifteen… Why are you telling me this?" said the other German soldier. Galene smirked, as she witnessed both of them argue over who was more stupid. It had felt like thirty minutes had gone by, so Galene used the spell again on the second soldier this time.

"Denbora tic toc denbora"- "Time tic toc time"

"It's three forty-three," he replied. This started a further argument. Galene sneaked off back to her bag and the broom which lay in the field. She knew the next train arriving would have the boy on board. Finding the carriage would be easy for her as she had- *Alice's looking glass* in her bag. Her Ma had taught her how to use the Glass. *"Wonder who Alice was?"* Galene remarked, as she read a label attached to the handle. The *Vision Spell* used with the spy glass would allow her to see the boy easily. The clanking noise as the train arrived could be heard from a quite a distance. Galene watched as they filled up the tank from the water tower. She saw Jewish people shovelling coal on-board the carriage. There were German soldiers swarming everywhere. A car had pulled up by the crossover of the track. The draping flags on the front of the bonnet, with its blacked out windows, appeared very familiar to Galene. As the driver stepped out of the car, she knew that it was the Soldier from the barn,

"This man is haunting me!" Galene remarked to her broom that was hovering at the side of her.

Heinz clambered out from the back of the seat. Frederick the driver gave him a black umbrella to shade him. Heinz peak cap- now covered his completely bald head. The dark sunglasses hid his eyes from view.

He was shouting instructions to the soldiers to tighten up security, as the girl that he was looking for was somewhere near here. All the Carriage doors were opened on the trains to allow the Jewish people to breathe fresh air, whilst the operation of water and coal filling took place. Even more Jewish people were being held by German soldiers in small groups, in readiness to be boarded onto the train, of what was already overcrowded.

"Force them onto the train, those that don't fit shoot them" shouted Heinz. Galene gasped.

"Now listen broom…you have to get me onto that train. You only have a few moments to do it! So you better fly as fast as a hummingbird" she said, gripping onto the broom.

"Kristalezko begi bilatzeko aurkitzeko bilatu. Jeremiah izeneko mutiko bat ! Erakutsi bat dela nire buruan da , beraz, sartu ahal izango dut Joango beharreko zion! -"Glass eye to seek, seek to find. A boy named Jeremiah! Show me the one that is in my mind, so I can join him to be entwined!

Galene chanted as she peered through the magnifying glass. She scanned each carriage until she arrived at carriage five.

"Arrrh, there you are." The magnifying glass showed a body glowing. Galene prepared herself ready for flight.

"Are you ready broom" she said, straddling over the top of it. The magnifying glass refracted the sun, towards Heinz who was standing by his car.

"There is the girl! GET HER NOW," he shouted. His voice was beginning to change in tone. It was becoming hoarse.

116

Numerous German Soldiers began running to the spot where Galene was. Galene waited until they got closer before she started her incantation of invisibility. The German soldiers stood by the spot where she was laying. They began waving back at the Captain Heinz. One German soldier shouted,

"She has disappeared, Captain"

Galene had but a few moments to fly into the carriage and for the broom to fly out to escape before becoming visible again. She threw herself off the broom onto the suitcases stacked high in the corner.

Oomph! - Was the sound as she hit the hard cases.

The broom flew back out towards the field and far beyond the soldiers, before it became visible again. Four soldiers returned from the field, Heinz removed his gun. He shot all four of them. They slumped together in a pile on the red dusty soil.

"Incompetent fools! Clear up this mess," he demanded, to the other German soldiers whilst reloading his gun with bullets. The doors of the carriages were slammed shut. The train began to move.

"Take me to Treblinka. I can now see that this girl is very cunning. She has escaped from me yet again!" Heinz stated, as Frederick opened the door of the car.

Chapter 8

Portal slide

Present day -03ʳᵈ August 1943

In the cellar room leading from the cave, just after escaping from
Treblinka... they had rested, before figuring out what to do next.
Suddenly there was a knock on the steel door leading directly
from the cave passageway.
Knock, Knock Knock!

> *Knock, Knock Knock!*

Asher looked back towards Galene and Jeremiah; they both just
shrugged their shoulders. Asher undid the bolt slowly.
He pushed outwards on the heavy metal door.
The door became slightly ajar....

> *Whoosh! ....Then it came in!*

"What the... Arrrh" Jeremiah screeched.

....

"How on earth did you find me?" Galene questioned, as
her broom flew through the open gap in the doorway.
Jeremiah was aghast,
"Are you a witch?" Is that what you are?" he said, choking
on his words. He watched the broom fall into Galene's
hand. Asher tugged the door to close it before scraping the
rusty bolt into place. He rejoined Galene on the blanket.
"Is it friendly... your broom?" he smiled whilst saying it,
with his hand reaching out to touch the bristles. The

bristles shook in disapproval. Asher pulled his hand back quickly. Galene laughed,

"I suppose you MAY think of me as some kind of *Witch* with a broom" she laughed, "But I am not so, it's a long story of how, and why I have it!"

Galene began pacing around the room. Jeremiah was so curious about Galene, Asher did not care too much as he was more fascinated with the broom, that was hovering up and down by the side of her.

"How do you know so much?" Jeremiah asked Galene.

"I don't… that is the point.…I know very little" Galene scrunched her face, "if only I could remember something of my past that is significant!" Preoccupied in thought, she was muttering to herself. She was so oblivious to Jeremiah talking.

"I need to think what Ma would do!" She muttered, before she sat on the blanket upon the floor, removing the spell book along with her stones from her bag. She was in deep thought. Asher tried once more to touch the broom. It shook, before brushing him into the corner of the room by the sink. The more he forced his feet into the ground, the harder the broom brushed against him. Galene just laughed, as Asher had no control over it.

"What is the plan?" Jeremiah asked,

"I am not quite sure, My Ma just told me to meet you before she *crystallised*… sorry I meant to say *died*!" Galene tried to analyse why she said *crystallised*, no more thoughts occurred about it, "…She never actually said why! I am supposed to figure that out for myself…"

"Why pick me and Asher, there were hundreds of others on that train?" Jeremiah stated looking bewildered.

"All I know is that MA said, that we all have a purpose to fulfil, to be honest, Asher was never in my vision" Galene pointed out, whilst staring at Asher pinned in the far corner of the room by the broom. Jeremiah sat upright; he crossed his legs as he would do in assembly at school. It was then he realised about the letter that he had removed from his jacket lining. He searched the blankets for the envelope. Galene watched as he opened it. The paper rustled as it was unfolded. He could smell his mother's perfume on the paper. Asher was still trying to get free from the broom.

"Who is it from? What does it say?" Galene said, waiting for him to read it out loud.

"It's from father" Jeremiahs mouth fell open, as he began to read it. "That cannot be so… how did they know all this?" totally shocked.

"What does it say?" Galene took the letter from Jeremiah's hand. He sat with a dumbfounded expression on his face. Galene began to read it out loud.

Jeremiah -Asher,

The tic toc has finally arrived after many,

Many of your earth years of waiting,

We have fulfilled our purpose on this land of yours, we must prepare for our return.

You are probably sitting with the "girl – Galene" this very moment.

You and the Galene will help us all to be finally free.

I know it must be all very strange for you.

But trust your instinct and the power that has been given downwards from generation after generation.

-From the many superiors... they state

The girl is now the key.

You must help each other.

Go to the Warsaw home to find the room.

You will need the Galene to find it.

She will know what to do…

She always does, that is… when she remembers.

Galene pay attention to:

ortografia 3 tic 8 toc 4 tic 5 toc

Erabili Green Crystal

, Father x

Asher finally found a way of escaping the brooms hold, *"Galene is leaving,"* he cried out, in sheer desperation. The broom rushed suddenly back to Galene's side. Asher crept back cautiously to the ruffled blankets. Jeremiah had the letter in his hand again. He read the words over and over to himself. Asher was transfixed on the broom. Galene, held Jeremiahs shoulder,

"Look, it would seem that we have to somehow go to Warsaw to find this *mysterious* room. It's the next step to solving this mystery. I am sure it is," she said.

Jeremiah tried to remain calm, tears ran down his face as he could not control his emotions any longer. Asher began to cry with him. Galene grabbed her bag. She pulled out the Spell book. The tears of Jeremiah and Asher suddenly stopped when she began to enlarge it.

"I don't understand... why all of us? What is so special about me and Asher?" Jeremiah muttered through his tears as he read the letter once more. Asher smiled at Galene as she kissed the metal clasp.

"Damn, there are yet more spells upon these pages!" Galene held her hand above the rather large opening page, she mumbled,

"Book thee, espazioan zehar diapositiba bat aurkitu behar. Egungo leku hau utzi behar dugu! "-"Book must find thee, a slide through space. We need to leave this current place!"

The pages of the book began flipping over, slowly at first. Within seconds, a gust of wind was created from the page flicking. The gust blew Jeremiah over onto his back. The pages stopped suddenly. The page stood upright, on its edge from the binding. Galene gently touched the page, and then watched it glide slowly down like a feather.

This spell needs fresh mud made with rainwater. It was written in the margin by Syeira, Galene recognised the handwriting instantly! She translated the spell to herself,

Spell 3 tic 1 toc 9 tic 1 toc.

Mud of the earth, water of the sky,

I create an escape from this place.

A point is known, so I drop it first.

Which I will leave no trace,

Doorway open,

Now let me in.

Let the transition begin.

Galene jumped to her feet. She grabbed her now dry clothing from the shelving. Upon dropping the sheet from her body, both Jeremiah and Asher turned away until she was fully dressed. Galene began throwing everything back into her bag, apart from the book for Galene began to memorise the spell. Jeremiah and Asher got dressed. Jeremiah placed the letter into his jacket pocket. Galene unbolted the metal door. It creaked open. The spell was fixed in her mind, as she shrank the book to place back in her bag. She repeated it to herself over and over, until she knew it fully.

"We need mud…The entrance of the cave where we came in yesterday was muddy! It was raining hard when we hid from the soldiers. We need to go back to that place" Galene stated with such confidence. Jeremiah checked the room to make sure that they had not left anything. Asher was already following the broom which had glided along by Galene's side. Jeremiah switched on the torch as the passage got narrow. His feet began to slip.

"This will do" Galene said, grabbing a handful of mud from the floor.

"Now what do we do?" Jeremiah asked

"I suppose we must make some kind of doorway from the mud" Galene had already begun sticking clumps of dark sloppy earth on the floor into the shape of a large circle. "We shall make it like a porthole on a *ship* as it is easier to make that shape"

Jeremiah began grabbing at the earth. He threw some at Ashers face. Asher laughed. Asher was pushing sludge towards the mound of wet soil. Eventually a circular shape was formed, the centre was sunken inwards.

"Now what?" Asher inquisitively remarked.

Galene stared at the mound of earth, she shrugged her shoulders. She then looked at Jeremiah hoping that he would know what to do. Galene grabbed a piece of material from her bag to wipe her hands on. She passed it to Asher, then Jeremiah.

"We need an address of where we are going one would suppose" Galene rummaged in her bag for a pencil, "Do you still have the letter with you Jeremiah?"

Jeremiah pulled out the letter from his pocket. Galene removed contents, but, she held onto the envelope.

"Here you are, write the address on the envelope" Galene handed the envelope and pencil to Jeremiah.

Jeremiah began to scribble. Firstly, he crossed out his name on the front. He wrote the address of the Warsaw home, before handing it back to Galene. Asher Held the heavy torch, he was shining the beam at Galene as she dropped the pencil back into her bag. Galene mumbled the spell to herself at first, before she was confident enough to say it.

"Both of you will have to be quiet whilst I do this, I cannot afford to make any mistakes." Galene began to recite the spell, but then she stopped halfway through. *"Of course,"* she said to herself. She began to dig a hole in the centre for the envelope to be posted in. She continued in a louder voice saying the spell out loud.

"Zuzenketa 3 tic 1 toc 9 tic 1 toc.

Lurraren Lokatza, zeruaren ura,

Toki hau ihes bat sortu dut.

A puntua ezaguna da, eta beraz, askatu nuen lehen.

Zein arrastorik ez utziko dut,
Atari irekia,
Orain utzi nigan.
Let trantsizio hasiko."

They all stood waiting for something to happen. Asher shone the torch at the circular mud creation. The envelope was sticking upwards out of the mud. Suddenly the envelope was sucked rapidly downwards into the mud. It disappeared out of sight. The centre of the circle dropped away. There was a loud popping noise as a bright light appeared in the hole.

"Looks like this is it" Galene grabbed the broom, she jumped into the centre. Sparks flew outwards as she slid downwards. Asher could hear the echo of *Ring a Ring o"* *Roses,* being hummed by Galene very faintly in the distance as he jumped in next. Jeremiah followed shortly afterwards. The circular mud began to swirl. It dissipated back to the floor, the light popped once more. The cave was once again in total darkness.

Chapter 9

Destine Rock

03rd August 1943, Evening

At the Warsaw home, *POP*...

A circular light appeared high up, on the stairway. An envelope glided out from the centre, a gust of wind blew it down the stairs until it landed on the dark, stained floorboards. *POP*... another circular light appeared; it opened up, midway on the stairs. Galene came through the light portal first. She bumped down the stairs before sliding along the hallway floor with such a force, hitting the umbrella stand, knocking it over. Her broom came to a sudden stop as it hit the wall. It fell to the floor beside her. One large black umbrella fell onto the floor where it opened up fully. Both Jeremiah and Asher came through at the same time. POP... The portal opened half way up the wall. Asher crashed into Galene whilst Jeremiah's leg hit the hall table flipping him around. He glided backwards until he came to a thumping stop at the front door. The sound echoed in the emptiness of the vast space. The letter box on the front door began to move. Galene grabbed the umbrella to hide her and Asher behind. Jeremiah lay flat against the door as a new draught excluder, so he could not be seen. The letter box flipped upwards, two eyes peered in.

"Hello is there anybody in there?" squeaked a very faint voice. They all remained still and silent. "Jeremiah… Is it you in there?" There was still silence as the letter box closed. Galene adjusted the umbrella, to see Jeremiah make an unknown, *shrugging of the shoulders* gesture towards her. Galene whispered,

"She knows your name!"

Jeremiah sat up; he gently pushed the letter-box flap open to be confronted with two eyes staring back at him. He fell backwards in horror.

"It's me... Isabella." She said, pushing the flap upwards again. Jeremiah jumped to his feet immediately. He undid the lock to open the door, to see Isabella standing on the doorstep.

"Quickly… come in" Jeremiah said, pulling her into the house.

"How did you find me? The German soldiers took you away in the truck?"

Galene closed the umbrella; Asher began standing in an upright position.

"I am Galene, and this is Asher, but I think that you already know who we all are." Galene held out her hand to shake Isabella's. As they touched, they both smiled, Galene sensed something rather calming about her. Isabella, replied to Galene, "Yes, I can".

"I have not asked the question yet!" Galene stated.

"Sorry, I always hear a voice asking it, so I reply."

"What question? This is getting confusing" Jeremiah was blushing yet again from seeing Isabella. Galene released her grip on her hand,

"Shall I answer that one for you? (Isabella nodded), Isabella can read people if she is near them. She can sense their inner thoughts and feelings. If she touches you she can read your mind more in-depth. My Ma told me that there are a few gifted around the world that can do this. *Ma* called them *Destine Rocks.* They will never tell you the right or wrong way of doing something. They ensure that every event is determined by your own actions. Yet they can see your very soul, and what you strive for. *Destine Rocks* will only guide you into your own decision, your own destination, whilst still remaining firmly grounded like a *rock* in the soil. I never ever thought I would meet a person who could do this"

"That is absolutely so Galene. I cannot help someone decide, but I can guide them in the thought process to an outcome" Isabella remarked, glancing intently at Jeremiah. It was then that Jeremiah realised, that she must have known about his feelings for her. His cheeks began to glow brighter, even sweat formed on his brow.

Asher tried to revive the *broom* that lay on the floor by the wall. He was shaking it vigorously. Asher's grip was tightened, as the *broom* took off, in flight up the staircase towards the bedrooms. Jeremiah was laughing.

"Jeremiah please save me, it won't let my hands go free. Galene, please save me" Asher cried out, as the broom had reached the top floor to begin its descent to the bottom again. Asher's feet knocked paintings off the wall, ornaments from cabinets, as the broom flew at such ferocity.

"Galene- Please Stop the broom, all that noise might attract the German soldiers" Isabella blurted out, in desperation of not being held captive again by the German soldiers.

"Broom, BROOM, here now!" Galene shouted.

The broom reached to the top of the stairway; Asher's hands were suddenly released. He fell against the balustrade, cracking one of the spindles in half. The broom flew back to Galene's side. Isabella grabbed the broom,

"Interesting… the broom would like to talk to you Galene" she said.

"Not now Isabella, we have to find the room mentioned, as…."

"… In the letter! I know everything" Isabella finished the sentence.

"How did you escape the German Soldiers Isabella?" Jeremiah stumbled over his words as he spoke out.

"I made them see that to set me free will do them good. As the truck veered around the corner from the shop, I made both soldiers see that I was of no threat. I set in motion thoughts about if they had children- would they help them! I asked him to stop for me. The German soldiers even waved me goodbye, after they helped me off the truck." Isabella calmly smiled. "I knew you would come here to this address as…."

"I know now…You read my mind, so you know everything!" Jeremiah stated.

Galene was pacing around the floor in thought, as Asher made his way down the staircase rubbing his lower back. The broom began shaking at Asher he walked by. Jeremiah and Isabella were just staring intensely at each other.

"The letter said to use the green crystal and a spell", Isabella blurted out. A vehicle had pulled up outside the house. A group of German voices could be heard directly outside the front door.

"Hide everybody, quickly!" Galene muttered. She opened the letter-box slowly to see a truck with a group of German soldiers outside the house. They were all jumping off the rear, laughing, smoking; some remained to clean their rifles.

"It's okay, I think they must be having a break, we must be extremely quiet" Galene said to the others, whilst staring at Asher. They all reappeared from hiding. From behind the furniture or under the white cloths, that covered the hall chairs.

"What do we do now?" Asher whispered.

"We need to find this *Green crystal*. Jeremiah and Isabella, both of you, search the two upper levels. Asher and I will search the lowest two. We will meet back here in about an hour. Remember... Be Quiet!"

They began to search each room in turn. Eventually they all met again in the dining room, which was in the middle of the house leading from the hallway. The room had a solid mahogany dining table in the centre. Surrounding the table were twelve dining chairs. Isabella pulled one away from the table to sit down. Asher proceeded to follow her suit by pulling another heavy chair from underneath. He plonked himself on the thick padded cushion that adorned the seat, he let out a sigh.

Jeremiah removed the letter from his jacket pocket again, to read what once more and it was then he realised, that they had been searching for no reason, as it asked Galene to use a spell firstly.

"What is this Spell 3 tic 8? If I am correct, you must use it to find the green crystal…" Isabella smiled knowingly.

Galene removed the book from her bag; she enlarged it on the table. Kneeling on the outer edge to reach the clasp, she kissed it. Isabella was fascinated by the book that she had to touch it. Her smile changed to tears. Jeremiah dragged her hand from the book,

"What is it, what's wrong Isabella? Why are you crying?" he said, holding her hand. Galene began frantically flicking the pages to get to the Spell. The broom hovered at her side.

"It is beautiful, but also so painful… I simply cannot remember why" Isabella commented, "I really don't know why I am crying. How silly of me," she said, wiping her cheeks.

"I have found the spell; this book is changing so fast that the spells are now all mixed up! *Ortografia 3 tic 8 toc 4 tic 5 toc"* Galene read the spell a couple of times, she then held her hands out to perform the spell.

"Errebelatu hori ezkutuko, ikuspegi batetik ikusmena, Erakutsi kristal errefraktoreak argia. - *Reveal that's hidden, from view, from sight, Show the crystal refracting light."*

Galene looked around the room to see if a crystal revealed itself. Absolutely nothing changed in the room. Everybody was looking at every wall, object to see if a crystal appeared. She shrank the book, to put back in her bag. She walked out of the room into the front room to perform the same spell. Still nothing! Jeremiah, Asher, Isabella and the broom followed closely behind her. Galene paraded down the stairway to the kitchen. She repeated the spell. Once again, nothing changed.

"Do you think we will ever find this room?" Asher asked in sheer frustration. Galene opened a door from the kitchen that lead to a small cold, storeroom. She stepped inside. The room was so small Galene dismissed it immediately. She stepped back out into the kitchen saying the spell as she walked,

"Errebelatu hori ezkutuko, ikuspegi batetik ikusmena, Erakutsi kristal errefraktoreak argia." She waited for anything to change or appear different. Nothing did. As she began to close the door, Isabella stopped her. She pulled the door back open.

"Look at the inside of the door," she said, pointing at a faint green glow which was behind a fake panel. Galene placed her hand on the edge of the panel; warmth came from the small gap. Jeremiah had removed his penknife from his pocket. He began prising the panel off the back of the door, the wood cracked. It splintered sending a shard of wood piercing deep in his hand,

"Arrrh" he cried out.

A splurge of blood ran down his arm. Jeremiah collapsed onto the floor, at the sight of his own blood.

"He's fainted" Isabella was wafting his face with her hand. Asher grabbed the piece of wood, which was shaped like a bread knife. He pulled it out slowly. As the last piece of it was removed, his hand began spurting blood everywhere. The wood had cut the vein. Asher panicked; he grabbed his hand to stop the fountain of blood coming out. His hands began to glow orange. Isabella watched as Jeremiah was healed so fast. She watched Jeremiah's skin stretch back over the wound, to the point where there was no injury.

"Let me touch your head" Isabella said to Asher. She placed her hands on his head. She smiled at him with such contentment.

"Oh… I now see what they have done with you," she said, releasing her grip from him.

Galene began pulling the remainder of the panel from the door. Hidden behind the panel was a painting of a green crystal. It had been painted on papyrus, hidden behind a fake panel on the door.

"It's not what I expected" Galene remarked, looking slightly bemused. Isabella began wafting her hands even more, for Jeremiah had begun to wake up from his fainting.

"You have been fixed by Asher" she widely grinned. She then bent over him to kiss his forehead. Asher had picked up his penknife, closing the blade back into the holster, he handed it back to Jeremiah.

"Thanks Asher"

....

A car had pulled up at the kerbside outside the house. Captain Heinz stepped out of the car. The German soldiers immediately stood to attention. He began shouting instructions to them,

"Search the houses; this is where the two boys were originally found." Heinz growled, adjusting the black leather gloves on his hands.

The German soldiers began running to all the houses. Crash... Windows smashed. Bang, Thud as the doors were kicked open by them. The door of the house slammed open hard upon the fallen umbrella stand.

"The German soldiers are here; surely it is best for all of us to hide in the mysterious room!" Isabella stated to Galene.

"Quick, everybody squeeze - into the cupboard, I have to figure this out. Asher helped Jeremiah to his feet. All four of them forced themselves to stand in the small space. Isabella giggled. The broom rustled as it was pinned in the middle of all four of them.

"Errebelatu hori ezkutuko, ikuspegi batetik ikusmena,

Erakutsi kristal errefraktoreak argia." Galene said once more. The green crystal painting began to glow, the crystal rose out from the surface. Galene grabbed it; she turned it upside down before letting go. It fell back into the painting. The emanating glow ceased, the small storeroom was in complete darkness.

"Nothing's happened" Asher indicated as he reached for the door knob. He let out a sigh of relief before pushing the door open. The room was different. The kitchen window had disappeared. Asher fumbled by the frame of the door, as he was being forced outwards by Isabella.

Clunk went the switch. Asher had found a light switch by the entrance and had accidentally knocked it on.

"Quickly close the door!" Galene stated as they all rushed into the room.

…………………………..

A German soldier began searching the kitchen. His hand grabbed the door knob to the store room. He pulled the door open. He rummaged through a few old decorating sheets on the floor in the corner, before stepping backwards to close the door again. He slipped, banging his head on the oak table. His hand touched the warm liquid on the floor before leaving.

SS-Sturmhauptführer Heinz was waiting by the car on the street. Frederick was polishing the chrome wheel trims with a piece of linen cloth, when Soldiers began to reappear from the houses. They all reported nothing. Jeremiahs house was the last house for the soldiers to exit. Each soldier in turn instructed that nothing was found.

Heinz sniffed each of the soldiers in turn as they passed by him.

"Stop right there," he said, holding out his arm to force the soldier to a standstill. "Show me your hands" Heinz could see blood on the palm of his hand from Jeremiah. "Come with me," he instructed, as he began glided back towards the house.

Upon entering the kitchen, Heinz switched on the light.

"Where did you find this blood?" he asked the soldier, who was already walking across to the far side of the table.

"Here Captain, this is where I fell."

The blood had gone, the floor was wet. A white cloth was in the sink soaking with detergent. Frederick entered the kitchen. He used some wooden tongs to grasp the white cloth. It was a blood stained cloth.

"Someone, clearly has cleaned up the area- Captain, It can only mean that they cannot be far away" Frederick stated dropping the cloth back into the water.

"That is so, leave the room... whilst I question the soldier more" Heinz instructed to Frederick.

Frederick stood directly outside the room. He pulled the door slightly ajar. Through a small gap he could see that was taking place between Heinz and the soldier. Heinz grabbed the soldier's hand. He pulled it to his face to look at it more. The soldier looked puzzled, but then scared as Heinz opened his mouth, his tongue came out, licking the blood with pure vulgarity. His tongue grew longer. It entwined around the soldier's arm. Frederick couldn't look anymore; He turned his back to the door. The soldier screamed in pain for what was a moment before there was complete silence.

....

"What about Jeremiah's blood on the floor" Isabella enquired.

They had all began to look around at the room that was never-ending. The door looked miniscule in the vast space filled with paper scrolls, books, artefacts, that spanned centuries of earth's history.

"You are right Isabella, I need to go back to clean it up" Galene remarked, pulling the closet door back open. Galene stepped inside the closet. She closed the door and then she reopened it. "All done, It's all clean," she said, as she stepped back into the room with the broken pieces of wood.

"That's impossible, you have not been gone at all" Asher commented, in such confusion.

"Time and space can be distorted by certain events or places" Galene commented, before she scrunched her face at what she had just said.

"This room on the inside probably has no outside time in it" Isabella mumbled as she picked up a small Egyptian urn from a table. Jeremiah was already looking at some of the handwritten book titles that filled one of the many hundreds of twelve foot book shelves throughout the room. Jeremiah read out some of the bindings

"Leonardo DI ser Piero da Vinci (Leonardo da Vinci), Μαρία ἡ Μαγδαληνή, (Mary Magdalene), Jehanne la Pucelle, (Joan of Arc)… Who are all these people?" he said, as he flipped the pages of Μαρία ἡ Μαγδαληνή. He placed the book back on the shelf. Asher had spotted a large sword embedded in a stone boulder. He tried to pull it out, but it remained firmly in place. Isabella was stroking a piece of fur stretched across a wooden frame. The fur released golden, orange crystals which fell to the floor; Asher's hand began to glow as the crystals fell.

"It must be the *Golden Fleece*" Isabella said, as her hand glowed from the touch as she began reading a brown label tied to the stand. She also glanced over at Asher and smiled at him. Galene approached a large round table directly under the single hanging light bulb. The table was carved with names. She began to walk around the table reading the names, Ιησοῦς, Μαρία, Ιωαννης, Παῦλος..."
She was also quite shocked that she knew each of the names in translation.

"Jesus, Maria (Mary), John, Paul... Mmmm! I thought the table was long not circular" she said, running her fingers into the carvings. There were numerous scrolls unravelled upon the wooden surface. Below by the foot of the table lay a few boxes with paper labels hanging from them.

"I think I have found something, there is a green crystal weighting this scroll on the table. I think we will be able to read it if I can find a spell to translate it." Galene pulled the small spell book from her bag.

Asher was fascinated with the sword. He kept trying to pull it out of the boulder. Jeremiah was still flicking through the many books filling the hundreds of bookcases,
"Who is *Joannes Gutenberg*? This book has got a Yellow cover? He must be important!"

Galene had enlarged the spell book on the floor, as it was easier to kiss the clasp. Using her *Find spell*, the pages began flicking, flipping over and over.

Isabella grabbed the yellow book from the Jeremiah's hands

"Let me see that." She stated, holding it in her hands, she flicked the pages. "Interesting, he was a printer from Germany, the Germany that is now burning all the books"

"How do you do that? It's very unnerving" Jeremiah grinned at Isabella, who had pulled yet another yellow book off the shelf,

"Ἀρχιμήδης - Archimedes - this is a book about a man" she flicked the pages before opening it onto the centre of the book where she placed her palm.

"He was a scientist, a mathematician. He changed how we view the world. He helped Galene, strange as it seems, they all helped... GALENE" Isabella dropped the book on the floor in shock. "That's impossible, how can this be, you did not hear what I just said Jeremiah, do not repeat it to anyone as it could change the new future, or is it the past. It is so confusing" she grabbed Jeremiahs hands, and held them tightly between her own,

"Promise me, this is our secret for now and eternity"
Jeremiah was unsure of Isabella's proposition, but he agreed with her anyway.

....

Galene began chanting her spell over the scroll on the table. Jeremiah, Asher and Isabella ran to the table to see what it was that she had found. Asher got a little too close to Galene; the broom knocked him off his feet.

The symbols on the scroll began changing temporarily, to readable text. Galene was shocked as she saw her name directly at the top of the scroll...

Chapter 10

Burning

03rd August 1943, 23:58.

SS-Sturmhauptführer Heinz Bieg-Brauchitsch departed the house, still tasting the blood of Jeremiah. He knew that the boy was still in the building somewhere.

"Surround the buildings, on my command you will burn them to the ground" He instructed. Three soldiers began spreading kerosene, over the wooden floors of each building. They drenched the furniture with the flammable liquid. In Jeremiah's house they tipped the kerosene down the stairwell to the lower ground floor, into the kitchen.

Heinz pulled a whistle from his pocket. He was unable to blow it due to his tongue was now obstructing the flow of air from his mouth. He gave the whistle to Frederick to blow. Heinz removed his dark sunglasses to see the event clearly. He raised his hand high in an attempt to signal Frederick to give the instruction. The three soldiers had finished dousing the buildings; Heinz dropped his hand, at the same time Frederick blew hard on the metal whistle. Numerous soldiers lit pieces of cloth to ignite when instructed.

Whoosh, the flames spread through the buildings so fast, that the glass in the windows, exploded from within.

"We shall see if those boys try to escape the flames, if they do I want them alive. Instruct the soldiers!" Heinz conveyed to

Frederick. The flames eventually hit the roof of the buildings, tiles slid off, smashing onto the ground below. All the soldiers waited for the boys to coming running out. The fire lit the night sky. The heat and light was so intense, that Heinz had to replace his sunglasses.

One hour passed by, the houses began to collapse; bricks fell from the high walls outwards onto the footpaths.

"That is enough; they could not have survived that fire. Take me back to Treblinka. The shambolic escape that took place there needs to be investigated. I will personally deal with those responsible- accordingly. I believe that there were also reports of the girl. She was seen by a soldier who said that she fell into a mine shaft, I need you to find me that soldier for questioning!" Heinz stated to Frederick who opened the car door. Black ash fell from the sky covering the bonnet, but was blown away as he drove off at speed.

....

The wood inside the houses was crackling with the intense fire, it whined as each piece of wood snapped in two. The floors tumbled down into the basements. The closet door in the basement of Jeremiahs house caught fire, as burning wood which lay up against it ignited the old timber. The crystal painting on the inside of the door began to bubble and blister from the heat. Eventually a flame appeared in the centre of the artwork. The crystal darkened before it disappeared from view. The painting had now been destroyed by the flames. The door was also destroyed.

The closet was gone.

Chapter 11

Tic Toc Ticker

The mysterious room held many artefacts from many centuries gone by. Jeremiah wanted to explore more of the vast space that stored them all. Isabella arrived at the table to view Galene's name clearly at the top of the scroll. Jeremiah had remained miffed at to how or why this could be. Asher never had a chance to see the scroll as the broom kept brushing him away. Instead, he went exploring some of the hidden treasures that lay about nearby, within the cavernous room. Suddenly, there was an almighty crash from somewhere further in the vault of a room. It echoed back towards the table,

"What on earth was that? I think somebody else must be in here with us. But surely that is not possible" Isabella whispered. Galene shrugged it off as she looked at the scroll,

Galene

You are probably used to all the surprises by now.

We have waited through many tics and toc's for this day to arrive. With your help, the journey will be finally complete. You see- the resolution is also the problem.

Once completed we will all be free.

The book as you know is incomplete.

Below this scroll on the table is a Tic Toc ticker.

You will figure out what it does… when you remember.

I have to go… we all wait!
Superior De#########

The remainder of the name was scribbled out and was unreadable! Galene lifted the scroll to see a small object.

Asher was still engrossed with the sword, which was firmly wedged within the rock boulder. He thought that he would give it another go that is to remove it. His efforts still remained the same. The sword would not budge from the rock. As he pulled extremely hard, he fell backwards onto the hard floor, catching a glimpse over his shoulder of the door that was burning.

"Jeremiah, quickly… the door… it's on fire" he yelled.

Jeremiah ran to see the final remains of the door being sucked into a swirling portal, similar to the one that they had travelled through from their Warsaw home. The door had gone. All that remained was the wall as a burping sound could be heard…

"How do we get out of here?" Asher started crying.

Isabella arrived to comfort him. She placed her arms around his body. Asher began to glow a golden orange, Isabella began to glow violet. Jeremiah shouted,

"Galene come here, quickly, you have to see this!"

Galene ran from the table. She stood staring at the colour's that came from them both. It was then she realized the door had disappeared.

"The door…Where is it?" she screamed, "What have you done?"

Isabella finally let go of Asher, her body returned to normal. Jeremiah spoke calmly,

"What happened...? Asher...? What happened to the door? Tell Galene, what you saw"

"It was burning, flames jumped from its surface. As I watched, it was pulled into one of those holes that- WE all went through!"

Galene began to pace back and forth, her hands rubbed over the wall where the door once was. "Mmmm," she mumbled, "we shall have to solve this problem sometime later. We have got to figure out what we need to do with this *Tic Toc Ticker*. She began walking back to the table, Jeremiah followed her. Isabella grabbed Asher's hand,

"Come with me, I saw why you are here" She said, as they both walked towards the sword.

"Remove it for me Asher. Take the sword out of the stone. Believe in yourself, believe in the power that you have. I want you to Imagine standing on the top of the mountain, then screaming that you finally did it. That is, you reach the top to save the world, and the satisfaction, plus the fact that its greatest achievement that you alone accomplished it" Isabella smiled, watching Asher who was stood on top of the boulder. His thoughts of confidence showed through his body posture. An orange halo suddenly appeared around his hands, the rock released the sword, and Asher fell backwards again, but this time with a rather large, cumbersome sword in his hand.

"See what I mean, you now believe in your own self, the sword also agrees with you"

Isabella began to walk slowly back towards the table,

"Are you coming?" she laughed inwardly.

Asher jumped to his feet. He could not lift the heavy sword. So he began to drag it along the floor. The sheer weight of it created sparks, which flew off the tip of the blade. Already at the table, was Jeremiah with Galene holding a very slim, paper thin clear object?

"What is it?" Isabella asked,

The noise of the sword being dragged along the floor made Jeremiah's teeth, grind together.

"Asher, put down the sword, you need to come on over here!" he said.

Asher dropped the sword, it crashed to the floor. The sound echoed throughout the space.

"Wowser, what is it?" Asher reached out his hand to touch it, but the broom flew over, slapping his arm away.

"It's very strange; we need to figure out what it is! It was underneath the scroll" Galene remarked, placing the object back on the table. The object see-through, but very shiny, it was the size of a small envelope, but light as a feather with no frame around the edging. Galene passed it to Isabella to see if she could feel anything. She just shrugged her shoulders, for she felt nothing from holding the object. Asher ran to Isabella, as she was about to pass it to Jeremiah,

"Let me have a look at it, please," he said, taking the object out of Isabella's hands. He turned it over viewed the others through it. Jeremiah took the object from him. He laid it flat on the scroll.

"I just wish they would have left instructions with this"

"I know it's now a stalemate. Until we figure out what or how to use it, we are now stranded" Galene stated.

Galene began to unroll more scrolls to see what they were about. They revealed historical facts about places or people. "It's like being in a Library" She said, "yet there is something quite strange and familiar about all these records"

"Strange... how very familiar?" Isabella said as she scrutinised Galene's statement.

"I have this uncanny feeling that I know what all of these are. These scrolls, books, artefacts that fill this room" Galene remarked, picking up a book on *Anne Boleyn*.

Asher was back with the sword, he was scraping it across the floor, pulling it towards the table.

Isabella grabbed Galene's hand. She held it tight as a source of comfort.

"I can only guide you, please remember that Galene. This room will happen for you -one day soon. That's all I can say at this moment as I cannot corrupt the future... our future"

Galene smiled back. She glanced around the endless space of artefacts before staring back down at the table.

"You are totally right Isabella. I need to focus on now, this very moment. I have to think what *'Ma'* would have done in this situation"

Jeremiah grabbed the sword from the hand of Asher. He helped him lift the sword near to the table. He noticed the handle had a large orange crystal inlaid in a clasp at the top...

"Give me your hand Asher" Jeremiah lunged for Asher's hand. He grabbed it tightly at his wrist.

"You glowed orange when you hugged Isabella earlier, maybe, just maybe!" Jeremiah placed Asher's hand, upon the crystal. It lit up. The warmth came through Asher's hand into his arm. The sword began to shrink as it floated off the floor. Asher's hand was pulled off the crystal, as it began to fly above his head. He stepped backwards, the sword dropped into his hand. It was now small enough for him to hold. Asher began to swish the sword in a childish, pretend combat. He knocked a challis off a pedestal. The challis made from Pewter hit the book shelf before falling to the ground.

"Please you two…. Be quiet! I am trying to think here" Galene shouted. Both of them made hushing noises to each other whilst smirking. Galene picked up the scroll yet again. She noticed at the far top right hand corner a symbol. It was a *Nonagon*. It was very faint, but still very much visible. She rubbed her finger over it twice.

"Interesting, I wonder what this mark is." She said.

Isabella moved closer to see the scribed mark. Smiling, she called Jeremiah over to the table. Galene was still looking at the scroll. Isabella nudged her, as she swiped her finger across the symbol yet again. Galene glanced upwards to see the same shape on Jeremiahs face illuminate a bright white.

"A key, you are the key Jeremiah to this *Ticker*. You need to do something to unlock this mystery of the *Tic Toc Ticker*" she said.

Jeremiah just laughed, as he thought it was utter nonsense, until Isabella held up the paper thin time *ticker* for him to see his reflection. The closer the ticker got to Jeremiah the more vibrant the symbol got on his face.

"Here hold this" Isabella gave the *Tic Toc ticker* to Jeremiah once again. "Do what you think is the right thing to do with it – don't think about anything, just do it!"

Another loud noise echoed through the room, this time it was close by. Asher shouted,

"Who's there, come out now!" Asher was still swishing the sword, knocking items from shelves. He had not noticed what was happening around the table. Jeremiah now had a hold of the *ticker,* at first he just held it in his hand, then he crumpled it into a ball, it unravelled. He rolled it like a newspaper, it unravelled itself again.

"I don't know what to do with it" He remarked, throwing it up in the air, back towards the table. The ticker glided downwards, it was as light as a feather. Then it stopped above the table. It was hovering, just waiting for something to happen. Nothing did happen, so it continued to fall once more, until it came to rest on the scroll.

Asher knocked even more items on the floor. He laid the sword on the floor to pick them up. A book named Ζεύς Zeus) followed by a book with the title Γαῖα (Gaia). Gaia, the cover was orange, the cover lit up like a beacon in the night, the beam of light shone upwards towards the ceiling. Jeremiah, Galene and Isabella turned around from the table. Asher dropped the book. He picked it up again, the book shone brightly once more.

"What is that book that you are holding onto?" Galene asked. Asher carried it to the table; he placed it in front of her, the glow stopped. Asher went back to playing with the sword. He was pretending to fight with some long embroidered gowns hanging on leather body mannequins. He was pretending to stab them. Another crashing noise was heard very close by but too far to explore to see what or where the noise was coming from.

 Galene picked up the book,

"*Gaia...* The mother of the earth, she was the mother of all the gods. I knew her well. My family...."

"You knew her well? My family?" Jeremiah was smirking whilst saying it.

"I don't know what made me say that, it's as if...."

Isabella placed her hand to Galene's mouth to shush her.

"The *time ticker*, you need to concentrate on the *time ticker*. The book is not important at this very moment," she said.

Galene once again picked up the ticker.

"Of course, it is so obvious. Why did I not realise this when Jeremiah was standing here. He is the key, well not him, but the symbol... the symbol is the key"

Jeremiah watched as Galene threw the ticker into the air again, she had just remembered about the Ticker. The symbol on Jeremiah's face glowed. Galene drew the symbol with her finger on the now floating ticker that was just above the table. Asher came running over to see what was happening. He was disappointed that it did not involve him, so he began to play fight once more with the mannequins. He arranged all three of them to face him.

"Three against one...eh- take that? We shall see who wins this battle..." He shouted at them, as he lunged forward with the sword.

The *ticker* stopped moving in mid-air just above the table. Numbers began to appear in bubbles above the ticker along with months of the year all in *Greek*. Galene pushed a number zero- the number appeared projected below the ticker. She continued to write *todays date* followed by the time of a few moments ago. She typed the place as *here*. It flashed up in bright light, the place *"here"* as *"Crystalaura04"*. A question appeared, "Save this place to the database? Yes or No" *(written in Greek)*. Galene pushed yes in the bubble as she understood the language quite clearly.

Galene held onto Jeremiah's and Isabella's hand.

"Are you ready? I just hope this is correct in what we are about to do." Galene took a firm grip on the *tickers* edge before throwing it high into the air. Galene, Jeremiah, Isabella, were pulled with it. The *ticker* size grew to a large size, as they were all dragged through the reflective panel. The last part of Galene's hand remained firmly gripped, stretched to the *ticker's* edge. It inverted itself before it flipped into the hole, with a popping bubble sound.

....

Asher was talking to the mannequins. He had not noticed that the others had disappeared. He turned to face the table to see that they had gone. Without warning Jeremiah grabbed his shoulder from behind him.

"Where did you come from?" Asher screamed out, dropping the sword which nearly pierced his foot.

"We have just left the vault, then we returned quite a few minutes ago, all that noise was us three crashing into things. It's very dimly lit further into this room" Jeremiah was brushing cobwebs from his clothing. Isabella emerged wiping the cobwebs from her face. Galene paraded out from the darkness wearing a black, long flowing cloak.

"Do you think this suits me?" It's real, fine silk. Look how it flows" she said, trying to see it clearly in the light. The material was finely embroidered with silk thread. The full length gown fitted Galene perfectly, covering the ripped trouser suit. It resembled that of a *headmaster's gown*. Her *tattoo* below was now clearly visible; it had grown in size across her arm!

"It makes sense now... all the other noises we heard were made by you three, when you returned to the room a few moments ago... So there is no one else in here, it was you all along" Asher wisely commented.

Isabella kissed Asher on his forehead,

"Cannot really say if we are alone Asher, it would take days, maybe months to explore it thoroughly. May I also add that you are learning fast? My help with your development will be short-lived, I would think"

Galene placed the *Tic Toc Ticker* back on the table. She lifted the scroll yet again, only to see that the text had converted back to the original hieroglyphic text. Jeremiah jumped up on the edge of the table to sit down. He sat upon the name Πέτρος – *(Simon)*. The table began to move, it spun towards the right. Galene grabbed the table edge to stop it moving. The centre of the table remained still, only the outer circumference with all the names moved. Galene pulled the table back to its original position. Isabella was by one of the bookshelves. She was flicking through the pages of *Florence Nightingale*. The cover was orange, so she took it over to Asher. She passed him the book, whilst he was in one of his deep fight sequences. Asher placed the sword down on the floor, before taking the book from Isabella's hand. The book glowed vibrant orange. Isabella took the book off him, before taking another green book from the shelf. Nothing happened with that book. So she removed a red book, still nothing happened. A bright light shone towards the ceiling when she picked up a purple covered book, the light was violet. Asher picked his sword up from the floor.

"Interesting to see all these books are colour coded" Isabella said, picking up another purple coloured book from the shelf. It began to glow violet as Isabella read the name from the cover for herself, *Daniel Douglas Home*.

Isabella picked up a green, yellow, red and blue book. She wanted to test both Galene and Jeremiah for their colours. Jeremiah was watching Galene near the table. Isabella placed all the three books on the rotating outer circumference. She then pushed the outer ring until all three books were in front of Galene. She picked up the Red book. Instantly, it was the brightest light seen so far. It pierced the cavernous rooftop, until it spread sideways highlighting all of the misshaped ceiling.

"Wow, you obviously have great strength. I can sense that your power is growing day by day" Isabella remarked stepping backwards from the light.

Galene placed the book on the table; she read the cover title out loud,

"*Harry Houdini* - Obviously, I see that you have figured something out about this archive of information. Do tell?" Galene asked, but Isabella remained silent as she turned the table further around to Jeremiah. Jeremiah picked up the green book, nothing happened, Isabella willed him to pick up the blue book as she had already read the title of the person upon it. Jeremiah's hand reached slowly for the book. His finger just touched the cover. A bolt of blue lightning hit the ceiling with such force that it thundered. Asher dropped the sword. Books fell from all the shelves.

"Stop Jeremiah… before you and your power destroy this place and all of us with it" Galene cried out.

Jeremiah removed his finger quickly from the cover. The thunder, along with the blue lightning ceased immediately. Jeremiah glanced over to read the title of the person on it.

"Ζεύς, I think it translates as Zeus"

"It does translate as Zeus, You have great power Jeremiah. You may not know it or know how to use it yet. In time you will figure out what you can use your power for" Isabella said, pulling the table back towards her to remove the books,

"We all have a gift, Jeremiah you have power, Galene you have strength, and this is also emphasized by your magic. Asher you have the healing capabilities, whilst I have

153

vision, the ability to see beyond our own thoughts. I know exactly how these books came to be. It's not fate that has brought us together... its destiny."

Galene called her broom with a wolf whistle, which had disappeared when the thunder started. The broom flew back to her side still shaking its bristles.

"Our future... It seems you may know, or have seen too much Isabella" Jeremiah commented. Isabella smiled at Jeremiah before taking the books back to the shelf, from where she had removed them. Asher Knocked a mannequin over, the cloak on the body caught on a hook before it fell over. It tore the cloth of the pocket allowing a small package to tumble to Asher's feet. Asher picked it up immediately, it had Galene's name etched on the smooth surface. He carried it to the table, placing it in front of Galene.

"Here- look what I have found" Asher stated.

Galene looked at the small box. She picked it up from the surface to inspect it closely. She ran her finger over the etching.

"The writing on the box is mine!" she recognised the signature. Jeremiah leant forward as she popped the lid off. Inside the box were seven small objects. She removed one for inspection. It was the size of a grain of rice. The object had a fine piece of hair protruding from one end.

"What on earth is it?" Jeremiah asked, as Galene handed the item to him. Galene removed a piece of paper from the lid of the box. It was marked as *Instruction*, it was written by her own hand in Greek... She read it out,

"Place the object within your ear whilst lying on your side. Hold onto the long strand until the item grips tightly. Once it is firmly in place… let go of the strand. The object will do the rest. The object is called a *Wiz-T*. It will help you understand every language. It will help you talk in every language."

"Wow that would be amazing if it was so!" Jeremiah gave the *Wiz-T* back to Galene. Galene tilted her head sideways before lowering the *Wiz-T* into her ear. Jeremiah stood back watching as the object lodged onto her inner ear. Galene let go of the *Wiz-T*. The fine strand began to grow. It wrapped itself around her earlobe, it entwined across the opening, back and forth, back and forth until the earlobe had completely been covered by what appeared to be a fine stitched cloth. The strand continued down towards the mouth, it made its way up through the nostril down her throat to her vocal box. It entwined around the vocal chords. In a matter of minutes Jeremiah had watched the object take over Galene's ear and face.

"It seems to have stopped growing" He said, as Galene raised her head upwards.

"Does it feel any different; can you feel it on your skin?"

"No, I can't feel it at all."

At that precise moment a clicking noise was heard by both of them, as the object turned itself on. Galene heard a faint buzzing noise at first, but that subsided as the *Wiz-T* began to camouflage itself against her own skin.

"I cannot see it anymore, it seems to have disappeared" Jeremiah said, trying to see if he could still touch it. "So what does it do?"

Galene picked up the scroll from the table, Galene began to read the hieroglyphics. A bright light appeared in her right eye with the text *Egyptian*. She heard herself speaking normally whilst Jeremiah heard her talking an unknown language to him, that being of Egyptian.

"You are speaking gobbledygook... I cannot understand a word of it!" Jeremiah tried his hardest to listen to the noises coming from Galene's mouth.

Galene spoke to Jeremiah,

"That's strange as I could see everything written on the scroll as normal translated text. Even when I spoke to you, it was perfectly natural. The object even told me what the language was. I could not hear any translation. This surely cannot be from this earth as it is way too advanced." She said, touching her ear to see if she could feel it. Isabella picked one up out the small box,

"Mmmm, it seems it is from earth, I can sense it. It's from the future. Maybe somebody retrieved it from the future! I cannot say too much as you know..." Isabella handed the lid to Galene, tapping her index finger on the name scribed upon to it.

Isabella then tilted her head to one side, before dropping one into her ear also. Galene had the opportunity of watching it expand before it fixed itself to her face. She also watched it become transparent. Isabella removed another one from the box,

156

"I shall make sure Asher gets this one," she said,
Galene had already begun to manoeuvre one gently into Jeremiahs ear. Isabella was shaking the tiny item in front of Asher's face, as she approached him. Asher slammed the sword into the bookcase so hard it pierced deep into the wood through to the other side, just missing a purple book on *levitation*. The book retracted itself from the blade point, pushing tightly against the other stacked books before it fell off the shelf. It began levitating upwards to the next shelf which had space for it to rest. Isabella removed the sword with three mighty tugs. She fell backwards onto the gown that Asher had knocked over from the mannequin.

Galene had retrieved her spell book once more from her bag. She had laid it on the large table before she enlarged it.

"What are you doing now?" Jeremiah enquired, as he was reading the Egyptian scroll to himself –it was now translated He quickly read out loud the translation projection on his retina to himself, *"Egyptian"*.

"I feel it's time for the book to tell us all what we need to do." She said, kissing the clasp. Flicking over the large pages with two hands with the aid of Jeremiah, who asked? "What spell are you looking for?"

"I will know when I see it" Galene said, as she turned to the centre page." Although, it's not looking very good at the moment… as you can see, I am already half way through!"

Isabella approached the table with Asher. They stood either side of the Galene as she turned the book to where the missing page was supposed to be. The ripped edge of the page still remained in the book,

"Wait... there is a page missing" Jeremiah indicated, placing his hands on the torn strip. Isabella reached out her hand to touch the torn strip as well.

"It's the starting point" Isabella whispered to Galene.

"Are you sure? How do you know? What if we are getting all this wrong? I wish my *Ma* was here to help!"

"She is with you all the time, just ask her Galene? Isabella whispered yet again.

Isabella guided Galene's hands, placing them firmly on the book. Jeremiah stepped backwards, removing his hands from the page.

"Just ask her Galene"

"Ma, I love you Ma! What am I to do? Do I need to find the missing page? Help me Ma" Galene asked as a teardrop ran down her cheek.

Jeremiah grabbed onto, Isabella's hand.

A ghostly figure rose from the open page. There was no face, just an outline. Galene removed her hand in shock, she stepped backwards very quickly. The ghostly figure disappeared.

"I think that you have to keep your hand on the page" Isabella remarked.

Galene placed her hand back on the page. She asked again. The ghostly figure appeared once more. It seemed to be looking around at all of them stood by the table. A stick appeared,

"Isn't that a broom?" Asher stated, trying to touch it.

The ghostly stick shook.

"What are we to do next Ma?" Galene asked yet again as she peered upwards at the figure. The ghostly stick pointed to the missing page. The torn edge flickered like a beacon upon a misty sea.

"So I see -we must retrieve the page. But how do we do so? Where is the page? Help me Ma…"

An image of the *Tic Toc Ticker* appeared as a ghostly form. It highlighted shadows of dates, times, places in clouds of smoke. The *Ticker* then disappeared in a cloud of swirling smoke. The book slammed shut, Galene just managed to pull her hand free from the page as it shrank to a small size without Galene's intervention.

"This book…. Sometimes, I think this book has a mind of its own!" She said, shaking her hands above the cover in disapproval. Isabella touched the cover, she began to frown.

Jeremiah tried to make sense of the clues, whilst Asher picked a book up off the floor by the table.

أبو القاسم ﷴ

The projection from the Wiz-T on his eye translated as - *Abu Muhammad.*

"This book has no colour, I wonder why that is? "Asher questioned Isabella. Isabella placed her hand on top of the outer cover, "Put it back Asher, it has no colour as it has not been placed in history as yet. Its history is still within this room only. Some items here are…" Isabella stopped herself from saying anymore.

"Are what? What are you trying to say Isabella?" Asher asked, as he bent over to put the book back in the same spot on the floor.

"It…it does not matter; all I will say is that this room has patience. Time means nothing! We have started… shall I dare to say at step six of the ladder, but seemed to have missed out the many steps that are below"

Isabella placed her hand on Asher's shoulder as he stood upright. Galene began to piece some of the clues together. Her thought process was interrupted by Isabella's own thoughts, as she could feel them, even hear them.

"Yes, Galene, at this current time it is about the book, I know all about the missing pieces just the same as you do." Isabella grabbed tightly onto Galene's hand, "We shall all do this together."

Jeremiah touched the cover of 'Zeus' once more where Isabella had returned it to the shelving. He wanted to see if it was just a fluke what happened earlier on. The thunderbolt shot to the ceiling, jolting many books off the shelving. It made Galene stumble forward,

"Jeremiah, you scared the life out of me. What on earth are you playing at?" She said, but Jeremiah was laughing.

"Sorry! I just couldn't resist."

CRASH!

"What on earth was that? It came from over there!" Asher pointed with his finger to a darkened area amongst a group of Roman Statues. Jeremiah, moved closer to see if he could see anything. Galene had already begun reciting a magic spell that she had memorised,

"Darkest gauean, distira hain distiratsua , buelta harri honen argitan "sartu"

"Darkest night, shine so bright, turn this rock into a light"

The spell confused everyone apart from Galene, who was saying it! The spell was never translated by the *Wiz-T*. Jeremiah thought the *Wiz-t* had stopped working. He began to bang on his ear ever so lightly to jolt the *Wiz-T* back into service.

"It's ok Jeremiah; mine is not translating it as well. I don't think that we are allowed to hear the translation, or know the spell" Isabella whispered, as she moved closer to Galene, who at the same time had touched the statue of *Julius Caesar* in front of her. *Caesar* began to illuminate, a radiant glow sent a light in towards the darkness to where the noise came from. As they searched they found nothing, apart from a faint smell of lilies. The scent wafted across Jeremiah's nose. Getting closer to a statue covered by a black material throw, he pulled the cover fast off the figure to reveal the statue of *Medusa (a woman with snake hair, her piercing stare would turn you to stone)*

"That perfume smells familiar..." Jeremiah was inhaling the cloth deeply, it smells like you Isabella"

"Sure it does, but it is not me as I am over here as you can plainly see" Isabella sniped.

Galene touched the light of Caesar to turn it off. The bright light began to fade slowly as they moved back towards the table. "This room is playing tricks upon us... I am sure of it!" Jeremiah stated.

Asher returned to the table with another item. He placed it on the circumference of the table for all to see.

"What is it Galene?" he asked as he spun it around to her.

Galene picked the item up. She tilted it sideways before passing it along for Jeremiah to look at. He then passed it to Isabella, to obtain information from it. She felt nothing. It was then passed back to Galene.

"Once again, it seems vaguely familiar. It's as if! But that would be impossible."

"What would be impossible?" Isabella winked at Galene.

"That it belongs to me that I have held this item before, even go as far as to say that I have used this item before"

Galene spun the item around in her hand. The cylindrical, tubular shape the size of a scrubbing brush had no markings. It was smooth to touch, grey in colour, it almost felt warm.

"Any ideas what it is?" Jeremiah asked

Asher got bored of waiting for an answer; he had spotted the fading light of the Caesar statue, so he drew his sword in readiness for combat.

Galene twisted the two ends of the tube. It clicked open in the middle. A small door allowed a mist to escape from the opening. Galene immediately dropped the item onto the table, "Step back, it could be poisonous" she yelled.

All three of them stepped backwards....The mist billowed out, but remained connected to the tube.

A shape formed from the mist...

Chapter 12

Upon Completion

04th August 1943

Treblinka was to be closed fully, as per instruction from the High officials at the Reich Headquarters in Berlin. German *SS-Obergruppenführer Schmidt* had also sent a message requesting an update regarding the girl from Heinz. All evidence that the camp ever existed was to be eliminated. Heinz made it his mission to dispose of those involved with the escape of the girl. He now found out, that she helped two boys escape on that very night. The *Austrian* soldier who watched his friend *Fritz* fall into the pit, spoke with such confidence that the children must have died in the fall as well. Heinz assured him of his error in assuming it all too easily. Frederick had to clean the room after Heinz had left it. All that remained was a charcoaled body surrounded by yellow crystals.

Fredrick walked with Heinz, as he made his way across the field to the mine shaft. Frederick saw the changes that had taken place over the months that he had assisted Captain Heinz.

Heinz transformation was nearing completion. He no longer walked, but seemed to glide across the ground. Frederick had to hop and skip to keep up with him. As much as it was extremely bizarre, Frederick obeyed his command in fear of his own life.

They finally reached the edge of the shaft. Frederick peered downwards, he felt dizzy through his fear of heights. Heinz carried on gliding above the precipice. He was hovering directly above the gaping hole. He began to lower himself into the hole, to where he saw the passageway. He sniffed deeply, he could smell Galene. Frederick watched him reappear above ground. He had removed his sunglasses; his eyes shone bright red. As a wolf in the night- he stared at Frederick.

"All of them were here; I need you to find, out- where that tunnel goes. Find me the map that shows this land" He growled before placing his sunglasses back on his face. Frederick began to run off in the direction of the camp.

Heinz landed by the edge of the pit. He raised his arms high. His skin began to fall to the ground from his face. The similarities of a snake shedding its skin on growth, so had Heinz. His eyes glowed vibrant red as he summoned from the pit the body of the German soldier, Heinz made a gesture to flip the broken body over.

"The girl, she was with other children, how many children was she with? Tell me so."

The dead body spoke, despite being rigid with rigormortis. The mouth cracked open.

"She was with two young boys; she helped them escape from the camp. That's all I know," he said.

"You have done well, I shall let you rest- forever" Heinz uttered whilst creating a fireball in his hand. He threw the ball with such force towards the body that it caught fire instantly. Heinz released the body back into the pit. There

was a thud as it hit the bottom. Smoke wafted out from the opening.

Heinz began to remove his clothing to let the skin from his body fall to the floor. His new body now resembled the smoothness of a dolphin but it also appeared as a silver metallic flexible coating. There was no imperfections, no kinks, no indentations, just a smooth outline of what appeared to be a man-shape. He threw his body skin into the pit.

Heinz managed to get fully dressed just as Frederick was running back towards the mine shaft with a map. Frederick saw Heinz, shiny grey face hidden behind the sunglasses. The peak cap never covered all of his head. Frederick was staring at the metallic looking grey sheen, he wanted to touch his body to see if it was metal, but he didn't dare. Frederick unrolled the map onto the grass pointing out the mine shaft in relation to *Treblinka Camp* to Heinz.

"So the tunnel... runs to a farm building close by" Heinz glided in the direction of the farm building, *"Bring the car to the farm, meet me there"* He firmly stated, smoothly floating off into the distance across the field towards some trees.

Heinz ran back the car, which was parked by the high fenced gates of *Treblinka.* The German soldiers had already begun dismantling the railway station building as the camp was going to be disbanded. It was going to be removed from existence in time, but not from memory. The smoke billowed from beyond, as two large fire pits blazed.

"Where is the Captain?" the German gate Guard enquired.

"He has gone ahead in search of a farmhouse, I shall join him soon" Frederick replied, *"Have you begun the eradication of the camp, as per instructed by the Captain?"*

"Yes, it has begun. It will inevitably take some time, due to the amount of prisoners that we have here. We keep receiving more and more each day. It's a daunting task, to which I don't agree, but I have to do for my country, the future of Germany, the future of all the German people!"

"Then let it be so" Frederick replied, opening the door of the car, *"May god have mercy on us all!"*

"Heil " the German-Austrian soldier replied, raising his hand high to salute.

As the car drove off into the distance, Frederick looked in the rear view mirror to see flames. Smoke from behind the fake railway station within the boundaries of the camp billowed upwards into the sky. When Frederick arrived at the farmhouse, Heinz had already arrived, just waiting by the disused, derelict building.

It did not take long for them both, to find the room below the barn. Down the tunnel, down towards the room was hidden by a feeding trough. The scraping on the floor of the trough being moved indicated fresh movement by someone. Frederick removed the torch from the glove box in the car. He approached Heinz warily. The beam of light shone into the tunnel which had many steps descending.

"You go first Frederick"

Frederick unclipped the safety harness. He removed a Black Handgun from the leather holster. He clicked off the safety catch to ensure the piece was live, holding the gun upwards as he descended. Heinz followed closely behind until they reached a door, which was slightly ajar. The light from the room shone through the gap. Frederick switched off the torch before pushing the door inwards. As he entered the room, a jar of apples fell from the shelf by the far wall.

BANG...

Frederick fired the gun. Heinz levitated in behind him.

"They have been here, I can smell them" Heinz said, sniffing really deeply to inhale the room. The faucet nozzle on the sink dripped water, rhythmically, drop by drop, before Frederick turned it anticlockwise to stop the noise. In the corner of the room, a pile of blankets began to move ever so slightly. Frederick grabbed the corner of the largest blanket. He pulled it vigorously. Beneath the cover was two children aged about twelve.

"What are you doing here?" Frederick asked, before realising they had Jewish stars stitched upon their clothing.

"Arrrh, they are escapees from the camp... Shoot them!" Heinz coldly remarked.

Frederick froze as he looked at the faces staring innocently back at him.

"Shoot them now that is... an order!"

Frederick closed his eyes, and then fired. The bullets lodged deep in the plaster wall, just above the children's heads. Both young girls screeched out, frightened.

'Please don't kill us, we have done no wrong'

Heinz grabbed the gun. He fired a bullet into each child. Both bodies slumped across each other. Heinz carried on searching the room for clues as to who Galene had become friends with. Frederick could not move, the shock of not being able to fire the gun made him freeze to the spot. He observed blood trickle slowly from one of the young Childs mouth. Before he turned around to assist Heinz, a tear ran down his cheek.

Teeth marks in this green apple. I will be able to see one of them" Heinz stated removing the apple from the jar.

"Frederick, come here now"

Frederick wiped his cheek. His feet crunched through a crystalline substance on the floor. Heinz placed the apple on the shelf as he removed his glove. There was a bite mark in the fruit to which Heinz placed his finger. A green glow came from Heinz eyes down his arm into the tip of his finger. The apple core began to illuminate, before growing outwards an image of Asher's head, followed by his body.

"I have you in my memory now. I now know what you look like. You will now lead me to the girl"

Frederick observed the image flickering in front of his eyes. Asher's image was as clear as a photograph, but in colour and three dimensional.

Frederick continued searching the room for any other items. He avoided the corner with the two dead children. Near to the sink he found the Jewish star, which Galene had ripped off her clothing. He picked it up carefully using two fingers. Heinz held out the palm of his hand as Frederick laid the cloth for him to inspect.

"It is her.... I cannot get an image as there is not enough body fluid within the fibre. I know that she is still alive... very much alive!" Heinz crumpled the star watching it catch fire. *"Our task here is done Frederick. We may have left the house in Warsaw a little -too hastily! Take me back to Warsaw. I want the remains of the house searched"*

Heinz had already begun floating towards the door. Frederick followed, but stopped to glance at the two dead children's bodies.

He switched the light off before pulling the door closed.

Chapter 14

Wepwawet Union

The mist gathered... changing shape continually.

It finally condensed to form- the shape of a body. A voice spoke out to Galene, who was holding back the others with her arms, in some sort of defence. The voice echoed in the vast room from the cylinders, gaseous cloud.

"It's been a while *Master*, how can I help thee?"

Jeremiah gripped Isabella's hand tightly. Isabella reassured Jeremiah, by pulling him closer to her body. His breath warmed her neck. Isabella blushed.

Galene was flabbergasted as the language *dēmotikós* was projected on to her right eye, temporally blinding her *(Ptolemaic demotic language 400-30BC)*. The language was spoken by the mist as it was taking shape. The demotic Egyptian spoken words were translated by the *Wiz-T.*

Galene blurted out towards the ghostly figure.

"I am your master? How is this so? What do I call you? Have I called you before...? This is all so confusing!

Galene began to throw her arms up I the air as she was having a mini tantrum.

"Yes, Master, you have called me to assist you many times before. You have always been alone when you have done this" the figure stated, as he viewed the others.

The ghostly figure had the body of a man but the head of a Jackal (*wild dog*). Galene suddenly referred to the creature as *"Wepwawet"* in a sudden subconscious outburst. Isabella understood immediately what she meant, she whispered to Jeremiah whilst shaking nervously.

"Wepwawet, it's another name for *Anubis.* My father always told me that *Anubis* would come and take me, if I did not behave as a child" She now gripped Jeremiah's hand, even tighter…Jeremiah tried to hide the pain of his knuckles being crunched… "But I thought that *Anubis* was a myth… until now that is! He represents all the dead of Egypt. He opens your soul to find your fears"

The creature scanned the room, he stared directly at Jeremiah and Isabella stood behind Galene. Asher bashed the statue of *Caesar* with his sword. *Wepwawet* turned suddenly to see Asher. He growled, not at Asher, but at the statue of *Medusa.*

"You have *Medusa* here. Do not let her escape again in this place, to wreak havoc once more. I see that she is in a deep sleep. Keep her that way."

Asher stopped what he was doing, as the roar of *Wepwawet* scared him so. His mouth fell open at seeing the dog head attached to the body of a man.

"So master, how can I help you?" *Wepwawet* asked yet again, whilst bowing over at Galene. Galene began to think. Her thoughts were being received by Isabella, who cried out,

"Ask for a new doorway to this room to be created"

The creature heard the comment from Isabella, but waited for Galene to speak.

171

"Create a new secret door to this room from the time and place that we originally entered from" Galene instructed.

Wepwawet lifted its spear high, before thrusting it in the air towards the clear, blank plastered wall. The wall sparked from the metal head as it pierced a small hole. The hole expanded outwards, until it was large enough for another door. Within seconds the door was in place, it slammed shut. The spear vaulted back into the hand of the *Wepwawet*. From the mist the *Wepwawet* retrieved a parchment with a green crystal painted onto it. He threw the painting towards Galene, who caught it.

"My task is complete Master, until next time…" The shape of the *Wepwawet* began to fade. The mist was drawn back into the silver tube. The small door of the tube closed. Galene opened the painting to reveal the green crystal. Jeremiah, Isabella came closer to view the painting. Asher turned suddenly towards the statue of *Medusa*; he thought that he had seen something move in the shadows. He turned his back to the movement. Then, using his sword, he viewed behind, with the edge of the blade as a reflective mirror. A figure moved yet again.

"Arrrh, I see you now" Asher turned around suddenly,

"Steady on! Asher" a voice replied.

Asher sighed, "How did you manage to get over here without me seeing you?"

Stepping out of the shadows into the fading light of *Caesar* was Isabella. Isabella's manner was somewhat different; she sunk her nails into Asher's arm.

"Ouch. You are hurting me" Asher squealed.

Jeremiah glanced across from the distance to see the Figure of Isabella by Asher. He then glanced at his side, to see Isabella stood beside him.

"You are here Isabella… so who is that over there with Asher?"

All three of them stared at the girl stood with Asher. She resembled Isabella.

Asher was in conversation with the girl, he had noticed she had a peculiar manner of pulling her hair forward across her face to hide her eyes. The girl tried to grab Asher's sword from his hand, but he resisted pushing her to the ground. It was then he realised this could not have been Isabella, for glancing over towards the table in the distance; he saw her standing by Jeremiah. Asher ran towards the table crying. The girl jumped to her feet in pursuit. Her eyes were revealed for the very first time. Red with rage, full of fire, she sent a flame ball towards Asher. The broom flew in from its stationary position from the table. It batted the ball of fire, back towards the girl who ducked to avoid it. Asher dived on the top of the table, knocking all the scrolls to the floor. The outer circumference spun him three hundred and sixty degrees. Galene held up her hands,

" Lurraren Gods, zeruaren Gods, encase piztia hau , bere etena egiteko "- "Gods of the earth, Gods of the sky, encase this beast, make her cease".

Galene whirled her hands, making a grabbing motion from above before throwing it towards the girl. From nowhere a gigantic glass bell jar fell on top of the girl. Splinters of glass chipped on the solid floor. She was trapped inside.

Galene stroked the outer glass. The girl inside the bell jar sat cowering on the dusty floor.

"Who are you? Where did you come from?" Galene asked, as Isabella placed both of her hands on the glass shell to view her. She sat trembling, pulling her hair.

"I'm Isobel; yes, that's who I am. I am Isobel"

She had read Isabella's thoughts as she peered through the glass. Isabella blocked her own thoughts immediately. Her face tightened as she did so.

"You can read minds too, I was just thinking how great it would have been to have a twin sister called Isobel" Isabella remarked amongst her now confusing thoughts. Isabella began to walk around the bell jar, towards the girl slumped on the floor. She signalled to Galene, with her hand to help her, before installing a thought into her head. Galene acknowledged the thought, by removing the book from her bag on the table. She began flipping through the large pages of the book to find a certain spell. Jeremiah was staring at Isobel through the glass, keeping her occupied. Asher was making noises as he lunged forward with the sword against a statue.

" *Kristalezkoa Sand, harea edalontzi - egin zure eskutik egokitzeko aldatu da* "- "*Sand of glass, glass of sand - make it change to suit thy hand*"

Galene reached out to touch part of the glass behind the girl. A hole formed, sand dropped to the floor like a waterfall from the opening. Isabella slipped her hand through the opening onto the Isobel's hair from the rear. The girl suddenly turned around. Her teeth were ready to

174

bite Isabella, who pulled her hand away fast. Galene released her hand from the glass. The sand reversed filling the hole quickly. It transformed back into thick glass.

"Well, did you manage to get the information Isabella? Was it long enough to find out who she is?" Galene enquired.

"Yes, I did so, she is me! I know that for sure. She is the evil part of me, which I keep suppressed. What I do know is that she has been here with us, all the time that we have been here in this room. She has been watching all of us. I have not figured out, how or why that she was separated from me yet. It must have been the *Tic Toc Ticker*. I am just guessing -Maybe, I am not supposed to figure that out, as it would corrupt our future"

Isabella touched the newly formed glass yet again, before walking back to the other side to view the reflected image of herself once more. "This is so damn freaky, knowing that part of me is in… this glass case"

Jeremiah placed his arm around Isabella's shoulder to comfort her. Galene was again, flicking the pages of the large spell book for answers. She turned once more to the centre where the page had been torn out.

"Look everybody, we must get back on track. We have to find this page. It may contain vital information as to why we were all brought together. We can deal with …Isobel later"

"You are right, Galene… Asher will you stop messing about with that statue, Get over here now!" Jeremiah shouted.

Asher ran past the glass dome, Isobel hissed as he did so. They all gathered around the table. Galene shrank the book to place back into her bag. She looked over at Isobel trapped in the glass dome.

"We cannot keep her trapped forever, we need to make a decision about her" Galene itched her brow, as she knew she would be the one to have to make the final decision. Asher spoke quietly,

"Let's send her through the door to *Warsaw*"

Asher had spoken so quietly, that Jeremiah had to ask him again to repeat what he had just said. Isabella replied,

"Yes. That may be the only solution at this present time. We cannot keep her prisoner, nor can we leave her here in this room of *magical artefacts*. She must be kept alive also, for I have not figured out, if she is supposed to be reunited with me at some point" Galene paced around the table, the broom followed, Asher began pacing behind her also, copying her movements exactly.

"Ok, I am not one hundred percent sure, but it is as you say- the only solution at this present time" Galene began to open the painting of the green crystal. We need to pin this on the inside of the door that was created by *Wepwawet*. We need some pins to do it. Asher ran to the clothing on the mannequins, to remove some pins pushed into the bodies. He handed them to Galene.

"Fantastic Asher, you are so helpful"

Asher blushed, but the broom brushed him backwards away from Galene.

Galene opened the door, she pinned the painting of the crystal on the back before closing the door again.

"Let's see if this works as the other door once did," she said, stepping into a newly formed closet. She closed the door, just after the broom had sneaked in with her." Galene began the spell

"Errebelatu hori ezkutuko, ikuspegi batetik ikusmena,

Erakutsi kristal errefraktoreak argia - Reveal the hidden, from the perspective of sight, Show crystals refracting light"

The crystal rose from the painting, she flipped it upside down before releasing it. She opened the door slowly from the closet.

"Where is this place? This is not the house"

Galene stepped outside the closet onto shards of broken glass. She now saw the door of the closet, it had been placed in the rear garden wall. She soon realised that it was the house, but it had been burnt to the ground. Galene inhaled deeply,

"So that's why the other door disappeared, it now makes sense why it caught fire, before disappearing. This will not do, the room is now too exposed to leave it fixed to a garden wall, we will only be able to use the doorway when needed... otherwise somebody else might figure out, how to get to *Crystalaura04*" Galene muttered to herself. The broom flew around the smouldering rubble... of what was the former house. Galene whistled for the broom to return to her side, before she stepped back inside the closet. As she closed the door to return back to the others, a car had pulled up on the roadside.

Galene stepped out of the closet back into Crystalaura04, she removed the painting. Isabella had somehow managed to climb high on top of a bookshelf to drop a book titled,

Max Nordau.

Tic toc 1849-1923 -Elder of Zion

Who had a gift of foresight?

Disputed – but true

She dropped into the opening at the top of the bell jar.

"What are you doing up there Isabella?" Galene shouted out, closing the door to the closet. Isabella dropped the book through the opening,

"Curiosity has got the better of me! I need to see if we are both the same," some of the pages of the book fell out of the binding on top of the glass casing, as she dropped it through the opening of the bell jar to the floor.

Isobel was hissing at Isabella perched on top of the bookcase. She saw the book on the floor. Galena watched as Isabel picked up the book. A blinding purple light shone up through the opening of the bell jar.

"I thought as much," Isabella blurted out, "we are the same apart from the light colour is of a different tone."

"But what does this prove? Why is it important?" Jeremiah shouted, upwards towards Isabella perched precariously on top of the shelving.

"I cannot answer that yet, I have not figured that part out. But somehow I know that we are all important. I hasten to say that... that includes Isabel as well!" she said, as she began her decent down the shelving. Isabella lost her footing, she slipped off the bookshelf. The ground was nearly fifty feet below. A book edged its way forward on the shelving. It began tapping on Isabella's hand to force her to let go ɪarɪs (Eris) the *Wiz-T* translated the book as Isabella glanced at the cover. The blinding light of the translation made her loose grip on the shelf. Books began to fall off the shelving, as she tried so desperately to grab on to something solid. Jeremiah began to run to the bottom of the shelving in a hope of catching her. Out of nowhere, from the darkness of the far room, the broom appeared. It swooped up Isabella's legs to prevent the fall. Isabella was now sat upon the stale. She gripped it tightly as it took her back to the table.

"Well done broom" Galene remarked, placing the green crystal painting back on the table.

Isabella's heart was pounding so fast. Jeremiah ran over to the table to comfort her.

Isobel had shredded the book in the bell jar. She sat upon the torn pages. A glowing purple haze of light sparkled above her head. Asher was taunting Isobel through the glass with his sword.

"I have seen the outside this room, the Warsaw house is destroyed. Our means of exit through the closet door, would give somebody an opportunity of finding this room" Galene remarked, pulling the *Tic Toc Ticker* from her bag,

"It seems our only means of getting out of this room at this present moment would be through this." Galene laid the *Ticker* on the table.

"But that will only take us to another time or place, and not our current time outside this room" Jeremiah stated, "as we cannot go to present time with It., Which means that we will no longer be able to search for my parents"

Isabella placed her arms around Jeremiah's waist,

"Galene will figure it out eventually... I am absolutely sure she will!" Isabella winked at Galene, who shyly nodded her head. Isobel began banging on the glass jar.

"She must be set free from the jar" Jeremiah pointed at Isobel. Asher hid himself behind Isabella. Galene remembered a spell from her book, which would make an invisible binding. This would enable for her to restrain Isobel upon release from the bell jar.

Isabella had already begun pinning the crystal painting back on the closet door.

"I will have to go in the closet with her to ensure she is released on the other side." Galene picked up the *Wepwawet* cylinder to aid her in her defence if anything should happen. She placed the cylinder inside her black robe. It was tucked neatly into her trouser suit. Galene moved closer to the jar before she began the spell from memory.

"Kristalezko alderantzizko ... ssalg - ssalg orain! "-

"Glass reverse... ssalg - ssalg now!" the glass jar began to disappear from the top opening. As it reached the height of Isobel, Galene began the next spell.-

"Whirling, aire- soka swirling , ongi objektu honi lotu, harrapaketa bat nire tranpa " en"-

"Whirling, swirling rope of air, binds this object tightly, Catch in my snare"

Galene began swinging her arms in the motion of a circle, before thrusting them forward towards Isobel, who was now trying to climb over the remainder of the jar. Isobel managed to climb over, she was running at Galene. A noose of light lassoed Isobel. Galene pulled hard on the light rope, only to see Isobel fall to the ground. She began hissing at Galene. Jeremiah ran to restrain Isobel on the hard floor. Isobel was lashing out, trying to break free.

Isabella approached, she stood above Isobel. Her thoughts were strong, as she bent over to touch Isobel's head.

"Sleep, you are feeling tired, sleep. Feel the trees sway in the breeze, feel the stream trickle to the sea, feel the warmth of the sun upon your face. You are tired. Your eyes are heavy, sleep"

Isabella was forcing the thoughts into Isobel's head. Isobel's eyes became heavy, she began to sleep. Her snoring made Asher laugh.

"How did you manage to do that?" Jeremiah was flummoxed. All he saw was Isabella touch Isobel's head.

"It was nothing. I told her that she was tired. It's no big deal," she replied smiling.

Galene brought the rope light in towards Isobel, who was now fast asleep on the floor.

"She will not be asleep for long, I have done this before. The sleep normally lasts for about ten minutes or so. That's all" Isabella commented, helping Galene pull the light rope onto Isobel.

"We must get her to the closet. On the count of three we shall all lift her... One - two - three."

As the closet was small it was difficult to manoeuvre Isobel's sleeping body inside, along with Jeremiah, Isabella and Galene. Asher was to remain in the room. He watched as they groaned, huffed at placing Isobel into an upright position. Asher forced the door closed. He saw the green crystal light appear from underneath the closet door. He stepped backwards, standing upon the brooms bristles. The broom was none too pleased; It brushed Asher off his feet onto the cold floor onto his backside.

....

Galene opened the closet door carefully, her head popped outside to see if the area was clear. There was nobody in sight, so she opened the door fully. As they carried Isobel out of the room, three, *"Arado Ar 96-B1"* (*unarmed German training pilot planes*) flew above their heads. They all ducked rapidly thinking that they were about to be fired upon. One of the pilots had spotted them, so he circled to fly back once more to see them, amongst the rubble of the burnt out houses.

"Quickly, we need to get out of here" Galene stated, out of breath from carrying Isobel.

They lay Isobel on a fallen piece of wall. She was beginning to wake up. Galene quickly removed the light rope,

"Argiaren Zuzenketa , free bistatik "-

"Spell of light, free from sight," she said, as she pulled on the rope light with a tug to release it. It disappeared as she did so. Isabella had already clambered over the rubble back

182

into the closet. She was followed quickly by Jeremiah. Galene began stumbling back across the broken red bricks when Isobel grabbed her ankle. She fell onto the charred smouldering remains of some clothing. Galene kicked out at Isobel, forcing her to release her grip. Galene clambered to her feet to run back to the closet. Just before she closed the door, she peered out to see that Isobel had stood upright, brushing off pieces of burnt wood from her dress. Galene pulled the door closed to return back to the room.

"She will be fine, I just know she will!" Isabella remarked, as Galene turned the green crystal.

Chapter 15

Warsaw Return

04th August 1943, Afternoon…

Heinz arrived back in Warsaw, where once stood a row of fine Jewish owned houses. Frederick opened the car door to let Heinz explore the area. His boots crunched over the broken glass, its charred slate, which had fallen from the burning buildings. His main priority was to explore the house that Jeremiah was last seen with his brother.

"Get some soldiers to search this area again!" Heinz growled at Frederick, "Do not have them leave here until they find something of importance. I shall wait in the car."

Frederick slammed the door closed upon the car, before he marched to the ruins of the house. He made his way through the remainder of the front doorway. Its carved stone pillars remained intact from the blaze. He stumbled upon loose bricks before reaching the centre of the house. Certain walls remained. The sitting room wall still had the pale blue paint visible on certain parts of the plastered wall. Smoke billowed up the shattered chimney breast to the opening at the top. Frederick ventured further to the rear yard of the property. Some of the stone slabs laid on a fine terrace garden, had cracked with the heat from the fire. As he scanned for clues as to the whereabouts of the girl, he noticed the door on the wall of the garden.

"How strange to have a door suspended on a garden wall!" he commented to himself. He heard a cracking of glass from behind him. Frederick spun around. He unclipped his gun holster at the same time. Stood directly behind him was Isobel, she was brushing her hair over her face to hide her eyes. A dirty soot mark streaked across her nose in true camouflage, military style.

"What are you doing here, where did you come from?" Frederick asked. Isobel never replied, she just kept pulling her long fringe over her eyes. She began humming the tune … *Ring O ring a Roses* to herself. Frederick approached her cautiously. He was standing near to her, when she hit him with a long silver cylinder.

....

Frederick saw a blurred image above him. A rumbling voice shouting commands from above him.

"Get up you fool, what are you doing down there?"

Frederick focussed to see Heinz stood above him.

"Can't you do anything, which is regarded as… simple?"

Frederick sat up; Heinz noticed blood running from an opening on top his scalp.

"Who hit you?"

"I remember a girl… she stood in front of me"

"Was it her, is it the girl we are looking for?" Heinz aggressively snapped –*"you let her escape!"*

"No… no, I don't think it was the girl, this one was strange. She was humming a song. I cannot remember the song now" Frederick touched his head, Blood covered his hand. Heinz pulled him to his feet using a strong force from his mind.

185

"*Let me see this wound,*" he said, spinning Frederick on the spot without touching him.

Heinz placed his hand over the bloodied skin. He sent a spark down his hand to the cut area. The area burned, the wound welded shut. Frederick tried desperately not to cry out in pain. Tears ran down his face.

"*It's fixed. Now tell me about the girl*"

"*I couldn't see her face, as she kept pulling her hair across it. Her hair was a mousy blond colour. That's how I know that it was not the girl that we are looking for.*" Frederick wiped the tears away from his face, "*She had this silver cylinder in her hand. That is what she hit me with*"

"*Let me see...*" Heinz reached his hand out yet again onto Frederick's head. Frederick began to fear that he might end up like the others, which Heinz had dealt with in the past. It was too late for debating this, as Heinz was already viewing the images of the girl for himself. He had projected them from Frederick's thoughts as a projected three -dimensional image. Frederick was watching it too.

"*She holds this cylinder in her right hand, I need to see it closely,*" Heinz pulled the image of the cylinder closer to his eyes. The image of the cylinder enlarged. "*It has some writing upon it... etched on the end of the cap. Galene Crystalaura04*" Heinz closed the image by removing his hand.

"*This must belong to the girl, we now know her name. We will now refer to her as Galene*"

Frederick was shaking, "*Yes Sir. So this girl who hit me, she must know of her whereabouts!*"

"Indeed so. She cannot have got far from here find here, get the troops from the camp to help you to search. I want that girl alive for me to interrogate. Go now!"

Frederick tried to run over the loose bricks to find that he slipped numerous times. He stopped by the stone doorway to see Heinz lifting rubble without touching it. The door in the garden wall made Heinz curious. Frederick ran across the park towards the Prisoner of war camp.

....

Isobel was sat in a tree in the park as Frederick ran past below her. She hissed. She was banging the cylinder on the tree. She had seen Galene use the cylinder, but did not know how it worked. Numerous times she twisted the ends of the tube, but it remained locked.

"If only I had read Galene's mind. I would know exactly how this works," she said out loud, whilst hissing.

....

Heinz opened the door on the wall. Behind the door was just an ordinary brick wall. He closed it shut, and then reopened it again rapidly. The brick wall was still there. He began looking at the door in detail. Its fixings were perfect, not a charred mark on the casing or the door. His cold hand touched the door. He sensed a vibration of Galene, but the image of her was blurred.

Frederick was running back across the rubble with four soldiers from the Prison. The four soldiers halted quickly when they saw the grotesque figure of Heinz in front of them. They began whispering, nudging each other as

Heinz lifted his head to view them standing, but a few feet in front of him.

"Frederick, take two of the men to search the rubble for any more clues or anything that seems out of the ordinary. The other two soldiers are to guard this door at all times"

"Yes Sir" Frederick indicated the two closest to him to stand by the door. He pointed to the area of rubble to be investigated. As the search began, Frederick noticed some trapped hair between two bricks.

"Captain, I think we may have something here," he shouted in the direction of Heinz, who was standing by the remainder of chimney breast, looking out towards the park.

Frederick had pulled the few strands of hair from the bricks. He ensured he did not contaminate the hair by placing his black leather gloves back on to his hands. Heinz eyes were averted to the park when birds flew out of the tree directly opposite. The birds were disturbed by something. Heinz held out the palm of his hand flat for Frederick to place the strands of hair. He began to clasp the strands tightly. His hand glowed,

"Another child it may seem, a young girl. This is not the girl I am looking for. However, she has been in contact with her-Galene" Heinz set fire to the strands, they disappeared into nothingness. The contact with the hair had highlighted an echo of Isobel from where she lay in the rubble. Heinz viewed a sparkling, shimmering glow through his dark sunglasses, which sat across his nose-less face. The luminescence of her feet ran from the brick rubble to the park.

"Frederick, Come with me"

Frederick paced, rapidly to keep up with Heinz, floating across the street to the park. On approaching the tree, more birds departed. Heinz pointed upwards into the highest branches.

"Get her down from there now"

Frederick removed his silver whistle from the top jacket pocket. He blew hard on the rattling pea inside. The two soldiers stopped searching at the remains of the house came running instantly.

"Yes Sir" they said in unison.

"Climb this tree," He pointed upwards, *"Bring me down the girl at once. No harm is to be done to her. Do I make myself clear... no harm?"*

The two soldiers began to clamber up the old tree. Golden orange autumn leaves began to fall as they did so. More birds flew from the branches.

"Captain, the girl.... She is!" a German soldier shouted downwards from the highest branches before he fell. His body cracked through every branch. Leaves fell with him. He hit the floor with such force, that he was killed instantly. Leaves kept falling upon his broken body. They covered him like a feather-down throw bedspread. Heinz inspected the body where it fell. He placed his hands on the dead corpse to retrieve an image of the last moments before death.

"Interesting, this girl can be of use to me" he stated.

The second soldier was thrown high above the tree. His arms were waving frantically in a motion of trying to fly.

Heinz pointed his hand at the soldier, a fireball hit the soldier. He exploded in mid-air.

"It is best that he does not suffer like the other one did" Heinz groaned, but in a quite calm tone of voice back at Frederick. Frederick gulped, pieces of German uniform showered down upon his head. Heinz began to hover upwards through all the branches of the tree to reach the top, where the Isobel was hiding.

"Hello child, I am here to help you. What is your name?" Heinz said quietly to Isobel, who was gripping extremely hard onto the very thin branches. The silver cylinder was tucked in the waistband of her dress. Heinz did not receive an answer. He asked again, but Isobel just hissed at him.

"Let me assure you, I want that girl Galene... Are you willing to help me get her?"

Isobel popped her head upon hearing the name Galene. Her eyes red with anger, viewed Heinz.

"Who are you? You don't look human?" Isobel asked as she stared coldly at Heinz. Heinz did not understand her but carried on talking anyway,

"I am here to capture that girl... Galene; we need her to aid our own war. That is the war of Germany against the world. Join me now, give me your hand" Heinz held out the silvery palm towards Isobel. Isobel pulled backwards, the branch cracked beneath her feet. She fell downwards, her left hand held on tight to the branch above.

"Give me your hand, let me save you, you can help me" Heinz said softly. Isobel forced her right hand forward. Heinz grabbed it tightly. Isobel let go of the tree.

Frederick watched as Heinz lowered himself down through the branches with Isobel. At the base of the tree Isobel stood, pulling her hair across her eyes. Frederick tried to get closer to her, but she hissed back at him. Frederick gently placed his hand upon Isobel's shoulder.

"Steady on you evil witch" he remarked, *"I work for Captain Heinz"*

Chapter 16

Berlin Radziwill Palace

04th August 1943

"Berlin"s Radziwill Palace, Reichskanzlei, Wilhelmstraße 77"

German SS-Obergruppenführer Schmidt was in the Telegram room.

" Nehmen Sie eine Nachricht . Schicken Sie es an SS - Sturmhaupt Heinz Quer Brauchitsch über Warschau Camp . Dies ist die letzte bekannte Kontakt wir mit ihm "-

"Take a message. Send it to- SS-Sturmhauptführer Heinz Bieg-Brauchitsch via Warsaw Camp. This is the last known contact we had with him" He said in his deep, smooth toned but subtle, German voice.

Lieutenant Schmidt paced up and down the small room. The stenographer began taking the shorthand notes on the message to be sent. She tried not to look up as he was making her dizzy. The scent of her perfume, *sweet lilies,* made Lieutenant Schmidt take in deep breaths.

"The perfume you are wearing is exquisite, it is making me lose concentration... on the matter in hand" He said coughing.

The stenographer was embarrassed by his remark. She just smiled, bowing her head even further into the notebook, which she had rested on her black long flowing dress. Lieutenant Schmidt began his dictation to the stenographer,

"Attention, SS-Sturmhauptführer Heinz. Stop.

Time is moving on, Stop. The German Reich Command would like a progress update, Stop. The Girl is required to heighten our German victory of this War. Stop. The situation is now classed as intense at this present time. Stop. This could be my last message to you. Stop. Next time I hear from you. Stop. I want a message to say the girl has been caught. The war needs her and her book. Stop, continue to burn the rest. Stop… insert my name, Stop."

Lieutenant Schmidt placed his hand on the young woman's head. He stroked her braided auburn hair. She blushed even more. Lieutenant Schmidt walked up to the taped up window. He peered out onto the dull grey, black 'n' white movie street below. He watched as a convoy of German tanks juddered by, upon the desolate street.

"That will be all for now. Ensure that the message is sent with the utmost urgency" Lieutenant Schmidt said, whilst indicating her departure with his index finger.

"I am sure that you have transformed by now Captain Heinz Bieg-Brauchitsch, as did all the others. It's now just a matter of time. I surely hope you have succeeded, where the others failed in conquering the changes that were forced upon you" Lieutenant Schmidt remarked to himself. His breath was misting over the pane of glass in the window.

"… It is probably too late for you now to transform back. It was necessary to transform you for our cause… He said, as he wiped his fingers through the condensation upon the glass."

Chapter 17

Crystalaura04

Asher had only just closed the door, when it was suddenly pushed open again.

"I thought you were taking Isobel to Warsaw?"

"We did... we have done!" Isabella remarked.

"But you cannot have. I have just closed the door on you all... that's impossible" Asher stuttered.

"Time is somewhat different on the outside compared to the inside of this vast room. Did I not already mention it before?" Isabella commented, grabbing Asher around the waist. She began tickling him. Asher was trying to break free, but was in fits of laughter.

"Enough you two... We may have only temporally got rid of Isobel. There is now another matter which may be of some concern- which could have possible consequences for all of us" Asher stopped laughing, as he ran away from Isabella's grip.

"What might that be?" Jeremiah asked.

"The *Wepwawet* cylinder, I think that I must have dropped it outside. If Isobel finds a way of using it, then she may be able to find a way of getting back in here. Or even track the whereabouts of all our actions" Galene slammed her hands upon the round table, "How careless am I to have let this happen!"

"Can't we go back for it?" Asher asked, as he sat upon the edge of the table.

"I do not think that it would be safe to open the door again to go back to Warsaw. The door is so visible now. Besides which, it is in the middle of the German war zone"

"So we just have to hope that she does not find the tube" Jeremiah remarked, turning the table with Asher sat upon it.

"Indeed, so… let us all hope she does not. She is part of me, so she would know information about me. She also knows about this room." Isabella stated.

Jeremiah sighed, as he pulled the table to the point of Μαρία (Maria, Mary). Asher jumped off the table onto the floor. He laid his sword upon the table. The broom flew in from the darkness to join all them, whilst they contemplated what they would be next. Asher found deep in his jacket pocket a bag of hard boiled candy. He shared the contents with everybody. The *Caesar* statue was still resonating light in the distance. Galene retrieved the Spell book from her bag. She removed all the scrolls from the centre before she enlarged it. She stroked the spine before kissing the clasp as part of her normal ritual.

"It is imperative that we have to retrieve the missing page for the centre of this book. It will shed some light as to why all this is happening around us" her hand ran down the ripped edge in the centre of the book.

"Once again, I see that the book has increased the Spells contained within"

Isabella touched the ripped page. Coldness ran through her body. She pulled her hand back quickly.

"There is something deathly about this book… I cannot get a true feeling from it" she said shuddering. Galene flicked through the pages to view some of the spells. Asher tried to touch the book, but the broom knocked his hand away.

"I have just had a thought! Do you think it is just the page that we have to find?" Jeremiah quizzed Galene.

"I am sorry to say Jeremiah, but there are numerous pieces missing from the Spell book, so, I cannot answer that one" Galene remarked, as she closed the Spell book with two hands. Her fingers ran over the book, where numerous missing pieces should have been, before she swirled them above. The book was shrinking.

Galene removed the *Tic Toc Ticker* from her bag. Asher was using his sword to alter the name Μαρία (Maria, Mary); he was digging out pieces of wood to add a *plus symbol* between her name and Ιησοῦς (Jesus).

"Asher -stop that at once! Do you not realise how old this table is?" Isabella gave Asher a stern face. Asher stopped immediately putting his sword by his side. His bottom lip began to quiver. The broom was angry; it hit Asher on the rear as a punishment, following Isabella's remarks. He jumped high, not expecting it. Jeremiah smiled, but then pulled Asher closer to him, to comfort him.

"Is there any chance we could explore this vast room Galene?" Jeremiah inquisitively asked.

Galene looked at Isabella, who shrugged her shoulders, for she did not know the answer to the question. Galene never replied to Jeremiah's question. She carried on looking at the spell book.

"Of course, why did I not think of it before… help me look for some liquid? Water would be ideal"

Isabella responded quite quickly,

"You have a plan? Why water?"

"It's a spell I can use to see into the near future. Water is part of it"

"We passed a water fountain when the *Tic Toc Ticker* sent us through time, back into the room earlier. Do you remember? We made our way to the light. The water was still in the basin, the small pipe features in the stone were trickling water."

"You have a good memory for something that was in partial darkness Jeremiah. How is this so?" Isabella enquired.

"Not so, the noise of the dripping water made me look towards the fountain when we passed by"

Galene created light wands for each of them to carry. The wands were made from tightly rolled up scrolls. She had used the *Letter enhancement spell*, which she had used once before to read the text in the dark. The scrolls were rolled so tightly, that the text shone through all the papyrus paper creating light. Galene gave each of them the wands to carry. She had only got a few paces towards Jeremiah, before realising that she forgot the *Tic Toc Ticker*,

"Broom – pass me the *Ticker*" she said, the broom swooped in batting the *Ticker* towards Galene who grabbed it.

"Thanks Broom. So Jeremiah, do you remember which direction the fountain was?"

Jeremiah was keen; he had already set off in the direction of the fountain. Asher followed, holding the wand in front of him, along with his sword.

"Keep together as we do not know what is in this room" Galene shouted, at Jeremiah, as he had paced too far in front of the rest of them. Jeremiah stood by a stuffed हिममानव. (Snowman, Yeti)

He was reading the tag which was hanging down from its arm, *Mountain man* also known as the *Yeti*, the label said after being translated by the *Wiz-T*. The label was in Galene's handwriting. Jeremiah waited for Galene to get near,

"Look, I have been captured by your creature" Jeremiah lay upon the huge foot of the giant hairy monster.

"Don't be silly, it's not my monster," she said, pulling the label towards the light of her wand. "Well, I will be damned, that's my handwriting" Galene scrutinised the label even more. She turned the label over to read –

Wiz- T translation, *Hindi* Language flashed in her eye…

Frozen Yeti

tic toc 1921

At the Lhagba La (windy gap) pass in the Tibet region not far from Mount Everest.

I rescued the Snow Man from the British Expedition who had stumbled upon the footprints in the snow.

Note: Not to be released until the tic toc 2097.

This tag is programmed to remind me to do so!

"Jeremiah, the creature is very much real- that you sit upon! It is alive, but in a deep sleep"

Jeremiah jumped to his feet immediately, he fell backwards upon the shelving knocking numerous books to the floor. He peered upwards at the creature's face covered in white coarse hair. The eyelids were closed tightly. Its mouth slightly ajar showed sharp pointed teeth. In the creature's hand was a stump of a tree shaped into a club hammer. Asher's jaw fell open, as he stared from its feet to the creature's head, which was twenty feet above him. Isabella touched the snowman to feel its emotional state.

"Oh dear Galene, the Snow man is not very happy with you for placing him in stasis. He wants to know if you got his partner as well" Isabella removed her hand from his leg.

Galene scanned the area with the light wand to see if another *Yeti* was visible. A large black material covered something in the distance caught her eye.

"Over there, what's that," she said as she pointed at the huge cover that was draped over an object. Jeremiah ran to the cover, he pulled hard on the cloth to remove it. Underneath was an egg shaped object standing thirty feet tall. It was completely metallic. It was floating about a foot off the floor. Jeremiah touched the egg shape, it quivered. On the floor lay the label.

Galene's handwriting yet again- Jeremiah read it out to the others, *Wiz –T* translation, *Auradom* language flashed in her eye,

"It says, *Danger: PP14432 Model, rescued from the War of the Worlds tic toc 3107, item never to be used in any part of earth's history prior tic toc 3107*" Jeremiah dropped the label before stepping back from the item, "Galene, it's your handwriting yet again! Is this room entirely yours?"

Isabella responded, as Galene appeared to be flummoxed at the question,

"Jeremiah, that is not important now, we need to find the fountain. Please carry on....lead the way"

Isabella placed her hand on Galene's shoulder for comfort. She whispered to her,

"You will remember sometime soon. All of it will make sense to you eventually! You are you and you will be many times over!" Galene, stretched her face in puzzlement?

Asher was stroking the foot of the *snow man*. The broom flew in to knock his hand away.

"Damn you… broom, stop doing that!" he snarled angrily.

Jeremiah continued walking, but the further they went the darker it became. They grouped together in a closer formation to make the wands shine brighter.

"Try not to touch anything as we do not know what most of these items are here for" Isabella remarked. They walked for what must have been ten to fifteen minutes or so before reaching a stone fountain. The basin of the fountain stood on a stone plinth. On top of the basin was another column with four sides trickling water from four metal outlets. The water was orange. A label lay at the base of the fountain. Asher picked it up off the floor. He began to read it to the others.

The Wiz-T translated, *Occitan* Language into the eye of Asher,

Lavabos Fountain
Le Thoronet Abbey, Provence,
tic toc 1862.
The water has special healing powers.
Note to oneself: replaced with an exact replica 1863 -with clear
water to prevent misuse of its power.

Asher placed the label back at the lower plinth of the grey stone, "Do you mean that if I place my hand in this fountain it will…?" Asher put his hand in the water, a bolt of bright orange light shot to the ceiling. It gave Jeremiah a chance to look at the other artefacts surrounding the fountain.

Statues, Books, furniture, animals were just a few of the items close by.

"Wow, this room is a treasure trove. Why are there so many objects of varied nature in here?" he said, spinning a three hundred and sixty degrees turn on the spot.

Asher removed his hand from the fountain.

"Galene will answer that when she is ready" Isabella added, wedging her wand of light into the crevice of the fountain.

"So Galene, what shall you be using this water for?"

Jeremiah stopped spinning, he also approached the fountain. He lit Isabella's face with his wand. Asher was drying his hand on his short trouser leg. Galene removed her book from her bag. She pulled up a Monkey stool (*a stool with a small central hole in the seat to allow the tail of the monkey to pass through*) that was nearby to sit upon. The others watched as the book began to enlarge. Galene kissed the clasp. She turned its heavy pages to find the *Clear Water* spell. Jeremiah gave Isabella his wand of light as he wanted to help turn the pages. Galene was mumbling to herself, trying to remember the spell. She just could not recall all the words. Eventually she found the spell on page one hundred and thirty three.

"Arrrh book... Stop moving the spells... there you are. Okay everyone, I need you all to find some dirt, dust for me. I need a small pile in front of the fountain. Isabella knelt on her knees brushing the floor with her hands to gather the dust nearby. Asher was doing the same. Jeremiah carried a cloth bag over from the book shelving.

"Will this do" he said, pulling a handful of soil from the bag.

Isabella got up off her knees. She wiped the dust from her palms onto her pretty dress. "What is that? Let me see," she said, pulling the label off the bag. She approached the fountain where she had wedged her light wand so she could read the label.

The Wiz-T translated, *Russian* Language,

Glinka Soil Collection

tic toc 1927

The Sample contains unknown crystal particles.

I removed this one sample as it has the highest concentration of crystals. It is too revealing to leave in place. P.T.O

This sample was taken by Konstantin D Glinka, Russian soil scientist of tic toc 1867.

He is a remarkable man way ahead of this time and century.
Isabella placed the card back with the hessian sack,
"I think it would be foolish, even dangerous to use this soil, as we do not know what the crystal particles represent or how they could react with your spells Galene"
"You are possibly right in your assumption Isabella, we shall stick to collecting dust from the floor" Galene remarked, continuing to mumble the spell to herself over and over in an attempt to memorise it.
The pile of dust by the fountain was ready for Galene to commence her spell. Asher was wiping the remainder of the dust from his sweaty palms onto his grey shorts. Jeremiah stood back from the dust next to Asher. Isabella retrieved her light wand that she had wedged into the crevice of the fountain. Galene approached, she had picked up a challis from a marble pedestal. She had not looked at the label hanging from the large cup. She scooped up the water from the bowl. The water was cold on her warm skin. She muttered to herself once more before placing the challis on the floor next to the dust mound.
"Okay, I think I can remember the spell now...Hopefully!" Galene smiled before winking at Isabella.
"Ur garbia dago, beraz, oraindik zutik ur garbi,
Altxa, swish eta biraka.
Bildu momentu , jartzailea zerua.
Jarrai hire begi bihurtu swirling .
Etorkizunean zer ekartzen ikusteko me.
Gida betiereko eraztunak bidez neuk
Sua, lurra eta ura ring A
Batzen

Utzi To tic toc aukeratzeko ,
Egin Betirako da eta betirako.
Spell 2 tic 6 toc 3 tic 5 toc.
Clear water, clear water- standing so still,
Rise up, swish and swirl.
Gather momentum, pierce the sky.
Keep swirling to become thy eye.
Let me see what the future brings.
Guide myself through the eternal rings
A ring of fire, earth and water
Come together
To let the tic toc choose,
Make it Eternal and forever.

Asher's mouth dropped open as the water from the challis began to rise upwards out of the cup. The water snake charmed its way towards the pile of dust that lay next to it. Galene continued with the spell by whirling her arms around and around. The water began swirling furiously around in a spiral, pulling the soil upwards. The soil was now standing four feet high, like a fencing stake. The orange water began to glow as it formed into a sphere, sparks, lightning bolts began shooting out in all directions. Images began to appear. Firstly a sign that said *Cairo*, followed by a camel. A signing register dated *1906, July 20th* with a name. The name was unclear. Jeremiah stepped closer to see if he could read the name, but the image changed into three dark figures with no faces. Jeremiah jumped backwards. Isabella commented,

"Look, is that the spell page from the book? It's the one that's missing. It's lay inside an open satchel bag in a hotel room"

Galene moved closer to see the page. It disappeared, changing into the three dark figures once more. The broom, saw Galene as being in danger, it swooped in from the high bookshelves. Its bristles batted the swirling water to destroy the evil being shown. The ball of water dispersed at such a rapid speed, that Asher was drenched. Water dripped of his mousy blond hair onto his grey jumper. He shuddered as it was cold. Isabella laughed. Jeremiah had stepped aside, just as the broom had commenced its sweep. He missed the fallout of water. Galene shouted,

"Broom, bad broom... What did you do that for?"

The broom flew off, hiding behind a material covered artefact.

"We now know where we have to go to -*Cairo, 1906*. It was definitely the missing spell page from the book... was it not Isabella? You saw it more closely, than I had the chance to."

Isabella ceased laughing; Asher was glowing orange from the water being in contact with his body. He glowed like a light bulb. His intense brightness highlighted all the area they were standing in.

"Yes, Galene, it was the page. I saw the page clearly. I would only imagine that we are now destined to retrieve it?"

Jeremiah was scanning the now lit room space. He noticed a large white cloth draped over what appeared to be a figure with the same build as him. He paced across to the figure quite casually. Asher placed his sword on the floor before he removed his jumper to dry his face. His hair was now ruffled from its normal side parting, as he rubbed the jumper across his head, which was also a glowing bright orange.

"You must have read my mind, Isabella, we need to retrieve the page, as it may contain some of the vital information that we need"

Jeremiah pulled on the fine white silk cloth. It slid to the floor.

"Whoa, this is freaky! Galene... Galene come here"

Galene ran over as Jeremiah had shouted to her, Isabella followed.

"Oh my word, it's you!" Isabella said flabbergasted.

"So it is..." Galene was running her fingers over the statue. She picked up the label from the plinth of the statue.

The Wiz-T translated, *Italian* language,

Jeremiah Dershowitz, Jewish Germany.

Jeremiah was sculpted by Michelangelo Buonarroti

tic toc 1515

Note: A record of the men in history that had great power. He worked day and night to create this statue along with one another – that of Moses.

Further Note: Jeremiah holds the staff of Moses as the Moses statue had already had most of the handwork completed.

Jeremiah grabbed the long wooden crook that was wedged in the hand of his statue. He began to prise it free from his own statue fingers. Galene put her handwritten card back on the plinth. Isabella reached out to touch the long wooden staff, just as Jeremiah finally got it free from the marble hand.

"It is that which the card states. It belonged to *Moses*," She paused, whilst she seemed to be watching images passing before her eyes," It is so powerful; I cannot believe that which I see. Jeremiah, it is... sorry was meant for to have. The statue was created to indicate this under Galene's instruction"

Jeremiah held the long piece of old wood in his right hand. He swirled it in the air, before slamming it on the floor. A thunderous noise vibrated from the stick. The room shook violently. Books began to fall from the shelves. His statue fell over breaking in half. Asher was thrown against the twenty foot bookshelf, as many books fell upon him. Isabella grabbed onto Galene to steady herself.

"Stop it now" Galene cried out, "Pull the *Moses staff* up off the floor!"

Jeremiah lifted the staff of wood off from the floor. The thunder ceased immediately. Asher was entrapped under numerous books. Orange light was shooting out in different directions as some orange covers touched his body. He emerged from the pile seemly unscathed,

"What happened, was it an earthquake?" he asked.

"Not an earthquake, it was Jeremiah. Galene you remembered how to stop the power from the *Moses staff*! Is your memory returning?" Isabella questioned, as she let go of Galene's body. Jeremiah was inspecting the staff of power. He could not believe that a piece of old wood could be so powerful.

"I feel sort of peculiar. It's as if I do know what it is, but then again, at the same time it is so vague. I seem to know the power of the *Moses Staff*. I also know it is even more powerful in Jeremiah's hands" Galene replied, as she began walking towards Asher. "The purpose of us all being together somehow seems familiar also"

Galene helped on removing books off-Asher's body. Eventually he was free. He was still glowing orange in small patches, as most of the water had now evaporated.

"Something is missing. I cannot quite put my finger upon it Isabella"

Isabella approached Galene, "It is so, but I am confident that you will remember what it is. So Galene is it *Cairo* that we are going to?"

Galene was thinking as she grabbed her bag from the floor. She stood over the broken statue of Jeremiah,

"Konpondu , twine, eta meld forma hau .
Horiek lotu gisa , hori hilaren web bat bezala ,
Altxa, stand behin gehiago.
Pieza ederren bat, lurrean "off igoko
Fix, twine, and meld this shape.
Bind as one, like a web that's spun,
Rise up, stand once more.
One fine piece, rise off the floor"

Galene was waving her hands above the broken pieces. The statue began to heal itself. The marble, carved stone rose off the floor. They welded themselves back together upon the plinth. The statue of Jeremiah stood by itself in one piece.

"I cannot go anywhere without repairing what is mine! I have done it again. I have said *what is mine*"

Isabella rubbed Galene's arm, as she lowered it from the spell. Jeremiah was also stood looking at the statue of himself on the plinth once more. Asher approached. He climbed up on the plinth, replacing the missing *Moses staff* with the rolled up papyrus paper.

"There at least it looks as though you are holding something. Galene can I ask you if you have a statue of me in here" Asher turned towards Galene waiting for an answer. The blade of his sword shimmered sending a blinding light into her eyes. Galene appeared somewhat surprised, before her expression changed when the light in her eyes triggered a memory,

"Oh my god – of course -Why did I not think of it before? Thanks Asher"

Chapter 18

Three Wishes Smashed

04th August 1943, late evening

Frederick kept his distance from Isobel. He felt she was extremely unstable. Heinz placed his arm around her as they stood by the foot of the tree. He held out his hand for the object, that she was holding onto so tightly. Isobel gave it freely to him, she felt at ease. Heinz examined the metal tube, which he had seen in the projected images earlier. He searched for the etching on the casing. His own metallic finger rubbed across the imprinted letters *Galene Crystalaura04*. The coldness of the metal against his own coldness prevented him from seeing any image of Galene.

A German soldier was running in their direction from the houses. He stopped short of Captain Heinz before saluting him,

"Heil" he firmly shouted, *"Captain, I think that we may have found something"* the German soldier bowed his head as he was speaking.

"Excellent, you shall be rewarded"

Frederick gulped, as Captain Heinz said the words.

"Lead the way. Show me what you have found" His voice was becoming more robotic.

Isobel was standing upon one foot of Heinz. As he began to hover across the fallen leaves in the park, they wafted upwards from the rapid movement. Isobel was clinging to the waist of Heinz. Frederick had to jog to keep up with them both. Heinz glided effortlessly across the fallen rubble of the burnt out houses, until he reached the other soldier who was left guarding the doorway. Frederick arrived momentarily after, extremely out of breath, very unfit.

The moon was reaching its full height in the night sky. The silence of the area penetrated the eardrum as a vibration.

"So, you have found something regarding the girl. Speak"

Isobel stepped down from the metal foot of Heinz, he moved closer to the soldier who stood by the door in the garden wall.

"Captain, the earth rumbled. We both fell to the floor" The German soldier spluttered out his words in the direction of Heinz. The other German soldier had now arrived back at the doorway. He was straightening his jacket from the jog the tight jacket buttons were stretched to the maximum. Any tighter they would have popped off.

"Heil" a slightly out of breath soldier announced, *"Yes, Captain, there was a rumble; we both fell to the ground. When it stopped, the door was slightly ajar. A small light was shining from within"*

The second soldier could not wait to interrupt,

"The light was coming from a small crack in the surface of a brick; we tried to peer inside but could not see anything"

"Open the door and let me see this light"

Still out of breath the soldier pulled the door open. The light was no longer. He tried to point out the broken brick, but somehow it had disappeared. The brick was no longer damaged. The second soldier was also dismayed at there being no light. His fingers were desperately poking at the bricks to see if he could find it.

"So you waste my time calling me here"

Isobel began hissing at both of them. She was clawing at another part of the wall, as well as hissing, then laughing at them.

"Get rid of them," she cried out between the hissing, "You no longer need them. I can help you dispose of them," she said, pulling her hair across her face. Heinz tried to understand some of the English words she was saying but failed miserably. Frederick spoke some English, so he translated,

"Captain, she would like you to dispose of them," he said in his native language -German.

Heinz called the unfit soldier towards him with his finger,

"Let me see your mind" Heinz threw the cap off the soldier to the floor, he grabbed tightly onto the soldiers head. The soldier began to writhe in pain, as Heinz rummaged through his thoughts to find the image of the light behind the door.

"Arrrh, there it is" Heinz watched the echo of time being played once more. "That will do, you shall now have your reward"

Heinz gripped tighter onto the soldier's skull. His arm shot a bolt of electricity, which sparked outwards down his arm. The soldier shook violently before Heinz released his grip. The soldier fell flat on his back totally lifeless. Frederick stepped backwards, whilst still watching. Isobel was hissing, and laughing hysterically as she clawed at the wall. The other soldier began to run across the rubble. He stumbled numerous times. The rubble, collapsed under his feet. He fell into the basement area of the house. Tons of brick fell upon him, as he lay looking upwards towards the gaping hole. Frederick peered into the hole once the dust had cleared. From the rubble protruded just an arm, gripping a small crucifix on a gold chain. It shimmered in the moonlight.

"He is dead Captain" Frederick called over to Heinz.

Heinz pulled the door open once more on the garden wall. His hand ran across the jagged bricks. Isobel copied him further down the wall.

"So my girl, how do we find this Ga-lene? Tell me what you know"

Frederick translated, Isobel the question. Isobel calmed herself before speaking.

"The room they hide in is filled with treasures. They all trapped me, before throwing me out here- to the wolves in the night" she hissed, then cackled.

Frederick tried to get too close to Isobel, she hissed again.

"It would seem Captain that she knows very little... dispose of her!"

Heinz pulled the silver metallic tube from under his jacket.

"Yes, I remember the tube. It has magical powers. There is a trapped wizard inside of it" Isobel remarked. "But I do not know how it works"

Frederick did his best at translating her comments to Heinz. He had to raise his voice an octave higher, as a group of German trucks with soldiers on board, rumbled by, crushing the broken bricks on the roadside. Heinz was examining the tubular shape. His hands twisted the ends of the tube simultaneously. It clicked open.

Smoke billowed outwards. Heinz dropped it into the rubble by his feet. Isobel came running over towards Heinz to watch, as the smoke took shape. Frederick moved closer as the *Wepwawet* appeared before them speaking Egyptian,

"You are not my master" He said, scanning all three of them. Heinz spoke abruptly in fluent German,

"I am now, you will do as I command," he dictated towards the creature. The *Wepwawet* howled, before growling back, as it now knew the language to reply to. The *Wepwawet* began to speak German.

"Where is my master? What have you done with her?"

Heinz held his hands above the fallen tube, they became magnetic. The tube jumped into his palm at a rapid speed.

"I will break this tube if you do not assist me in my quest. I must find the girl - GALENE. I am your master now"

The *Wepwawet* observed as the tube began to glow red hot from the heat generated by Heinz hand. The tube began to distort its shape.

"STOP! I will help you. I can only grant you three wishes! But I warn you now, that on the third wish being completed, my container will disappear"

Heinz ceased heating the tube, Isobel was laughing. Frederick stumbled over broken bricks, until he fell over. His wrist cracked as his body landed on his arm. He yelled out in pain. He began screaming out loud once he sat upright. His wrist had a bone protruding from the skin. It began to swell. Blood filled the area quickly. His screams of pain got louder.

"I wish you would stop all that silly noise, it is only pain. Learn to control it" Captain Heinz angrily remarked.

"Your wish is granted" the *Wepwawet* raised his hand, a bolt of lightning shot from his fingers to Frederick's wrist. Within a matter of moments the wrist was fixed. Frederick's wailing also stopped. He smiled examining the now repaired hand.

"I did not mean for the 'wish' to be his wrist, it seems you are very cunning with your wishes" Heinz was somewhat annoyed at the loss of a wish. Isobel ran over to Frederick, she grabbed his hand to examine the repair. Her teeth sank deep,

"Ouch, you...." Frederick kicked her backwards to the ground. "You evil..."

"Enough you two, stop this childish behaviour, I have two wishes remaining. I need to find the girl. It seems if I would wish for that, then I would be somewhat deceived. I need suggestions on how to use the wishes effectively"

Frederick stood up from the floor. He began to brush the brick dust off his military attire. Isobel stayed low to the ground. She was pulling her hair across her face.

"I think you need to wish for an entrance to the room that's hidden" Frederick stated, pulling his jacket downwards with both hands to straighten it against his body.

The *Wepwawet* was waiting for the other wishes to be asked. It was scanning the area for people.

"Of course, I could resolve this situation in one swoop, I would be able to obtain the girl if I could enter the room" Heinz was speaking out loud the thoughts he was thinking *"So my second wish will be to have access to the secret room that Galene has been in. I wish to have a door to enter Galene's secret room"*

The *Wepwawet* raised his spear; he pointed it, before throwing it at the garden wall. A bright light appeared in the centre of one brick as the spear hit and sparked, the light increased in size. Eventually, it reached the size of a door. The door slammed shut. The spear flew back to *Wepwawet*. There were now two doors in the garden wall, side by side. The *Wepwawet* began to turn into a cloud before whooshing back into the silver, tubular cylinder in Heinz hand. Frederick opened the door, a small closet was inside.

"Shame we never asked for instructions," he snidely remarked in English.

Isobel stood up, "I managed to read Isabella's mind. I saw how the door works, but then she blocked me from getting any more information about her."

Isobel pushed Frederick aside. The closet that was filled with brooms, mops plus many other items for cleaning, Isobel searched for the crystal painting. She had totally missed that the painting was on the back of the door. Captain Heinz glided across to the doorway.

"What are you looking for" he asked, as Isobel, who was throwing cleaning items out of the closet. The crashes of the mop buckets on the rubble echoed into the night air.

"A painting of a crystal" she cried out, "I need to find the painting" Frederick was constantly translating the comments of Isobel back to Heinz.

"The painting is here on the door" Frederick said, laughing.

Isobel stood up; her face was covered in dirt from the small room. She hissed at Frederick.

"That's it" she said "We all need to stand in the closet to enter the secret room" Frederick moved into the closet followed by Heinz. Isobel closed the door. All three of them were crammed tightly together. From memory Isobel recited.

"Errebelatu hori ezkutuko, ikuspegi batetik ikusmena,

Erakutsi kristal errefraktoreak argia.

 - *Reveal that's hidden, from view, from sight, Show the crystal refracting light.*"

The crystal from the door glowed. It appeared to rise out from the paper. Isobel turned the crystal upside down before releasing her hand. The crystal fell back to the page. The room became dark. Isobel kicked Frederick in the shin, before opening the door.

"We are now in the room" Isobel stepped out of the closet. Frederick followed, rubbing his lower leg. Heinz began rolling a fireball in his hand. He threw it up in the air to the highest point to see the extent of the room. The light lit the area that they were standing in. Object after object filled the space. Bookshelves thirty, forty, fifty feet tall, stood continually hiding more objects beyond the flaming light.

"It would take an eternity to search a room of this magnitude" Heinz stated,*" Why is the room in darkness if the girl is already here? She did not expect me to enter."*

Heinz removed the Cylinder from his jacket. He twisted the ends of the tube until the *Wepwawet* appeared before them. He threw the cylinder upon the floor

"You summoned me for your third wish?" the *Wepwawet* said, in German.

Heinz hovered around the *Wepwawet*, looking for a weakness. *"May I inquire if this is the room that Galene is in?"* The *Wepwawet* began turning to follow, Heinz face as he hovered around the *Wepwawet* ghostly figure,

"You did not ask to be taken to the room that Galene was in, you asked to be taken to a secret room that Galene had been in. Galene refers to this room as Crystalaura07" the *Wepwawet* replied.

Heinz was so angry, that his hands had fire falling from them. His eyes raged red. The constant gliding around the Wepwawet meant Isobel and Frederick kept their distance.

"You are constantly deceiving me. You will provide me with the knowledge of the Galene's whereabouts. You will cease to stop playing games with me. I will destroy you if do not comply" Heinz threw a firebomb at the cylinder on the floor. It moved further away from him. The *Wepwawet* was pulled with it. Heinz threw another fireball. The cylinder hit the wall with the door upon it.

"Stop, your third wish! I will help you one more time with your final wish"

Heinz stopped throwing the fireballs. Frederick was looking at the large fireball that Heinz had thrown high above into the room. It had fallen at least forty feet. Soon it would be on top of the wooden bookshelves.

Isobel had opened the doorway to the closet ready to leave. *"I want you to tell me the best wish, which I could do to achieve my result of finding that girl -Galene?"* Heinz asked the *Wepwawet* quite calmly. The *Wepwawet* was holding the spear out in front of him in readiness to fight off any oncoming fireball.

Frederick watched, but stepping closer to the closet as the highest bookshelf caught fire. The flames began to spread rapidly through the thousands of books stacked up on the shelves.

"Captain, the room it is now on fire. We need to leave immediately" Frederick anxiously commented.

"We will leave... when this wizard tells me what I want to know"

The *Wepwawet* was billowing- in and out of the tubular cylinder to find an answer to Heinz.

"You could wish for a tracker"

"Tell me more. How will this help me locate Galene?" Heinz moved closer to the *Wepwawet*, which was pressed against the wall.

The room was getting brighter from the every increasing fire that was spreading from artefact to artefact. Screams, wailing could be heard from the burning artefacts.

"It will help you to know where she is in all of time. It will provide you with the knowledge of her whereabouts. It is the best I can advise you on. You are supposed to make the wishes, I merely will grant them." The *Wepwawet* waited for the wish

to be said. Heinz began to think about what the *Wepwawet* had just said. Frederick had now also stepped back into the closet anxiously waiting,

"Captain, the fire is spreading fast" Frederick pulled his hat further over his face to avoid the intense heat.

"I wish for the tracker that you have spoken about, wizard. Grant me my wish!"

Without hesitation the *Wepwawet* granted the wish, the tracker object appeared in Heinz hand. The *Wepwawet* quickly shrunk back into the cylinder. Heinz threw a fireball at the canister on the floor, but it was too late, for the canister had disappeared before the fireball had any chance to do damage. Heinz stepped back into the closet.

Isobel performed the spell.

……………………………..

05th August 1943, 05:22

Standing back in the rubble of the burnt out houses, Frederick watched the door catch fire upon the wall. It was pulled into a small circular fire, before all that remained was the brick wall again. The original door to *Crystalaura04* was still in place.

Heinz was inspecting the tracker device. The object was a bracelet made from what could have been metal. The silver alloy, blended exactly with the colour of Heinz body. Heinz slipped the clip bracelet onto his wrist. It merged with his metallic skin. The bracelet was now part of him. He could not remove it. As it welded to his wrist, an influx of data filled his brain, from glowing cables that spread across his body. The information was on the operation of the tracker. Heinz pressed the tracker's face, it lit up with bright green writing. The writing began to project outwards, to a space in front of him. He asked the tracker a question.

"Where is Frederick my driver at this current time?"

The tracker projected a map with Frederick pinpointed by a red dot. It showed his exact location. It also showed the date, time of his location. *"This is marvellous; it will be easy to find the girl with this!"*

Frederick took a moment to push Isobel over onto the rubble. She fell, but hissed back at him. Heinz glanced to see the beam of a torch approaching from the roadside.

"Telegram for SS-Sturmhauptführer Heinz Bieg-Brauchitsch from the Third Reich Headquarters, Berlin"

Heinz lowered his floating body to the ground,

"That is me, is it important?"

"Heil" the German soldier replied, staring at the alien figure in front of him. He held his arm upwards in the air in front of himself. *"Sign here Captain"* the soldier clicked the heels of his boots together as he handed the telegram over. He stumbled into doing so upon the rubble. The soldier tried his hardest not to stare at Captain Heinz, but it was somewhat impossible. The Captain's silvery figure reflected the light from the torch back into his face.

"You may go" Heinz remarked, opening the telegram letter. The soldier fell a few times onto the hard rubble, for he could not resist turning around to stare at the strange robotic figure of Heinz.

"*Take the girl back to the car, wait for me there*" Heinz said whilst reading the telegram to himself.

"*Yes, Captain.* You with me" Frederick said, pointing his finger at Isobel. She groaned, back at him, but then proceeded to follow.

Captain Heinz,

We would like to commend you for all your work with the closing of the Treblinka camp. Stop. It is imperative that you capture the girl quickly. Stop. Once captured" stop. *Bring her to Berlin for questioning. Stop. She needs to be alive to open the book. Stop. The war is in vain if we cannot secure her power. Stop.*

Lieutenant General Schmidt.

....

Heinz created a flame as he blew the letter off his hand. It burnt to a smouldering black, lightweight ash.

Touching the *tracker* on his wrist, he asked for the location of Galene. He waited to see what was projected in front of his silver eyes.

"*Damn you wizard, DAMN YOU!*" he wailed, as the image showed the earth, with Galene popping up everywhere possible.

The time showed zeros, the date showed zeros and the place- showed everywhere possible!

Chapter 19

Galene's haystack

"Oh my god – Why did I not think of it before", Galene repeated it yet again, glancing around the room. "Objects, from this room are all about specific powers associated with people. You all have some special power so that means you will all have an object that is specific to you! Do you not see Isabella?"

Isabella smiled at Galene,

"I knew all the time; you just had to remember it for yourself Galene, as I cannot interfere with this timeline"

Jeremiah was holding the *Moses staff*; Asher was swiping the fabled *sword of King Arthur* as Galene pulled up her long flowing gown from the floor. She yelled,

"Come with me, I know where your item is kept. I filled this room… I know where everything is now!" she said, scrunching her face, looking unsure!

Galene began jogging through the darkened aisles between the all the bookshelves. Her bag was hooked across her shoulder, banging against her waist as she ran. In one hand she held the gown whilst in the other she held a papyrus light wand. Isabella was at her side as they reached a space that was filled with thousands of various sized wooden boxes.

"Everybody, we are looking for box 385. They are all labelled. Please be wary and do not open any of the boxes as they could be dangerous"

Isabella picked up a very small box. She pulled the label forward to read it.

Box 984

Crystal hairpin

Murasaki Shikibu tic toc.984

The Tale of Genji, A love of words

Note: Knowledge – power

Colour: Yellow

Isabella placed the box exactly upon the clear space that she had removed it from. Jeremiah was looking at the big boxes within the room. He walked around the box to find a label,

Box 2184

Antoine Louis tic toc.1785

Prototype of a Head-chopper

Later - become known as Guillotine

Warning: Dangerous- power of death

Colour: unclassified

Asher was reading label after label, just looking for the number 385. He wanted desperately to find it as Isabella had helped him retrieve the sword from the rock. Box after box was looked at, none of them could find the label 385.

"Galene, we have searched now for what seems like hours. Are you sure that the box is here?" Jeremiah said, in sheer frustration, "You said you knew where everything is…!"

Galene was still reading labels,

"I do know where everything is, well, sort of… except I was not that organised when I stored them here. It is here. I know it is" Even Galene was getting frustrated at not being able to find the box. Isabella was curious as to a box labelled with the colour violet. It was labelled 1541.

Box 1541

Galileo Galilei tic toc.1638

Crystal ring – mind vision

Colour: Violet

Note: Seeing is to believe

Isabella secretly opened the lid of the box to remove the ring from a purple velvet cloth. The silver banded ring held a large crystal rock. The crystal was smooth to touch. She placed the ring on her finger. The crystal glowed purple. Small purple veins began to flow from the crystal into Isabella's head. They pierced her skull. Flashing images of times in history from past, present and future filled her mind. Some of the history that she had never even imagined was now being shown to her in the form of a dream. Without warning, she collapsed onto the floor. The dreams continued. Jeremiah was the first to notice that Isabella was lying on the floor, so he came running over. He placed the *Moses Staff* beside her.

"Galene, quickly… Isabella, she has collapsed. What shall I do?" Jeremiah picked up Isabella's head to place it on his lap. He began stroking her hair as a tear fell from his eye onto her cheek. Galene dropped box 5621 on the floor to see what was happening. The contents spilled out, four *locusts* ran to the bookshelves in sequence, for cover. Asher picked up the empty box that lay by Isabella. He was reading the label. Galene arrived, Out of breath,

"What has happened, tell me quickly"

Asher gave her the empty box.

"It's the ring on her hand" Galene stated, placing the box on the floor. Jeremiah pulled her hand from under her body to see the ring glowing purple. He immediately began to remove the ring,

"Stop Jeremiah, it's not that simple. You cannot just remove the object from the person. It could do more harm. This object does not belong to her. It never will" Galene stated, frantically. "I somehow need to stop her seeing whatever it is- she is seeing" Galene began to pace up and down. Jeremiah watched Galene, before noticing that Isabella was ageing.

"Hurry Galene, Isabella is changing... She is ageing rapidly"

Galene thought frantically to find a solution. Asher stepped forward, placing his hands on Isabella's hand, she began to glow orange as his healing powers stopped the ageing process.

"Thank you Asher" Jeremiah stated,

He then saw that Asher was beginning to age. He had begun to drain Isabella of the power of the *crystal ring* upon healing her.

Galene stopped pacing. She held her hands above Isabella. She began muttering to herself, before finally committing to a spell.

"Hire gorputz gainean objektu,

Power tiraka eure arima batetik,
Itzali hori, hau hasi duzu,
Let kendu dit , zuk erdibitu egingo da"
Object upon thy body,
Pulling power from thy soul,
Turn off that, which you have started,
Let me remove you, you will be parted.

Galene swished her hands above Isabella. Red particle dust fell from her fingers onto the hand with the ring

"… Now Jeremiah, remove the ring quickly before it starts again" Jeremiah grabbed the ring on Isabella's index finger, he pulled it vigorously, as it was stuck above her knuckle. Asher quickly spit on her finger as he saw Jeremiah struggling to remove it. The ring slid off her hand. Jeremiah was finally holding the crystal ring. The purple glow dissipated from the crystal. Asher picked up the small wooden box- for Jeremiah to drop the ring back in. Galene smiled at herself. She had remembered the spell without the book. She was even more surprised, at the fact that most of the spells from the book were actually written by her.

"What's going on? Why are you all gathered around me?" Isabella questioned, sitting upright against one of the large boxes.

"I told you Isabella not to touch any object as you do not know its power. I have also to tell you Isabella that I remember… I can remember even more about this room. I even know that it is one of many! Although, I am not quite sure how many"

Isabella stood up on her feet, but wavered a little, so Jeremiah placed his arm around her waist. Asher opened the box for her to see the ring.

"You put this ring on your finger Isabella, then you collapsed" Asher snapped the box shut.

"I remember seeing lots of images. One vivid one kept reappearing. It was of a silver manlike figure. He was everywhere as we journeyed through history. He was with Isobel" Jeremiah released his grip on Isabella, when she became rather excited at one image. She pulled away from his arms. She raised hers to exaggerate the sky.

"It was beautiful... lots of moving colour across the sky. I felt at peace, relaxed, somewhat frozen. Galene I was totally mesmerised. I kept hearing you sing... But I cannot remember what the song was now"

Galene was looking upwards trying to imagine the colours in the sky. Jeremiah picked up the *Moses Staff* off the floor to lean upon. Asher tried to get close to Galene to see if he could imagine what she was imagining.

Slap!

"Ouch, I didn't touch her" Asher dropped his sword on the floor. Its noise reverberated through the space before echoing back. The broom had whacked Asher on the backside. Galene turned around,

"BROOM! Behave yourself"

Galene pulled up the long gown from the floor. She began to walk back in the direction of the round table.

"Come on, It will take forever to find that box. I am sure I will remember where I put it at some point, let's go back to the table"

Isabella picked up a papyrus light wand. She pulled Asher close to her. Asher was rubbing his backside. Jeremiah followed, but turned around to look at the endless boxes. The area was left in total darkness as they all departed. A couple of locusts ran across the darkness, following the light, Box 5621 lay opened on the floor, its label read,

Box 5621

Great Famine upon Tutankhamen

Locust infestation sent by Mother Gaia

Warning: Dangerous- power of death

Colour: black

....

Galene arrived firstly at the table. The single light bulb above flickered. She threw her bag on top of the outer circle. It moved ever so slightly to the right.

Asher was playing with the sword yet again; He knocked more books off the shelving on passing by them. Isabella was humming to herself... *"Ring a ring O' roses.*

Jeremiah began humming it too. Galene joined in.

"That song just haunts me... there is something about it, but I just cannot put my finger upon what it is" Galene said, stopping her humming as she removed the *Tic toc ticker* from her bag. Jeremiah placed the *Moses Staff* across the table gently. Isabella paced her hands flat on the table.

"That is the song I heard when I was dreaming. I remember it now that is definitely the song. The silver man with Isobel, along with that annoying, but beautiful nursery rhyme"

Galene responded, whilst searching through her bag,

"It only became a nursery rhyme in earth's time, but let me assure you it is not... Why did I say that?" Galene dropped the handles of the bag onto the table, whilst she tried to think to herself. The harder she tried to remember, the more her mind blocked her thoughts. Asher's stomach was rumbling once again, "I'm hungry; it was ages ago when we ate some food" he said rubbing his aching stomach.

"You are totally right Asher, We need to leave this place to find food. We know the time, the place that we should be going to. So, do you think we should go?" Galene stared at Isabella firstly,

"Of Course Galene"

"I am up for that, I like adventures" Jeremiah stated.

Asher jumped up and down in excitement,

"Yay, food is on its way. Jeremiah, what food do they cook in Egypt?" Asher was pushing the sword into his belt whilst he asked the question.

"Whatever they have, it will have to be *Kosher* meat" Isabella stated, "My father was very strict with food. He triple checked everything that he bought to ensure it was fresh. He always bought his meat from a *Kosher* Butcher!"

Asher approached the table; He pulled a box from underneath to be able to climb onto the table with his sword. The circumference of the table moved again, Isabella steadied it with the hand as Asher sat down. A metal cylinder rolled off onto the floor on the opposite side, where Asher was sitting. Jeremiah walked around to pick up the cylinder,

"Isn't this the Tube that you lost Galene?" he asked, as he read the scribed letters.

Galene took the cylinder from Jeremiah. She rolled it around in her hand.

"It most certainly is. How curious. I wonder how it got back here"

Isabella took the metallic tube, off her. She closed her eyes, whilst she concentrated on the tube.

"The *Wepwawet* was talking to the silver man figure... Isobel was also present. I can see them clearly" Isabella handed the cylinder back to Galene, "It appears that they were granted wishes by the creature"

"Is that so, the wishes should never have been granted without my permission" Galene twisted the metallic tube to open it. Smoke billowed from the opening. The *Wepwawet* was standing before her.

"Yes, master, you require my assistance once more?"

"You granted wishes to a silver man like figure, tell me more? What did he ask for?"

"Master, I can only apologise. He forced me into giving him wishes. He would have destroyed my container if I did not do so" The *Wepwawet* bowed down onto one knee, "please forgive me, do not punish me yet again"

Galene looked bewildered, "Punish you? Why would I do that?"

"You have done it before, especially if I did not comply with any request that you made" The *Wepwawet* removed a large bracelet that covered his right arm. He turned his arm over for her to see. Galene gasped. Isabella turned away as she felt sick. Jeremiah held his hand to his mouth to stop himself being sick.

"I did this to you? Why would I? How could I?" Galene was stammering all the words outwards.

"You have changed Master; you now seem calmer, much happier. Before you were violent, aggressive"

Asher moved closer to the *Wepwawet*, he kneeled with his head bowed. He was staring at the large infected abrasions' on the *Wepwawet* arm. The cuts were bleeding; puss was oozing out from the large sores. Asher grabbed the *Wepwawet* arm. He began to glow orange. Within moments the sore, cuts had healed on the *Wepwawet*.

"Why do you do this for me?" the creature said, before howling. "Thank you Master"

Galene was shocked that she had done this to *Wepwawet*. She was relieved to see Asher heal him so.

Isabella placed her arm around Asher, as he stepped back from *Wepwawet*. The *Wepwawet* rolled the large gold bracelet towards Asher,

"Wear it, for one day it will protect you"

Asher placed the bracelet on his arm, it shrank to fit.

Galene asked, "So, this silver man was with a girl? What did they want with you?"

Wepwawet replied instantly,

"Yes Master, he was with a girl. But they were also with another man. They wanted you... He wanted you" bowing his head yet again towards Galene, he continued, "I did not give him what they wanted Master, I tricked him. The wishes were useless. I gave him a *tracker* to find you, but it does not work. You appear everywhere at every point in history"

Galene placed the cylinder on the table. She was in deep thought whilst doing so.

"Did he use the *tracker* to find me?"

Wepwawet paused, whilst he rewound time to view Heinz use the tracker attached to his wrist.

"It did not work Master. I have watched him use it"

Galene was not totally convinced by *Wepwawet* answer. "Is it possible that it did not work, merely for the fact I am in this room, which you know has no time or place on earth?"

Wepwawet bowed yet again,

"I am sorry, Master, It could be so" *Wepwawet* held out his spear, a ball of light appeared which only he could see. It showed Captain Heinz, using the device in the not so distant future. The device was working. "When you leave this room, he may be able to track you, but there will always be a delay in him tracking of you,"

Galene was angry, "You have failed me so. I do not need you anymore. Return to your tube" Galene angrily stated.

Wepwawet howled, whilst being drawn back into the cylinder. Galene slammed her hands on the table.

"DAMN"

Asher jumped off the edge startled. When he did so, he knocked the boxes over underneath.

"Sorry Galene, it was an accident," he said.

The broom flew in out of nowhere; it began sweeping Asher away from the table. It was sweeping him away from the overturned boxes which could have been dangerous.

Jeremiah began picking up the boxes...

Chapter 20

The Silver Crystal

04th August 1943, 06:38am

Frederick closed the door of the car. Heinz sat comfortably upon the cold leather seat. Isobel was sitting in the front of the car with Frederick. The small box with the crystal was digging uncomfortably into the side of Heinz waist. He removed it from his pocket. He was rolling the box in his hand. Frederick caught a glimpse of him in the rear view mirror. Heinz removed his dark sunglasses. Frederick looked again in the mirror,

"Where would you like me to drive you Captain?" Frederick asked. He finally saw the full face of Heinz as he asked the question. Frederick gasped at his glowing red eyes. He averted his own to avoid seeing any more of the Captain staring back at him. Frederick uncontrollably yawned. He had not slept for quite some hours.

"You are tired... you will rest whilst I think. I need to somehow work out how to capture that girl... Galene... by surprise" Heinz opened the car door by himself. He removed his hat placing it on the seat.

The day was appearing rather fast. The brightness made Heinz replace the sunglasses back on his nose less face. The small bump that remained allowed him to rest the ridge of the sunglasses on it. He began to glide across the park. Frederick could not keep his eyes open any longer. His eyelids flickered closed, then open, just enough to see Heinz enter the park. Isobel curled up on the hard seat. She began to sleep like a cat. Occasionally she hissed without realising.

Heinz was in the park. Leaves fell quickly onto the damp dew on the ground. In the distance, he saw the wall of the *Warsaw Ghetto*. German Soldiers were being marched to its entrance.

Heinz opened the small box. The crystal changed colour from white to silver. He removed it from the padded lining. Holding it up in the air, he watched it shimmer in the morning sun through his darkened shades.

Two German soldiers marched by him without him even realising. They stared intensely at him holding the crystal. They never saw his Captain's uniform as the sun was blinding their eyes, One German soldier remarked,

"Look at the freak!"

The other German soldier rubbed his eyes under his round rimmed spectacles to glimpse Heinz viewing the crystal.

"Yah, it is a freak show. Weirdo's always congregate in the park," marching quickly on by. Heinz never quite heard their remarks. He willed for them to repeat what they had said once again, so he could listen this time. His body juddered, whilst his eyesight blurred momentarily. The crystal spun in the palm of his hand.

-Two German soldiers marched on by. Only this time he was aware of them. One German soldier remarked,

"Look at the freak!"

The other soldier was about to comment about him when Heinz placed the crystal back in his pocket. He created two fireballs in his hands. He blew one fire ball towards the first soldier, who instantaneously caught fire. The soldier began to run away in flames, before exploding. The other tried to run. Heinz blew the other fireball at the other soldier who also exploded. A cloud of dark dust rained down from the trees, followed by an abundance of golden leaves. Heinz removed the silver crystal from his jacket pocket once more. He placed it back in his palm. He began to think of the two soldiers just moments ago. The crystal began to spin in his palm.

-Two German soldiers marched passed him. One German soldier remarked,

"Look at the freak!

The other German soldier rubbed his eyes under his round rimmed spectacles to glimpse Heinz.

"Yah, it is a freak show. Weirdo's always congregate in the park," he said, marching quickly on by.

Heinz let them carry on walking this time. He was more fascinated with the fact that, the crystal could alter time by using his thoughts projected towards it. He stared at it once more in his hand. A *face* reflected in the front facet. Heinz peered around to his rear to see if someone was standing behind him. No one was there. He stared at the crystal once more.

"No one there, my mind is playing tricks upon me... But I am sure that there was a face in this crystal...." He said to himself. Heinz placed the silver crystal back into its box, before

dropping it into his pocket. He peered down at the tracker on his wrist. It still showed Galene all across the globe. Heinz tried to remove the tracker from his metallic wrist, but it was welded tightly against his arm. The sun was bearing down upon him, his skin was getting hot. Heinz glided into the shade of a tree. He bowed his head to rest. Hovering from the ground, his body rested against the rough bark of the tree. He became transparent. The tree shone through him. Heinz had disappeared from view. His skin adapted to the environment when he slept. Just like a chameleon blending to its own environment.

Isobel was fighting with Frederick. Their squabbling started within Frederick's car, parked by the burnt out houses. Their loud voices could be heard by Heinz. It woke him from his resting place. He became visible.

Heinz arrived back at the car to witness both of them rolling around on the stone pavement. He stood above them watching. He glided closer to see why they were fighting. Frederick's hand touched his foot as he hovered above them. Isobel stopped instantly, viewing the statuesque figure above her.

"What are you two are fighting for?"

"She took my gold locket, from my pocket whilst I was asleep" Frederick stated, pointing at the locket in Isobel's hand. Both of them stood upright to face Heinz.

"Give it to me now" Heinz held out his silvery palm towards Isobel. Isobel reluctantly gave it to him. Heinz examined the gold item with fine engraving upon the exterior. He clicked the spring button to open it,

"Who is she? Who is the girl Frederick?" Heinz asked

Isobel hissed at Frederick, before running to see the image in the locket. "That's Galene!" Isobel screamed out in excitement. Heinz understood her scream of excitement over the photo of Galene.

"So this is Galene. How did you come by this locket?"

Frederick was embarrassed at the situation. He placed his hand back into his jacket pocket to feel the other gold jewellery that he had. One of the rings in his pocket, he gripped tightly, as his thoughts were re-living the day that he shot the woman, *Syeira Angelica*. He looked at his boots, for he could visualise the circular marks that she had made with her blood-stained finger.

"It was from the woman traveller with the trailer. We stopped there many, many months ago at Malkinia Gorna. We questioned her about where she was travelling too?"

"She travelled alone? Why have you got this locket?"

Frederick let go of the ring in his pocket. Isobel mimed the sentence yet again at Frederick, who was looking very uneasy with the situation.

"She had died; I took the jewellery to sell at a later date"

"So you never saw the girl travelling with her?"

"No Captain… but on the night I visited her, I was absolutely sure that there was someone else nearby. But then I dismissed it," Frederick bit into his lip as he was nervous.

"Isobel… Is it a recent image of the girl - Galene?"

Frederick had to translate the question to Isobel.

"Yes it is…" she hissed at Frederick once more.

"Frederick. Get this small image relayed to all Heads of command in Berlin. Use the Warsaw Prison facilities to aid you. We need a publication of this girl- with a reward for her capture" Heinz pulled the small Black & White photo from the locket. He gave the locket back to Frederick, who immediately dropped it back in his pocket with the other gold items. Isobel tried to place her hand in his pocket to remove the locket again. Frederick hit her hand with his knuckles.

"Hiss!" Frederick ran across the park, relieved, whilst Isobel watched Heinz remove the silver crystal from its box. Isobel reached out to touch the silver crystal. Her finger came in contact with it ever so slightly. She saw the face looking at her.

"Who are you?" she said.

"Who are you talking too?" Heinz asked her.

"The face in the crystal, I saw the face looking at me"

Heinz rubbed the crystal on his jacket to polish it. He stared directly at the crystal. The face was staring back at him.

"Who are you?" Heinz asked. His own silver face was being duplicated in the many other facets of the stone. The face spoke to Heinz. Isobel stood on Heinz hovering feet to see more.

"I am *Graumus. Zaude?"* - *"I am Graumus. You are?"*

"Captain Heinz Bieg-Brauchitsch of the Third Reich"

The crystal listened to Heinz voice, analysing the language, before next replying in *German.*

"So Captain Heinz Bieg-Brauchitsch of the Third Reich - answer my question... What Tic Toc is this?" The face came closer to

the facet. Just an eye was staring back at him through the crystal surface.

"What Tic Toc? I do not understand the question"

"Tic Toc, Time, Year in your language or understanding," the crystal said, oblivious to others apart from his own race.

"August 1943. Who are you? Why do you need to know this?" Heinz changed the direction of his body as the sunlight was refracting light from the crystal into his eyes.

"You have changed I see, you have grown into my body. I search for a girl with the spell book also. Her name is Galene. Do you know of her?" The crystal showed a mouth whilst speaking; it had no lips, but sharp, filed teeth visible in conversation. Two openings under the eyes that let out a fine mist each time the mouth opened. The mist moistened the forever open eyes. Heinz could not wait to reply,

"We search for the same girl. I know of her whereabouts, but I cannot seem to reach her"

The crystal eye was viewing from the facet once again.

"You are not alone I see, that creature with you... explain?" Heinz placed his arm around Isobel; she gripped onto his jacket to avoid falling off his feet.

"This is Isobel, she knows of Galene. She knows how devious Galene is in avoiding capture"

Isobel responded by hissing.

"You say that you know the girl's whereabouts, tell me as I can help in her capture. She needs to be stopped before it is all too late" The crystal received no reply as Isobel never understood German.

Heinz showed the crystal the *tracker* upon his arm. At the present time Galene appeared to be everywhere. The crystal watched the tracker, turn on, then off, flashing numerous places, times, dates as it did so.

"The tracker will not work whilst she is in one of the hidden rooms. I know this is so. I helped her create them many tic toc's ago. Once she leaves the room- then we will see where she is"

Heinz for the first time, smiled.

....

04th August 1943, 12:09pm

Frederick had given clear instruction to the *Warsaw Ghetto* commander with regards to the photograph. An exact copy in pen and ink was being drawn by an artist, before going to print. Frederick instructed them, that he would call back later to review the finished newsletter. He had also said that the first print was to be sent to the *Reich headquarters command Offices in Berlin*. With his hand upon the gold in his pocket, Frederick made is way to the central district of Warsaw. A pawn shop that was marked *"Schmuck gekauft - Jewellery bought"* had already been raided by the *Reich army.*

The shop window had been smashed, its doors left wide open. Frederick glanced inside, before stepping onto the broken glass.

"You won't find any gold in there, The Reich Army has it all" a small, German woman said, passing by the shop. Frederick's feet crunched upon the broken shards of glass as he stepped out from the shop.

"Is there anywhere I can sell my gold?" Frederick removed a few pieces from his pocket to show her.

"Not anymore, The Nazi Party want's it all to fund the war. You could donate it to them," she laughed, as she carried on walking up the street.

Four German trucks drove by. Frederick stood on the deserted street, glancing at either side. He saw a Jewish man jump from the rear of the truck trying to escape. The German soldier fired a gunshot from the truck as he was running. The Jewish man stopped in slow motion, he slumped to the ground. The trucks carried on towards the *Warsaw Ghetto*. The fallen Jewish man was surrounded by a pale blue crystalline powder. The powder gathered momentum into a tornado shape before it shot upwards into the sky.

Frederick released his grip on the gold in his pocket. The sky suddenly darkened. Frederick felt a chill through his body. His feet had a mound of black crystals forming around them. He tried to step out, but he just couldn't move. At the far end of the street, a ghostly figure floated towards him. The figure was moving rapidly. It was a woman. She held a knife in her hand.

"You are dead, I shot you!" Frederick shouted.

The figure of *Syeira Angelica* moved in closer. Frederick removed his gun. He began firing the bullets one after the other. The gun ran out, so he threw the gun at her. He watched her figure rise up above him to the three orbs that hung outside the shop. The screws holding the metal orbs in place began to slowly unscrew ever slowly. In sheer panic, Frederick began tugging at his legs, but they were firmly stuck to the floor. One screw fell on top of Frederick's head. The second screw fell beside him along with the third. The fourth and final screw released the three globes from way up high on the exterior wall of the shop. It Fell…

"Arrrrhhhhh" he screamed, throwing his arms up above his head.

… Silence…

One of the globes rolled into the road covered in blood, before rolling back towards the body of Frederick on the pavement. The globe rolled onto the bloodstained boot. The drawn markings that *Syeira Angelica* had made on the black leather began to pulsate. The drawing of the three circles with four dots began to glow. . The curse was now complete. The black crystals dissipated from the pavement.

The ghostly figure of *Syeira Angelica,* disappeared.

The old German woman saw Frederick lay upon the pavement on her return about an hour later.

"Unfortunate soul, Justice comes to all eventually, in one way or another…!" she said, stepping over his bloody body, but laughing.

Chapter 21

A Book with Verse?

The broom had brushed Asher further away from the table. Jeremiah commented,

"Galene, look there are boxes at the base of the table. One of those wouldn't by any coincidence, be box 385?"

Galene bent over pulling the small boxes towards her, reading the labels as she did so.

"Well, I will be damned, it's here Isabella. Box 385". Isabella moved closer to the table, Galene lifted the box onto it. She read the label…

The Wiz-T translated, *Italian* language

Box 385

Lisa del Giocondo tic toc. 1506

The Headscarf modelled in painting.

Fine silk.

See reverse: note

Colour. Violet

Galene flipped the card over to the reverse side to read the following out to everybody.

Lisa — business woman, mother, wife

Had vivid dreams of the world, very surreal

As captured by the artist – Leonardo- in the painting.

Scarf: Will give great thinking power to "those" who wears it.

Updated note: renamed Mona Lisa

Galene placed the label on the table whilst she pulled the lid off the box. Inside laid the fine silk, dark purple headscarf. Isabella touched the silk, but on doing so part of the scarf shimmered with light. Small glitter dust particles, adorned Isabella's fingertips.

"It's so beautiful," she placed the scarf over her head to see what would happen, but was weary after the last incident with the ring.

"It will be fine Isabella, we are all here if you need us" Galene said, watching the scarf lay flat on top of Isabella's hair. The scarf twinkled. A halo formed above Isabella's head, before it disappeared from sight into the shape of her hairline.

"Where has it gone? Asher enquired, getting closer to Isabella. "It's completely disappeared, I cannot see it anymore"

Isabella placed her hand up to her hairline; she could feel it resting upon her head.

"I don't feel any different, is it supposed to do something?" Isabella remained calm. Galene grabbed her hand tightly,

"Close your eyes... Read me, what am I now thinking of" Galene then let go of her hand before she began thinking of a certain food.

"Pumpkin, you are thinking of Pumpkin pie"

"That is correct, if I had asked you before to see what I am thinking you, would have had to reach out and touch me to do so. Is that correct?"

"That is correct," but I was not touching you was I?, I could see everything that you were thinking, including your thoughts on Egypt with its large green Olives"

"I had forgotten how powerful this head scarf is. I remember that when *Lisa* wore it, she had strange dreams of many imaginary places, but I can assure you some were not imaginary After she had been painted by *Leonardo,* she gave it to me for safe keeping, but alas, she never asked for it back" Galene could not believe that she had remembered something else, which had happened to her in the past.

"That's impossible! How could you have met all these people throughout history? That would make you thousands of years old?" Jeremiah stated, examining her face, looking for wrinkles upon her smooth skin.

"I don't really know, I cannot remember anything else. Just on occasion, something seems to jog my memory. I remember her very well. She was extremely nice to me. I remember that I was but a child myself. I was ten earth years old, but over two thousand tic *toc's* in reality"

Isabella sighed. She placed her hand on Galena's shoulder.

"It would seem you're remembering lots more each passing minute that we spend together. You now have to remember why you forgot it all in the first place!" Isabella's hand remained firmly on Galene's shoulder. It was then that Galene's subconscious mind, told Isabella why she was forced to forget. Isabella gasped at the sight she saw. She thought of letting go of Galene so the image would stop. It did not stop; the headscarf heightened her sensory perception. She saw all, in quick succession, image after image.

"Oh my word... You were bad. Oh my... the anger... the hatred!" Isabella pulled the scarf from her hair. "I don't want to see anymore. This is not the person I see before me"

Jeremiah and Asher just watched as Isabella threw the scarf upon the table.

"What is it Isabella, What did you see about Galene that shocked you?" Jeremiah inquisitively asked.

Asher stepped closer to Isabella for he wanted to know as well. "I don't think it will change any timeline in history. So I can say... Galene, the Spell book is not what it seems. It changed you into something evil. This room... came about because of that book, along with the other eight rooms. I saw a shape connecting all the rooms with lines. A nine sided shape... like that on Jeremiah's face" Isabella pointed at the nonagon shape made by the flying buttons.

Galene removed the book from her bag. She placed the small trinket size leather bound hardback on the table. She stroked the spine cautiously. It grew bigger, as she waved her hand above it. It began to push the scrolls off the table onto the floor. Jeremiah had just enough time to grab the *Moses staff* to prevent it falling.

"I don't understand Isabella, how? Why was I evil? What has happened to me?" she said, as the book enlarged, to a size that filled the table. Isabella touched the book once more. She picked up the headscarf to lay it flat on her head, resting against her shiny hair. As she did so, she saw more about the book.

"Show me, why you want Galene so much?" she asked the book in thought.

The book played images in Isabella's mind. What was just a few seconds was somewhat longer for Isabella. She viewed different parts of the history all at once. A multi-channel of images was installed in her brain.

"I was right, Galene" Isabella quickly let her hand fall away from the leather cover, "the book needs you, in fact it needs all of us. We are not yet complete. You are the Key. It told me- *Galene key* over and over. Does that make sense?"

Galene remembered the missing page, she kissed the clasp, "Yes, the book says *Galene Key* where the page was removed" Galene opened the book to the centre pages. Jeremiah and Asher stepped closer to see Galene flip the pages to point out the words *Galene key*.

"But you said I was evil? What happened to me?"

Isabella pulled the scarf from her hair once more. She tucked it into a small pocket in her dress.

"All I know is the book forced you to do something that you did not agree with. It would not show me what it was. You refused to become part of the its plan. The spell cast upon you was quite recent, give or take a few centuries from what I can see. You cast this spell upon yourself to escape remembering. Except, what you did not realise is that the spell would make you forget everything, including who you are... Every time you get too close to any people or remember too much, your spell makes you forget again.

You need to remember which spell it was to reverse it, before you forget all of us" Isabella instinctively remarked. Asher was at Galene's side when the broom swooped in from behind, lifting him up high into the air. He gripped the broom stale firmly as it flew above the bookshelves.

"Broom, that's enough of your fooling around. Bring Asher back here now this instant!" Galene shouted, which she followed with a high pitch whistling sound. The broom flew back towards the table. But it landed a few feet away from Galene. Asher jumped off the broom smiling. He pulled his sword out to attack. As he swung the blade forward, to jab the bristles of the broom- it shot off rapidly. Asher stumbled over onto the floor. Jeremiah laughed.

"Isabella I need to ask you something. I want to know the truth. Is Ma- *Syeira Angelica* my real mother? Please tell me as I need to know?"

Jeremiah stopped laughing instantly. He hushed Asher, who was making combat fighting noises. Isabella placed her hand, unintentionally on the spell book,

"I cannot tell you that. I do not know" the spell book answered the question to Isabella. Her bottom lip quivered ever so slightly.

Galene responded by slamming the book closed, and then shrinking the book. Her frustration created such haste. She threw it back into her bag.

"Let's go, we need to get out of here, before it drives us all insane. I have never spent this much time in any of *these* rooms by myself, as I wanted to be with people. Besides which- I know someone is hungry," she looked in the direction of Asher. Isabella whispered to Jeremiah,

"She has just remembered more without realising"

Galene reached for the *Tic Toc Ticker*. She began programming the destination of *Egypt, Cairo 1906* with the date on the illuminated letters and numbers. All four of them stood in a line, holding each other's hand. Jeremiah laid the *Moses staff* on the floor as it was too large to take. Galene shouted,

"Are we all already? Hold on tight and whatever you do this time Isabella, Don't let go!"

Galene launched the *Tic Toc Ticker* into the air. The opening appeared just to the side of Galene. Asher jumped in first; he pulled Isabella next, along with Jeremiah. Galene followed last. She grabbed the *Ticker*. She held on extremely tight to it so she could drag it through the time portal.

Whoosh! The broom followed just in the time... *pop!*

Chapter 22

Vanishing Point

04th August 1943, 15:39pm

The tracker on Heinz arm began flashing. A message appeared on the brightly lit tracker in glowing red letters, *Galene- Egypt, Cairo 1906, July 25th, 04.46am*

Isobel was excited at the tracker showing the whereabouts of Galene. She began skipping sideways; humming *"Ring a Ring O' Roses"* Heinz began to wonder where Frederick had got to. His impatience was showing by the way he hovered behind Isobel, circling.

"I cannot wait any longer. We must catch that girl – Galene. The crystal will help us achieve this goal," he said to Isobel, who did not understand his German.

Heinz pulled out the crystal box from his pocket. He removed the silver crystal from the silk lining.

"Crystal, the girl Galene has appeared in Egypt, Cairo... ~Look at my tracker"

An eye appeared in the crystal facet, it stared at the tracker embedded in Heinz wrist. Heinz faced the crystal face as Isobel climbed onto his foot.

"At last I will have the girl. We must go. I need you to capture her for me. Once you have her, give her my face crystal. She will instantly know how to use it" the crystal cut surfaces, began to expand. Shooting strings of lights encompassed Heinz with Isobel. The strands formed a bubble of light, which

shrunk to the smallest miniscule size before it vanished. The crystal held Heinz, Isobel in complete darkness, as it searched for the exit to the new time, new place. Isobel clung on tighter to Heinz jacket for a fear of falling into nothingness. A small light was visible in the distance, the vanishing point grew larger. They were being pulled towards it.

Before they exited Isobel commented,

"Whoa, this place is hot! Is this Egypt?" she said, as they began to resize back to the original height, down a small alleyway, in Egypt's, Cairo. It was night-time. It was a full moon that was shining down upon them.

Heinz began to tap on the tracker with his silvery finger. It showed Galene not far away. Isobel jumped off Heinz boot. She wafted her face with the palm of her hand to cool down. Heinz remained cold, his skin resembled frozen metal.

"So crystal what do you want me to do with her when I have her? As I need the girl safe, with the book intact, for my superiors would like to question her" Heinz held the crystal directly in front of his face. The crystal face came into view. The mouth came closer to the facet face.

"I need her alive too, She needs to restore me to my former glory. I need to finish off what I stopped many tic toc's ago"

The face disappeared back into the crystal. Heinz placed it back in the box in his pocket. Isobel watched Heinz view the Tracker once more. He began to follow the drawn out map that was projected towards the flashing dot of Galene.

"At last the Reich will be proud of my achievement. I will be promoted to the highest command once I capture her.

Chapter 23

Shepheard Hotel, Cairo

Cairo, Egypt – 1906, February 22nd, 03.30 am

They all fell out of the *Tic Toc Ticker*, into numerous large wicker baskets that stood side by side. Galene was the last to fall. Her grip on the *Tic Toc Ticker* inverted back as her hand slipped through the portal opening that hovered in mid-air. The broom just managed to fly through before the gap began swirling like a tornado, closing with a loud popping noise. Asher stood up slowly, showing his head out of the top of the basket. It was night-time. Stars filled the sky, upon what was a very hot, dry night. Galene's head sneaked over the top of the largest basket,

"Phew! It's mighty hot in this place," she said, rolling the basket onto its side, so she could climb out. She began peering in all the other baskets to find Isabella and Jeremiah. Jeremiah glanced over the top of the far basket, which lay against a mud plaster made wall. A makeshift canopy, partly covered a stone carved bath, filled with water. A camel was drinking from it.

A male approached from the distance. He acknowledged Galene as he walked on by. Galene suddenly had a thought,

"Excuse me, Sir, What date is this? What year?" she said.

The reply from the man was somewhat scary as he began shouting,

"Stop being so ridiculous, you know what year this is?... Go away. You are irritating little children" The Wiz-T began to translate, *Arabic* language, the man held up his fists up in anger, he was mumbling to himself.

"He was scary," Isabella remarked, tipping the basket on its side to climb out. Asher tried his hardest to roll the basket, it just would not move as it was weighted down with a large quantity of coconuts. Jeremiah had already climbed out of his, so he pulled Asher free. Galene looked at the *Tic Toc Ticker*, it was flashing on and off.

"I think the Ticker is trying to communicate with me," she said, pushing the flashing red light on the very thin panel. The image was blurred due to the brightness of the moonlight.

"We need somewhere darker to view this"

"Here inside this passageway" Jeremiah stated, pointing towards the passageway which had a covered arch above it. It was ideal, since it was completed shaded, if not hotter. Asher was already changing colour. His face was becoming flushed with blood, as the heat of *Cairo* was making him sweat.

They all made their way under the arched passage, Galene hit the button again, and an image of a building flashed up. It was projected onto the mud wall. It showed a huge building. Using her fingers, she flipped the projection one hundred and eighty degrees to see the other side. A name appeared,

"Shepheard Hotel! It's a hotel, but why a hotel? "Isabella stated, "What is the significance of this hotel with the *crystals...* sorry I meant to say with our mission to find the missing *Spell book* page?"

The Shepheard Hotel was a leading Hotel in Cairo in the nineteenth century. It was originally called the Hotel de Anglais until an eccentric entrepreneur from Northamptonshire took over the hotel in the 1841. He named the hotel after himself once he, and his shared partner separated, (Samuel) Shepheard. He sold the hotel in 1861 when he retired, but the name remained in place, as the reputation of the hotel standards had spread far and wide. It was renowned for being- opulent with such grandeur. The hotel was destroyed by fire in 1952 during the anti-British riots.

The camel began to make grunting noises, Asher could not resist in replying. He began a conversation as the *Wiz-T* began to translate his noises into camel dialect.

"I agree with you, it is mighty hot here, what if… I will cool you down with some water?" He said to the camel. Asher began splashing the camel's head with water from the drinking bath. Galene closed the *Ticker* down by pressing a white light located in the top right hand corner, before throwing it into her bag.

"We need to blend in with the people here! Our outfits are from the future. I noticed that there was some clothing in one of the baskets"

Jeremiah was already in the process of tipping the other baskets over to retrieve the clothing. Asher was getting rather excited at the prospect of dressing up in costume. Isabella tucked her hair under the *keffiyeh.*

Keffiyeh - (a square piece of cloth wrapped around the head to protect from the sun).

Asher's robe was extremely long. Galene removed a pair of scissors from her bag to shorten the length. She cut vigorously through the cotton material. The broom kept brushing Asher's hands away, as he tried to support himself on Galene as she cut away at the cloth. Jeremiah was patting the back of the camel, the coarse hair released dust into the air, which made him sneeze. Galene kept her black robe on. She tied it around the waist with a piece of rope so it looked like a *qaftân-(A long robe garment used in hot countries).*

"Broom..." she said, "fly above up into the sky, find the *Shepheards Hotel*"

The broom shot off into the night. It veered from side to side, in search of the hotel. It flew over the rooftops of Cairo. Asher lifted his robe, so he could pull the sword from his inner short trouser leg. He had sneaked it through when the others were not looking. Isabella gasped,

"You fool, that blade could have cut you to pieces" she then thought about what she had just said, "How silly of me, you would have healed yourself" Isabella smiled whilst ruffling his hair.

The broom returned quite quickly, it zoomed down from the starry sky towards Galene. Galene jumped upon the broom,

"I won't be too long, I shall be shown the way by the broom" she said. Using the *"Invisibility spell,"* she and the broom shot off into the night.

Asher needed to know more about the sword. He wanted Isabella to tell him more.

"Isabella, I have been thinking about this sword" Asher held the sword upwards. It glistened in the moonlight, "If I have the power to heal, then why have I got a sword that can kill?"

Isabella touched the hand of Asher that held the sword tightly. She removed her *Keffiyeh* so she could place the *Lisa headscarf* on to her hair. Jeremiah held the *Keffiyeh* whilst she did so.

"Well, Asher, it seems the sword was meant for you. Although fabled to be the sword of *King Arthur*, I can now confirm it was no fable, it was his. It was bonded to the stone as a test of faith, not strength, as most people would think the latter. Only a true believer could have removed it from the large boulder that it was embedded in. The bond that the sword and you have is a perfect match. The sword was not meant for killing. It gives the one who holds it greater confidence, an ability to choose whether death is, or can be the only option. You are a healer. The sword will protect the healer from death" Isabella removed the scarf from her hair. She crumpled it back into her pocket. Asher looked more relieved at the thought of not having to kill someone.

The broom whooshed down beside Jeremiah. Galene became visible.

"It's not far guys," she jumped off the broom. She stroked the broom a few times. Its bristles shivered, before it flew away into the sky once more. "Come on, it will probably take about fifteen *toc's* or so"

Isabella replaced her *Keffiyeh* back on her head. Jeremiah adjusted the band that held it in place. Asher was already walking out of the dark alley, following Galene. Isabella lifted the long robe that was dragging on the dusty, sandy floor so she could sprint a little to catch up.

Eventually they arrived at a huge building -that never seemed to end. On finding the entrance they all huddled together under the canopy across the street. They viewed the hotel from the *Bazaar markets*, under the many archways. The street was busy, despite it now being 06:05am. The small terrace at the front entrance had numerous tables occupied with gentlemen smoking pipes. The waiters were smartly dressed in white robes tied with dark belts as they served iced tea. The name *"SHEPHEARD"* was stitched in black lettering on the front, to ensure everybody knew that they worked for the hotel. The wicker furniture with its plush red cushions attracted attention from people who passed by on donkeys, camels or even horse drawn coaches. Jeremiah rubbed his hand on the crumbling mud plastered wall to ensure that it would not fall, before he leant against it. They could see the entrance was a hive of activity, people passing to and from the hotel. The only problem was that they never saw any children, just adults. Isabella watched as people just walked into the hotel without being questioned.

"Galene, it cannot be difficult to enter the building like everybody else is doing. We need to try it to see"

Galene was unsure about it, but agreed to try. They all approached the steps up onto the front terrace. The terrace on either side of the doors was busy. One Arab member of staff was watering the shrubs.

"Walk normally with me into the hotel" Isabella stated, as she paraded up the stairway to the large glass door entrance. Adorned with palm trees, she pushed the door inwards, it was held open by a male Egyptian doorman. Isabella nodded before thanking him. The Wiz-t translated her speech.

"Wow, this place is just as huge inside" Asher cried out, his mouth fell open as he stared at all the marble columns. Large palms grew in ornate pots on the brightly coloured floor tiles. They progressed further inwards into the long hallway. The *Cook & Son* stall was open for business this early in the morning selling tours around the *Pyramids,* or into the desert by camel. Posters with chalkboards advertised the prices below each one. The hotel was busy with people checking in, or checking out at the long ornate carved, reception desk.

"So where do we go from here?" Jeremiah enquired, staring at men dressed in suits, women dressed in full length dresses entering the restaurant for breakfast. "I think we are slightly underdressed for the restaurant," he said, pointing at the people being shown to their tables inside.

"To the kitchens" Galene stated, "Asher needs food, but firstly, we need to find where the kitchens are!" Isabella saw the Englishman on the *Cook stall* giving advice to a couple wishing to venture on a trip up the *Nile*. The couple was reading the leaflet. Isabella asked whilst they were doing so,

"Excuse me, sir, Could you point me in the direction of the kitchens please?"

The male behind the stall, smiled politely at her. He grabbed Isabella's arm to guide her to show her a different view point of the hotel.

"You need to go through that doorway, keep walking down a sky lit corridor before you reach the kitchen it is on the opposite side of the restaurant" he said pointing at the closed door. Isabella thanked him, but told him to *"hold on to his dream, as it will happen"* Isabella had read everything about him from the touch of his hand onto hers.

"Well, did you find out how to get there?" Galene asked, throwing the cloth bag over her shoulder.

"Yes, the kind man said, through that door down a long corridor. It's on the opposite far side of the restaurant. Jeremiah opened the door after scanning around for any staff that may have stopped him. All four of them ran into the corridor. They began to sprint down the corridor towards the door at the end. Asher looked upwards to see the stars in the sky as he passed each sky light. As they arrived at the door, it flung open. Two waiters came out holding trays with croissants, jam, granary toast, and butter upon them. Asher saw the trays,

"I could eat a horse," he said, his stomach rumbled. Jeremiah stepped into the kitchen. It was busy with chefs, waiters preparing food of all types. Asher eyes were enticed by a table that had large green olives in a spicy tomato sauce.

"Scrumptious food," he said, stuffing one in his mouth. Galene also grabbed one from the dish. Isabella had spotted French toast; she dipped it into the silver marmalade dish. A large dollop fell onto the table top. Jeremiah picked up a large slice of watermelon. As he ate it, he spat the seeds in an empty fine bone china cup.

Galene was grabbed on the shoulder by the head chef.

"So what have we here then? Thieves in the night... Come with me" The Wiz –T translated *Arabic* language in her eye. He began to pull her across the crowded kitchen to a storeroom. Jeremiah, Isabella and Asher were also forced into the store by the other staff members assisting him, "you will be dealt with when the police officials arrive" he said, slamming the door shut upon them.

Galene picked up an Orange. She peeled it whilst she paced the large storeroom. Asher had found some sweet biscuits in an open wooden crate. He placed some of them in his pocket as he feasted upon a banana. Jeremiah began laughing, Isabella questioned him so,

"Why are you laughing? Don't you realise we could be arrested?"

"Yes, we could be, but that won't happen, as we have Galene to help all of us to get out of here"

Galene was thinking as she placed a segment of orange in her mouth. The tartness of the orange made her cringe.

"Whoa... that's very sour!" she winced.

"If someone enters, then we shall escape. Jeremiah will you please look out for when the door is about to be opened" she stated, searching through more open boxes of food.

"Here Isabella, eat this its lovely" Asher handed Isabella a cake covered with dark chocolate. The cake had moist fruit with large dates inside, smothered with a whipped gooey fruit puree oozing out from the centre.

"Oh my, that is divine!" Isabella said, taking a large bite out of the cake. She even pushed some into Jeremiahs mouth as he stood by the door. The fruit puree ran down into his dimple on his chin.

....

Both Heinz and Isobel had made their way along the small passageways in the older part of Cairo. Isobel was concerned about Heinz.. His hovering above the pavement, along with his shiny silver skin, could attract attention from people. Hanging from the fencing at the rear of the *Shepheard hotel,* on numerous cables, was long robes with the name *Shepheard* emblazoned on the front. Isobel grabbed two of them; she began pulling one over her head. She gave the other to Heinz, who did the same. He placed the German Peaked cap back on his head afterwards. The *German swastika* symbol would mean nothing to anybody in Cairo. The long robe now had hidden the fact that Heinz was gliding. Isobel ripped her robe shorter as it was too long. They entered the hotel through the delivery door at the rear. Isobel gave Heinz a wooden box with moist dates into carry, so they would not arouse any suspicion. She carried another of the boxes, but ate some on the way in.

Heinz pulled the robe away from the tracker on his arm. It was still flashing.

"Have you located them…Hiss!" Isobel asked.

"Not sure if you understand my language, but it appears that they are extremely close by. Tell me how many will be with her Isobel?" Heinz held up his hand, he pointed to the door, *"how many people indoors?"* Heinz said, hoping Isobel had understood. He then waited for Isobel to respond after she had swallowed the *juicy black date* in her mouth.

"Think you might want to know how many? Galene, my sister Isabella and probably two boys, but I cannot be certain" Isobel held up four digits on her right hand.

Heinz listened, absorbing the numbers that were helping Galene. He began to move closer to another door. Isobel skipped out behind him, humming *"ring a ring O roses,"* the door was marked "Storeroom" in Arabic. Heinz could not...

– مـخـزن –

… Translate the door marking. He opened the key lock before he pulled the door open slowly.

....

Jeremiah whispered loudly,

"Galene The door its opening, what shall we do?"

Galene grabbed Isabella's hand tightly, Isabella read her mind instantly, she grabbed on to Asher's hand. Isabella whispered to Asher,

"Grab your brother's hand… quickly"

Asher Grabbed Jeremiahs hand just as Galene had begun to mumble the *invisibility spell*. The door opened fully,

Isobel came skipping through the doorway into the storeroom, followed by Heinz.

"That's impossible, it shows them quite clearly as being in here" Heinz was knocking the tracker on his wrist against the door. Isobel was sniffing the air, she could smell Isabella.

"She has been here, I can smell my sister" Isobel was so close to touching Isabella that Isabella gasped. Isobel sniffed the air again. "Mmmm, I wonder…" she said out loud, as she began grabbing at thin air. Isabella had stepped aside as she did so. Heinz removed the crystal from his pocket; the crystal face appeared in the stone. Galene gasped as she saw the face. She now partly remembered why she had used the memory loss spell. Isabella read Galene's mind. She gasped also. Galene dragged Isabella, who in turn pulled the others to follow as they stepped outside the room. Jeremiah slammed the door shut, locking it. Isobel was banging on the door,

"I know you're here… Open the door at once" She screamed, she began to lunge at the door with her fists. Heinz stared at the crystal face.

"You had them once again, why did you let them go?" The crystal asked angrily. Heinz was very frustrated. He created a large fireball in the other palm of his hand to throw in the door.

"You idiot, what use will that be against a heavy metal door. Are you trying to burn the hotel down?" The crystal laughed, *"The time for a fire in the hotel as not yet arrived. Put out the flame. We must be patient"*

Heinz clenched his hand to extinguish the fire. They could do nothing but wait for the door to open.

Chapter 24

Mr Baum

Cairo, Egypt – February 22nd 1906- 10:45am

In the lounge of the hotel, a small man with a dark moustache was reading to a group of children. They had arrived at the hotel for a book session, from all the other hotels nearby. The children listened intently; he was reading from a book that he had written. Even some of the English hotel guests smiled, watching the children's faces become enthralled with the story of a *rainbow and its magical far off land*. The man reading the book portrayed all the voices of each of the characters.

Jeremiah released his grip on Asher's hand. He became visible. He felt a kiss on his cheek. Isabella let go of Galene's hand. Jeremiah blushed as Isabella winked at him. Galene stopped reciting the invisibility spell.

"What now Galene, How do we find this -*missing spell page?*" Jeremiah asked.

"We were led here by the *Tic Toc Ticker*. It must know where it is or just maybe…"

"Just maybe what… What are you trying to say? I felt and even saw everything that you did, especially when you saw the crystal in the silver man's hand" Isabella scrunched her face,

"But I am not going to judge you for that, as you stopped all of the other future events from happening"

Galene pulled the Spell book from her bag. She stroked the spine before kissing the clasp. It enlarged on the marble floor. Asher had to move aside to let it expand. Galene flipped the pages with the help of Jeremiah. On reaching the centre of the book where the missing page was from, she asked,

"Book... you will show me where the missing page is right now in real *Tic Toc*?"

The book projected an image onto an empty space upon a plastered wall. It showed a man in the lounge with a briefcase with a group of people, children, even staff focussing on this one man. Galene shrank the book. She placed it back in her bag.

....

"She has found part of the book in this hotel, she must be stopped. The merging, must not happen!" the crystal face shouted at Heinz,

"You must stop her before she places the missing page back into the centre of the Book"

The crystal began spinning in Heinz hand. It became hot. Flames began jumping from the stone outwards onto the dry wooden crates. Isobel was throwing *moist dates* on top of the small fires to put them out. Heinz stopped the crystal,

"I will stop her when I get out of here. Can you get us both out of here?" Heinz calmly said.

"No, that is impossible. I brought you to this time. Once we leave we cannot come back to the same time exactly. We could arrive

moments after an event or even weeks before. This in itself will then give Galene time to change this part of history"

Heinz paced to the heavy metal door.

"There is no alternative," he began knocking on the door...

"Open this door... Anybody... Open this door" He shouted, in his husky, stern voice.

Isobel hissed. "Open the door! Anybody?"

....

The muffled sounds coming from the storeroom could be heard by Galene,

"Just ignore the cries... I know that I have to get the spell page. But I also have a strange feeling that it must happen before they get out of this store. Why does it all seem so very familiar....?"

Isabella nodded in agreement as she took charge of the situation,

"Okay, Asher and I will enquire at the desk as to whom the man is reading the book, we will search his room. You and Jeremiah, find the lounge in case he has the page with him. We don't have much time"

Asher ran with Isabella towards the long corridor to which they arrived at the kitchen. It took them back to the main reception area. Galene took Jeremiah in the opposite direction; a sign on the wall had been translated by the *Wiz-t* from an Arabic text -*Lounge* - with an arrow pointing in the opposite direction. Galene acknowledged staff on the way along a passageway. Eventually they arrived at the lounge.

"Are you ready Jeremiah? Keep your eyes open for anything that resembles the page from the book" Galene stated, flinging the door inwards. The solid wood door swung rapidly. It was caught by a *Shepheards hotel* staff member with the palm of his hand. Jeremiah entered first, followed by Galene. The room was of great proportion. Its chandeliers were lit despite it being daylight. Opulent table lamps of crystal glass were strategically placed on small tables, amongst the winged legged purple, red velvet covered sofas. There were many private seating areas within the room. Large palm trees that created overhead shading, Jeremiah *wowed* every item he passed by. Galene couldn't resist on touching items. Galene had a *'déjà vu'* moment regarding the many hidden rooms that she had filled with artefacts. Jeremiah could hear children laughing just further in the distance. As they got closer, they could see a male figure sat upon a chair facing them. He was small, very smartly dressed, reading from a book to ten children or so. He had half-cut reading glasses perched precariously on the tip of his nose. Two women sat directly behind the children were wafting hand fans rapidly in sync, cooling their faces. Galene began to scan the book he was reading. She moved closer. The book was printed, but leather bound. It was obvious to Galene that the *Spell page* was not attached to that. Jeremiah was lost for a moment in his characterisation of the book. He began to see the *dark forest with the yellow winding cobbled pathway* through it. He nudged Galene with his arm, discreetly pointing to his briefcase satchel at the side of his feet. Galene nodded.

Jeremiah sat on a chair, its sumptuous cushion seat, hugged him so. His legs ached from all the standing, and the walking that he had done. Galene stood staring at the Satchel. She whispered to Jeremiah in desperation,

"Get ready to make a distraction when I shout out -*Silver man*" she said.

....

Asher had arrived at the Reception Desk with Isabella. There was numerous staff working frantically as new guests arrived to check-in.

"How are we going to find out what room the man and his wife are staying in? We don't even know his name..." Asher asked Isabella. Isabella saw the poster advertising the reading on an easel stand by the side of a large potted palm tree.

"Of course we know the man's name... Look over there!" Isabella pointed to the poster, "Let's just say he is our grandfather. We may get lucky... Right Asher – I want you to cry for me"

Asher started laughing. The suggestion of crying had made him laugh. Isabella grabbed Asher by the arm, dragging him towards the desk. She dug her nails deep into the soft flesh on his arm. Tears streamed down his face.

"Ouch, you're hurting me," he wailed.

"Excuse me... Excuse me, sir" Isabella shouted, "I need to return this boy to its owner" A reception clerk arrived promptly to see Asher crying,

"What seems to be the problem? Can I be of assistance?"

Isabella changed her voice to a very posh English voice,

"Yes, you may help me; I need to return this boy to his Grandpapa and *erm*… Grand-mamma! I think they are staying here in this hotel. Their name is Mr and Mrs Baum…!"

The receptionist began flipping through a large ledger diary upon the desk.

"Arrrh… yes… that will be Mr and Mrs Baum staying in room 198. We can send a mail boy to the room to call them for you if you wish"

The tears from Asher's eyes had stopped. Isabella replied,

"No thank you, I shall wait for them in the Lounge" Isabella nodded in appreciation, stepping slowly back away from the desk. She pulled Asher with her. Once they were out of sight they ran towards the wide carpeted staircase. At floor one - they observed the wall plaque with directional arrows to rooms 1 to 30 in one direction. In the opposite direction was 31 to 68. Asher paused at level two as he was out of breath.

"It's like being at home," he wheezed.

"Come on, hurry, if the silver man escapes the room, he could get the page before us" Isabella snapped, as she made him climb up another set of stairs to the next level. At level three, she stopped waiting for Asher.

"This way is 170 to room 200; I think the receptionist said room 198 was Mr and Mrs Baum"

Asher's face was beaming red, as his cheeks had filled with blood to cool down is plump face.

………………………………………

Sergeant Uddin of the Egyptian Police arrived at the Kitchen accompanied by two officers. They were met by the Head Chef who shook his hand.

"This Way" the chef said, taking them to the storeroom, "I caught them stealing food from the kitchen. Little thieves need to be punished"

He opened the lock on the storeroom door. The Head chef, the three officers stepped inside to witness Heinz and Isobel who were waiting to get out. The *Shepheards* robes still covering their own clothing as the Head Chef scanned them, he was shocked that the four children had gone.

"Where are they? The children that I locked in here, the little thieves?"

Heinz was still angry from being locked in the room, he watched as Isobel opened her mouth before running towards the Chef. She took a bite into his arm. The Chef pushed Isobel backwards onto the floor. The two officers were sent to grab her by the Sergeant. Heinz eyes began to light up with burning rage. He stopped the two officers with his hands. He sent a pulse of hot light into their bodies, they both evaporated. A cloud of dust billowed to the ceiling. The Chef was holding his arm, he tried to run. But Heinz sent a bolt of fire into his body. The chef fell to the floor before exploding into a fine dust. The Sergeant gulped,

"Please. I beg you, I have... a family to look after," he said in partial English. Heinz shrugged his shoulders, as he did not understand. Isobel stood up from the floor, she was

hissing at him. She moved closer to him. Heinz had a fireball swirling in his hand.

"My friend speaks German only. DO you speak German?" Isobel stated to him as she snarled, gnashing her teeth at him.

"Yes… Yes… I speak German… Bitte... Bitte... nicht mich töten. Ich kann Ihnen helfen, Ich spreche fünf Sprachen"

Please... Please... don't kill me. I can assist you, I speak five languages."

Heinz dispersed the fireball back into his palm. The Sergeant dropped to his knees, which crunched in a green crystal powder that had formed on the floor. This was left by the two officer's instantaneous death. Isobel was standing on the red crystal dust where the Head Chef had stood.

Heinz spoke in German to him,

"You can assist me. What is your name?"

"It's Kalef Uddin. Sergeant Kalef Uddin of the Egyptian Police"

He bowed his head to Heinz. Isobel was disappointed at Heinz not killing him.

Kalef Uddin was a tall, thin man. His skin darkened by the sun's rays. He wore a *Keffiyeh* which had a police badge attached to it. His short legged trouser suit in blue had shiny brass buttons on the front. His name Kalef was stitched across the pocket.

"You can call me Captain Heinz. I want those children alive, you will help me catch them now" Heinz instructed Kalef quite firmly.

"Yes, I will help you, but please spare my life o' mighty one"
Kalef nodded his head in acknowledgment.

Isobel had already made her way into the corridor. She waited for instruction from Heinz as to the direction of Galene. Heinz glanced at the tracker, before he set off in the direction of the Lounge, followed by Isobel and Kalef.

....

In the lounge Galene was getting ready to search the bag by the foot of Mr Baum. She moved closer every time he changed his voice to create the characters. Finally, she stood by the bag, but was hiding behind a tall palm tree pot. She screamed at the children,

"Watch out... it's the Silver man"

There were screams from the children; Galene recited the *Invisibility Spell* to herself. Jeremiah witnessed the bag fall over onto the floor, it was then turned upside down... being shook by what appeared to be no one. Pencils, papers fell out of the bag. Mr Baum stood up from his seat,

"It's alright children; calm down it was just someone being silly"

As the children began to sit back down upon the floor, a girl aged nine screamed yet again. The rest of the children screamed with her. Mr Baum turned around to see a silver man to the side of him.

"Oh my word... this is the utmost... bizarre... encounter... situation... that I have ever seen. Is it really you, *Tin Man?*"

In shock, he dropped the book to the floor. It opened upon the page of a drawing of a shiny silver *Tin man*. The children began to run from the room screaming, Galene was still invisible. She made her way around to the opposite side of the room to grab Jeremiah by the arm –he became invisible also. She whispered to him,

"Quickly, we need to get out of here"

Amidst the chaos both of them exited with the running children. Galene stopped reciting the spell outside the room. They had now entered into the dining room. They carried on running through the seated guests who were enjoying luncheon. Jeremiah tripped on a Persian rug. He began sliding on the polished marble floor towards a large pot elephant. Galene spoke out loud raising her hands high up into the sky,

""Stop, gelditu ehotzeko , arreta stand , gorputza jolt bat emango "

"Stop, grind to a halt, stand to attention, give the body a jolt"

Jeremiah stopped sliding; his body was thrust upwards into the running position once more.

Both Galene and Jeremiah carried on running towards the Main Reception.

Heinz stood with Kalef on one side of him, Isobel on the other. Mrs Baum stepped forward. She was very brash,

"Who are you? Coming in here ruining my husband's book reading?"

Isobel laughed, Kalef tried to make a gesture for them both to leave immediately. Heinz spoke via Kalef,

"Why has this man got a picture of a Silver man in his book?"

Heinz held his hand above the book; it rose upwards into his palm. Kalef asked Mr Baum about the book before translating his reply in German,

"It's a book for children; it is a fantasy about a scarecrow, tin man, lion and a girl. A witch is involved. The man wants to know if he can leave with his book." Mr Baum held out his hand for the book. Kalef snatched it from Heinz. Kalef began pushing Mr Baum towards the door. He also grabbed the jacket of Mrs Baum. Mr and Mrs Baum tried to stay longer to observe this *tin man* standing in front of their very own eyes.

"Go… your life is in danger!" Kalef stated.

"I have told them to leave as they are not required any longer. That is ok to do so, Master?" Kalef relayed his sincerity to Heinz in his own German translation before he then bowed his head,

"We still need to find these children… They cannot be that far away from here. They have not had much time to escape"

....

Isabella arrived at the bedroom first, the door was open. A maid was placing clean towels upon the bed. Isabella barged into the room with such confidence,

"Thank you for the towels. That will be all for now!" she said.

Asher had arrived behind her, somewhat out of breath. The maid stepped aside to let him pass her by.

"Quickly shut the door Asher. We need to search the room, before the maid realises that it is not our room!"

Isabella had already opened the dark carved oak chest of drawers to search through some very fine cotton, embroidered blouses. Asher pulled the large travelling trunk from against the wall to flip the lid open. He rummaged through numerous items before dropping the lid shut.

"Shh!"

Isabella removed a ladies satchel bag from the bottom drawer; she placed it on the white linen bed sheets. Asher watched as she released the twist catch. Inside was a velvet cloth to which she removed, placing the cloth on the bed. She folded back the corners of the fine material. It was the missing *Spell page*.

It had a drawing of a rainbow on it, with a witch on a broomstick flying through it, towards what can only be described as a green crystal. Isabella could not read the very few words upon the page. The *Wiz-T* would not translate it for her.

"What are we to do now, Isabella? What if Galene and Jeremiah have been captured by the *silver man*?"

Asher touched the page with his finger. His finger glowed orange. Isabella touched her finger on the page it also glowed, but this time in violet.

"How bizarre to see this happen in one object, I wonder if Jeremiah and Galene would have the same reaction if they touched it too?" she said, lifting the velvet cloth higher to view the images.

"That surely cannot be Galene in the drawing…or can it?" Isabella questioned herself, focussing intently at the drawing of the witch. Asher tried to see as well, but Isabella held it close to her face.

"I am positive it is"

"Let me see. Let me see!" Asher was extremely keen to view the image. Isabella placed the page back on the bed cover. Asher leant over to scan the drawing. The drawing of the witch began to move, it flew closer on the page, her face became visible as she turned to view them both standing there in the bedroom. The drawing spoke,

"Hurry up you two, we have to get out of this time. It's another step closer to *Saviour Angel* –the *tic toc*...! Bring the *Spell Page* now, hurry!" the drawing of Galene on the page-flew back towards the rainbow. Asher was rubbing his eyes in disbelief. Isabella wrapped the precious page back in the velvet cloth once more,

"That is most peculiar. How did she know we would find it? I thought I knew everything about her. Asher place the satchel back in the drawer" Isabella locked the clasp on the bag before she handed it to Asher. Asher pushed the stiff wooden drawer back into the cabinet.

"If I am not mistaken Asher we are three floors directly above the lounge. That would make sense of the projection showing the page in the lounge earlier. We have to find Galene. I feel that she is in danger"

Asher pulled out his sword ready for battle,

"I am ready for anything, let me at them," he said, making thrusting movements in the air.

....

Galene and Jeremiah stood in the *Main Reception* waiting for Isabella and Asher. They hid behind a *Cook's Travel Poster Board* at the bottom of the stairway.

Heinz, Isobel and Kalef came through to the Reception from the dining room. Heinz was tapping his wrist with his finger.

"They are here somewhere. Search this area now"

Kalef translated it to Isobel before they both separated in opposite directions in a frantic search.

PING!

PING!

The reception bell kept pinging.

"Porter, here, now, take these bags up to room 162" the Head Receptionist shouted in *Arabic* to Heinz who was standing close by. Heinz had forgotten that he was still wearing the *Shepheard Hotel* robe. Heinz glided closer to the desk. He summoned the Head Receptionist clerk with his finger to come towards him.

"Yes?" The receptionist said.

Heinz reached out his hand; he grabbed him by the collarbone. The life drained away from the receptionist. His body slumped on the floor before disappearing in a cloud of dark smoke. All that remained was a heap dark smouldering ash surrounded by clear crystals.

Galene and Jeremiah watched from behind the large poster.

"Did you see what he did Galene?"

"Yes, I did, he is getting power from somewhere to do that. If I am not mistaken that is a *Captains* hat from *World War Two*. That's where we came from. He and his uniform are totally out of place here. Something or someone is helping him chase me through time"

Suddenly, without warning both Galene and Jeremiah were grabbed on the shoulder from behind.

....

Mr and Mrs Baum entered their bedroom on the third floor just as the light through the window was beginning to dim.

"My feet are killing me in this heat" Mrs Baum whined as she took off her dusty shoes. Mr Baum noticed that the drawer of the cabinet had been pushed further inwards.

"Look here, my dear, I think someone has been in the drawer?"

Mrs Baum pulled the drawer open. She hastily grabbed the satchel to view the contents.

"It's gone! The page that has brought you good luck in your writing has gone! Someone has stolen it," she said, shaking the bag upside down to show Mr Baum.

Mr Baum appeared contented. His face had a huge grin. He turned towards the sunset visible from the large open windows, which lead to a balcony.

"That's not important dearest, come and view this wonderful sunset"

Mrs Baum huffed and puffed, as she waltzed her stocking feet towards Mr Baum,

"Not important indeed. How many books have you wrote with the aid of that *magical page*?"

The silence from Mr Baum summed up his feeling about the matter. He just stared at the red glow from the sun as it shrank above the white plastered buildings shadowed by large palm trees. Mrs Baum stood beside him. He gave her a sneaky peck on the cheek with his lips.

'I think we have enough photos of our trip to Egypt to make a new travel book' Mr Baum remarked. His hand fell into Mrs Baum's hand, "At least we got to see the *Tin Man*. The stories I have written are somewhat true… my loveliness"

Mrs Baum finally smiled,

"I know…Who would have thought it?"

………………………………….

"Hurry Galene, let's get out of here, we have the missing *Spell page*" Isabella said hurriedly, holding onto Galene's shoulder from behind. Jeremiah was just about to hit the person who was behind him, before he realised that it was Asher. Galene tugged Isabella lower to the ground as did Jeremiah with Asher,

"Look, it's the *silver man*," Galene said, pointing at him through a leafy fern, at the side of the Poster.

"I need you to get closer to him if you can, to find out why he is chasing me?" Galene stated, gripping Isabella's hand, "but it could be somewhat dangerous from what I have just seen"

Isabella saw the images pass through her mind of the silver man with the Head Receptionist. She looked horrified.

"Oh my word, is he really capable of doing that?" She said, as she let go of Galene's hand.

Asher sat closer to Jeremiah with his sword in his hand. He was rubbing the shiny metal part of the blade with the sleeve of his shirt, to see his own reflection. In the blade edge, Isobel was creeping towards him. He nudged Jeremiah to look at the reflection. Jeremiah jumped up to his feet.

"Leave her to me," he said, pulling Asher on the opposite side of him. Asher bumped into Galene. Jeremiah stepped out from the poster. Isobel was now aware that she had been seen, she began a sprint towards Jeremiah, hissing at him. Jeremiah was in such a rage that his body went into a spasm. His hands glowed vibrant blue, as he thrust them forward towards Isobel, releasing a bolt of pure energy from his fingertips. Isobel was catapulted backwards into the linen room door.

Crack!

Thud!

The force pushed her through the door where she landed in a pile of towels. She banged her head on the wall, knocking herself out. The glow of blue from Jeremiah's hands began to spread further up his arms into his body,

"Calm down now Jeremiah…. It's me Galene. It's all ok now!" Galene whispered in a quiet soothing voice. *"Now I know why you need the Moses staff, it will control your power,"* she said to herself, the glow receded back into his hands. Jeremiah could not remember what had just happened. He saw Isobel inside the broken door of the Linen room.

"Did I do that?" he enquired of Galene, who was holding his hands, pulling them downwards to his side. Isabella was stroking Jeremiahs hair to soothe him.

"At last, I now have you, grab her Kalef!" Heinz shouted. The *Wiz-T* translated it from German. Kalef gripped Galene tightly around her waist restraining her arms. Her bag fell to the floor. Isabella, Jeremiah and Asher stood facing Heinz, who had created a swirling fireball in the palm of his hand.

"Where is the book? My leaders need it to ensure victory in Europe!" Heinz stated. Kalef was translating it into English towards Galene, but she stopped him so.

"I understand what he said; I understand all languages" the *Wiz-T* began its task of converting her voice into German. *"What book? I do not understand the question?"*

"The Magical book, with the missing page, which you have just found here in this hotel today along with your escapee Jewish colleagues" Heinz eyes were turning red, the fireball grew larger.

Asher held tightly on to the sword behind his back. Isabella retrieved the fine lace cloth of *Mona Lisa* from her pocket. She threw it up in the air. She watched it unravel before stepping slightly forward for it to fall upon her head. Galene was kicking hard against Kalef's legs in an attempt to break free. Jeremiah could feel his anger building up inside of him. His fingertips were changing to the colour of blue once again.

"I will not ask again, the book- where is it?"

"I will never tell you… Isabella did you get the information I need?" Galene asked calmly whilst struggling with Kalef.

"Yes Galene, all of it. Well, at least I think it's all of it"

"Good, are you ready, read my mind?" She said, with a smile. Suddenly Galene kicked her bag towards Isabella, who pulled out the book. She waved it directly at Heinz, taunting him so. Galene muttered a spell,

"Ezkutua energia direla benetakoak altuera duena, inguratzen nauen horma bat bezala"

"Shield of energy that stands real tall, surround me like a wall"

Galene was suddenly released from Kalef's grip as a wall of light shot up from the ground. Galene ran forward towards Isabella, Jeremiah and Asher surrounded by her protective shield. Heinz released the fireball from his hand thrusting it towards Jeremiah. Jeremiah had no time to duck from the fireball as it was nearly touching his body. Asher jumped forward with the sword; he hit the fiery ball with the blade....

Whiz!

It then shot off in the direction of Kalef, who dived behind a pot plant. The fireball hit a marble statue of *Tutankhamen*, which exploded into many pieces. Heinz glided towards Isabella, who had the book in her hand. He snatched it from her. The book began to emanate a white pulsating light. Galene placed her hands inside the wall of light to part the wall whilst the others climbed inside.

"The book, Galene... He has the book!" Jeremiah shouted above the loud humming of the barricade that had been created.

"Not for long... Isabella, get the *Tic Toc Ticker*. Also, where is the page? Is it safe?" she said, as she turned around to face Heinz, who had removed a small box from his pocket. Isabella replied,

"Yes, Galene as per instruction"

They all stood within the protective wall, watching as Heinz opened the box. They witnessed the talking crystal that spoke in German.

"You have Galene? You have the book?"

"I have the book... Galene is here. Look!" Heinz pointed the crystal towards Galene.

"At last Galene we meet again after all the *Tic Toc's*. We can do great work together. Come join with me now to complete your task" the crystal face moved closer to show just a mouth full of sharp teeth in the front facing facet.

"I will never come with you, who are you? What do you want with me?" Galene screamed at the crystal "program, it now Isabella, hurry"

Isabella was standing directly behind Galene and Jeremiah. She was hidden from view as she began to program the *Tic Toc Ticker*. Asher moved forward to stand at the opposite side of Galene,

"Light boterea duten dirdira bat da , erortzen da, beraz, guardia me ezkutuaren "

"Power of light that is a glow, drop the shield that guards me so" she said. The wall collapsed before her eyes. Heinz tried to hover closer, but they all stepped backwards, Asher held his sword upwards in the air ready to fight.

"Now listen to me Galene. You cannot deny your future, the one that is with me. It was already planned by the gods" the crystal said calmly.

"I can do whatever I like, history can and will be changed. I think I have changed part of it already. I WILL remember everything soon. Hopefully, all the past or is it future that I will erase, especially with the help of my new friends" Galene gripped Jeremiahs hand. She then grabbed onto Asher's, hand tightly.

"It is not so, you belong to me, you will always belong to me. You cannot escape. Look, I have the book", the crystal was now shouting at her.

Heinz glided further forward; Kalef was hidden behind the large terracotta pot.

"Now Isabella" Galene shouted, "Throw the *Ticker* up in the air!"

Isabella pressed the button that was flashing on the *Ticker*. She released her grip with a mighty swoop of the hand. Everybody glanced upwards as the *Ticker* began to fall downwards from the ornate roof of the hotel. Isabella caught the *Ticker* as the vortex opening appeared. Galene pulled her hand away from Asher's. She joined his hand with Jeremiah's. Isabella held on tight to the *Ticker* as she jumped into the dark opening directly above them.

Whoosh ...Isabella was dragged into the opening. Galene called the book sweetly from Heinz,

"Book me sartzen zara, batu nirekin orain"

"Book you belong to me, join with me now"

Jeremiah was now being pulled into the opening, followed by Asher,

"Hurry Galene we are leaving" Asher shouted.

The book was forcing itself free from Heinz grip, it shot across the air, dropping into Galene's right hand, before she jumped upwards grabbing onto Asher's sword handle with her left hand.

She disappeared into the swirling dark cloud.

"Where is the broom?" Asher yelled.

Heinz hovered extremely fast towards the vortex, with the crystal.

"Don't let them escape," the crystal cried out.

Heinz gripped onto Galene's black robe. She tugged it hard to make him lose his hold on it. His arm was in the vortex as it began to close.

"NO....You cannot escape me", shrieked the crystal, "I will catch you Galene. You are mine!"

It was too late the vortex closed.

Chapter 25

Berlin's Radziwill Palace, 1943

04th August 1943, 16:45pm

Berlin's Radziwill Palace, Reichskanzlei, Wilhelmstraße 77

There was an eerie silence within the building as all the Stenographers began to cover the typewriters, in readiness for their time to go home. Last one out of the building was the head of the typewriting pool team. She made her way along the corridor to the *Winter Garden* with a Brown file tied with red ribbon. The ribbon was sealed with golden wax. The wax was emblazoned with the symbol of an eagle. She noticed a change in temperature as she walked from the corridor into the *Winter Garden*, the air felt warmer, more relaxed from the hustle and bustle of her own work environment. She approached a desk by the large windows overlooking a dismal courtyard garden. *SS-Obergruppenführer* Schmidt was sitting at the desk, rubber stamping, signing documents before placing them in an out tray upon the polished wooden desk.

"You requested this file from the Vault. Will that be all you need from me, as I am about to leave?" the head secretary asked in a tired, droning German voice.

SS-Obergruppenführer Schmidt, glanced upwards at her, He removed the file from her hands, placing it on the desk,

"Yes, that will be all! Secure the building before you leave"

He watched the pencil drawn seam on her naked legs crease, as she exited the two double doors back into the corridor. She pulled both doors closed. Lieutenant Schmidt removed a large pair of steel scissors to cut the silk ribbon. The label on the file stated,

Top Secret für die Augen der SS - Obergruppenführer Schmidt nur "- "Top Secret for the eyes of SS-Obergruppenführer Schmidt only"

Lieutenant Schmidt peered upwards to the clock on the wall showing the time. It was 16:56. He pulled away the ribbon before flipping open the file on the desk spreading numerous photographic pictures. Each one was greyed out. They were over exposed photographic sheets. Lieutenant Schmidt began spreading the blank photos across the desk. There were five in total.

"So let me see, the girl was kind enough to misplace these in 1912" he said to himself. He turned over the last blank photo to see a message,

William Albert Henry Fox tic toc. 1841

First photographic paper with all processes complete

Colour: Violet

Note: Ask and thee shall see

As he slid each of the blank photos across the table, he could see that there was still nothing on them.

"Show me the end of the War that started in 1939?"

The clock now showed 17:01.

Lieutenant Schmidt stood up to pour himself a coffee from a jug by a row of dull, grey filing cabinets. The hot jug of coffee was on top of a small coal heater by the window. He spilled some on one of the cabinets as he poured. It ran as blood would run from a dead body. On returning to the desk, one photo had begun to change. It was no longer grey. The photo had begun to develop. He saw a celebration in a school playground. A date appeared in the bottom right-hand corner.

Talbot Process. 01ˢᵗ September 1945

Picking up the photo, he saw women, children laying small amounts of food upon rows of wooden trestle tables in the playground.

Lieutenant Schmidt could not figure out whether it was German or English within the photo. None of the other photos had developed. They still remained grey. As this photo developed, its images became more intense. In the top left of the photo, he could see bunting streaming across a tree to the downpipe of the school building. The mini flags were somewhat still indistinguishable. They appeared as small grey flags. Lieutenant Schmidt sipped on the hot coffee as he waited for the bunting to become visible. He dropped his coffee in shock onto the tiled floor as a blackbird flew into the window directly behind him. Coffee splattered up his trouser leg. The bird was stunned as it patrolled on the stone slabs outside the window. Lieutenant Schmidt grabbed the stove cloth, which was used to hold the poker whilst stoking the coal in the fire. He patted the grey material of his legs on the suit.

"Is that a coincidence or an omen" he thought to himself, picking up the photo once more.

Opening the top drawer of the desk, Lieutenant Schmidt removed a large magnifying glass, so he could see the flags more closely.

At last he could see the flags clearly.

The flags intensified revealing the nation that won the war. Lieutenant Schmidt spoke to himself as he analysed the photo in depth,

"Did Germany win the war...? Are we victorious at the end? Will the future history be changed or be forced to change by the Silver man, and the captured girl with her magical book?"

...

His questions were answered... as he viewed the flags.

Chapter 26

The Eternity Spell

Cairo, Egypt – Shepheard Hotel, 1906, late evening

Heinz fell backwards upon the marble tiled floor. The crystal fell from the box rolling towards Kalef's feet. He stopped it rolling with his sandal. The crystal spoke out to Kalef in *Arabic*,

"It was you who let the girl escape. I shall ensure that you receive your punishment very soon"

Kalef kicked the crystal across the floor. It catapulted against the staircase, then behind a Poster of a trip to the *Valley of the Kings* arranged by *Cook's Travel.*

A crowd of people had gathered around Heinz, who lay holding his shoulder. His arm was missing. There was no blood. Heinz felt no pain. He stood to his feet without realising that his arm had gone.

"Stop staring at me, BE GONE" he shouted aggressively, before calming down again. *"Everybody just carry- on as normal,"* he said in a deep, hypnotic, voice. He watched as the crowd dissipated, they seemed to forget what they had just seen. It was then, that he noticed that his arm was missing.

"No! This cannot BE!" he yelled.

Kalef tried to sneak away from the large pot.

"Kalef, I can see you... You made a promise to serve me. Come here now!"

"Yes Master" Kalef stated, approaching but constantly bowing his head. Kalef kneeled in front of Heinz. He retrieved the empty box by his feet. Heinz began searching for the crystal.

"Graumus, Graumus! Where are you?

A beam of light shone upwards, towards the decorative plastered ceiling from behind the poster stand. Heinz pushed the poster into the wall as he bent over to pick up the crystal. Kalef was still kneeling when Heinz returned.

"Deal with this fool, we no longer require him!" Graumus instructed. Heinz eyes were piercing Kalef, who was pleading for mercy! Isobel stumbled through the broken door back into the Reception area.

"NO, I need him Graumus; he can assist me in translation" Heinz replied, *"I will deal with him, only when I have to and not before"*

Isobel hissed loudly at Kalef from behind, she kicked him as she got closer to Heinz.

"Where have you been?" Heinz was furious with her. Kalef translated, as he rose to his feet to Isobel.

"That boy... he has strong powers. He used his own magic to throw me into the cupboard" Kalef relayed her words back in German. Heinz was removing the *Shepheard Hotel* robe. His German grey Suit was visible once more. Isobel pulled the robe from her body. It fell in a heap. She ripped out a square piece of the cloth, to cover the gaping hole where Heinz arm, would have been.

Heinz looked at his remaining arm with the tracker. It was beeping. It showed Galene everywhere, yet again.

"The girl Galene, She as returned to normal time... We still have an opportunity to catch her. We now know what we are up against. We shall remain here until we know where she will travel to next" Graumus said to Heinz, as Heinz replaced the crystal back inside the silk lined box.

Kalef Paced in a circle,

"Heinz... Master – I need to eat... I cannot go on without food" He stuttered in German.

Heinz dropped the box back in his pocket, before walking towards the dining room doors.

"Eat you shall, Isobel will eat too. I will gather my thoughts in the process" Heinz said, swinging the doors open.

....

POP... The swirling vortex closed.

"Where is the broom?" Jeremiah asked, brushing the dust from his shirt.

"Don't worry about the broom, it can fend for itself! We have the page now... Isabella let me see the page" Galene stated, dropping her bag to the floor by the round table. Isabella pulled the velvet wrapped page from her pocket, along with the *Mona Lisa Headscarf*. She placed both items on the table edge, before she pushed the circumference of the table towards Galene. Jeremiah moved closer to see the page, as Galene uncovered it. There was no text, except numerous sketches. Galene spoke out her thoughts,

"This cannot be the page; the book shows text prior to the page in the spell book, so one would imagine that text would be on this page!" She began to scratch her head with one hand, whilst flipping the page over with the other. The page contained colourful drawings of a green crystal and a silver man.

"Where is the witch Isabella? - Look at the page... the witch has gone!" Asher blurted out.

Isabella leant across the table, her fingers rested in the carved name of Ἰούδας (Judas).

"So she has... the witch has disappeared from the page. Galene the witch in the drawing was you!" Isabella remarked, her fingers slipped from the carved name, "Ouch, damn! I got a splinter from the wood now"

Jeremiah used his teeth to remove the splinter from Isabella's finger. She blushed.

"Thanks Jeremiah"

Galene was still miffed about the page. The lack of text made her doubt that this was the *spell page*. She lifted the cloth off the surface of the table to reveal the name Θωμᾶς (*Thomas*). The *Wiz-T* translated yet again, her eye was blinded by the translation.

"Of course, *Doubting Thomas*... How silly of me! He's making me doubt it now. Thomas once said to me -*that he must believe... and that he will believe no matter what*... I will believe – that this is the page. I am sure of it" Galene spun the table to the name Φίλιππος (*Phillip*), to remove her doubts. Jeremiah picked up the *Moses Staff* at the same time as Galene retrieved the book from her. Jeremiah began playing with the small blue crystal fastened to the top of the pole. He pushed it ever so gently. The crystal clicked inwards,

Whoosh!

The pole shrank inside the crystal. What remained was the crystal with a dark leather strap that you could tie around your wrist. Asher's mouth fell open. Isabella laughed at Jeremiah, who thought that he had broken it.

"Push the crystal again Jeremiah" Isabella said. Jeremiah did so.

Whoosh!

The Pole reformed.

Meanwhile, Galene had enlarged the book on the table.

"Here goes, everybody... Let's see what happens!" she said, placing the small ripped page upon the large spell book.

Suddenly the page began to swirl. It enlarged, as it did so, Galene stepped backwards. Her hair was blowing in the wind created by the fast movement of the page spinning. Once the page reached its full size, the ripped seam began to sparkle. The missing page was pulled in to join with the book. Galene began to rise up from the floor. Her gown was still blowing from the movement of the air. She held out her hands forward - towards the book.

"Liburua , bete zeregin . Zure lotura " barruan orria zigilatu"
"Book, Fulfil the task. Seal the page within your binding"
Galene yelled, through a tornado of wind and noise.

Asher ran towards Jeremiah, he gasped as Galene was lifted off the floor above the book. Her legs were left dangling in mid-air. Rays of light shot out into the vast room, as the page finished melding together with the ripped seam. A ray of light shot into her eyes, her head rocked backwards. Her body was pushed away from the table at a rapid speed. She hit a large bookcase. Her body slumped to the ground with an almighty thud. Book after book tumbled from the shelving upon her.

"NO, this is not supposed to happen!" Isabella screamed out, "Quickly Jeremiah, Asher, dig through the books, we must find her"

In a frantic rush for the mass of books on the floor, they began throwing each one to the side of them. Some glowed as they touched their corresponding colour.

Galene's leg was visible from a group of *orange coloured books*. Asher removed each one in turn. All the books that fell around Galene were orange. Asher touched one cover, all the covers glowed. The books had formed a protective barrier around her limp body. Galene was unconscious as the last book was thrown off to the side. Jeremiah, was gently calling her, Asher touched her hand. In doing so-the small cuts on her face healed instantly.

"I remember. I remember!   Galene was so excited. She cried out the words, "Isabella, Jeremiah and my lovely Asher, I remember what is to happen next!"

....

At the exact same moment -that the page was merged with the book, Heinz was jolted by a strong electricity volt, which was released from the crystal in his pocket. His body was thrown across the dining room of the Hotel. He came to rest by a tea trolley.

A maid bent over,

"You ok Sir? Would you like some English Tea?"

Isobel ran across from the table, from which they were sitting- eating. She was immediately followed by Kalef.

"You ok Master?" Kalef asked, as he leant forward to help him up. Heinz removed a glove from his suit pocket. He slapped Kalef across the face with the glove,

"Idiot, of course I am alright" Heinz body suddenly became rigid; his body, then flipped to an upright position. The crystal- *Graumus* was shouting from within the box. Heinz clicked open the clasp.

"Galene has merged the spell page with the book. She CANNOT- she must NOT be allowed to find any of the other missing pieces. Heinz you have failed me. You have let her escape with the book. IT MUST NOT HAPPEN AGAIN!" Graumus angrily shouted. Isobel began hissing at the crystal. Heinz slammed the lid closed on the box, but then he re-opened it slowly.

"You need me, as much as I need you to get the girl with her spell book. I cannot escape this year without your help, nor can you capture the girl without mine" Heinz said calmly to the crystal. The eye of Graumus came to the front facet. His voice was calm whilst he spoke,

"You are correct with what you say. It is time to return to your present time of 1943. We shall await Galene's next move. I am sure she will reappear" Graumus replied, *"Are you ready to leave?"*

"Yes, we are ALL ready!" Heinz gripped Kalef's gun belt so he could not escape. The crystal began to create a diversion within the lobby of the hotel. The doors blew inwards followed by a mass of sand. Chaos ensued as the staff

began to run frantically to close the doors. The storm only allowed the staff to look down at the floor, in an attempt to stop the sand blasting into their eyes.

"Now we shall go…" Graumus shouted. Isobel jumped on to Heinz feet. She held onto his grey suit tightly. Heinz gripped to Kalef's belt so he could not escape.

....

Jeremiah helped Galene to her feet. She stood for a moment just staring at all three of them. Her mind was somewhere else. Isabella touched her hand to see what she was thinking about.

The history that Galene herself had encountered flashed through Isabella's mind. Isabella finally saw the alternative path that Galene previously took. Somehow the memory loss spell had spanned many of earth centuries. Each time the spell reset itself. She tried so desperately to change her future. It lasted different lengths of time, enabling Galene to collect artefact after artefact. Each time she was returned to a different time that is until her *Ma-Syeira Angelica* appeared in her life. Galene was brought back to the same time for many of earth's years by the Superior of the *Aurora,* with the aid of the many crystals.

Galene had now realised that she could not do it alone.

"I saw it all too Galene, The other children are needed, we must find them. You were so aggressive in the past! In fact, so evil! What has changed?" Isabella remarked, knowing what she had seen.

"I don't know!" Galene scrunched her face up, as images of her *Ma – Syeira Angelica* appeared in her mind. "Yes, I do. I know what happened- I met a wonderful woman, my *Ma*. She made me feel, to love, to see the world differently. But it seems that I have met her so many times, in different places!"

Isabella held Galene's hand, as a tear ran down her face.

"Now she is gone"

"I miss my mother and father too" Asher began to cry also. Jeremiah comforted him.

"Sorry, I forgot! How selfish of me. We have all lost someone dear in our lives. I know now what must be done. I need all of your help to achieve it. I can't do it alone – This is something that I have now realised. Are you with me?" Galene smiled, wiping the tears from her cheeks. She thrust her hand forward waiting for the others to do so as well,

"Yes, Galene, to a new future… I am so glad that you have remembered" Isabella coughed nervously, "I was scared that I might slip up at some point, and tell you what must be done!" Isabella placed her hand on top of Galene's. Jeremiah reached out to grip both of their hands,

"We shall do what is necessary in helping you Galene. As we may find our parents too at some point"

Asher sniffled as he tucked his sword in his belt. He gently placed his hand on top of Jeremiah's.

"Count me in. I miss my Mother and Father!"

As Asher placed his hand on top of the others, it began to glow. Jeremiah's hand lit up, followed by Isabella's. Finally Galene's lit up. They all watched as a cloud of green swirling light moved up above their heads. The light flowed back and forth until it faded.

"That looks familiar. I remember when I was younger seeing this same light in the sky. Father took me to see it in *Tromsö, Northern Norway*. I also remember him holding my hand, telling me that this will one day- be the new future!" Jeremiah recounted, "Father referred to it as an *Aurora*, dancing lights in the sky. Do you think its important Galene?"

Tromsö, Northern Norway is 350kilometres from the Arctic Circle. A Northern Lights (Aurora Borealis) observatory was founded in 1927. The temperature can drop to minus 19 degrees Celsius. In winter daylight can last but a few hours only.

Aurora (Sunrise) Borealis is the dancing lights in the sky, supposedly' caused by magnetic fields from the solar winds of the Sun.

Isabella ducked her head down towards the floor. She did not want to give her guilty face away.

"All I can tell you at this stage," she said, "yes it is important. It seems Galene did not remember all of it as one would have expected!" Isabella remarked quietly.

"You mean there is more?" Galene tried to remember more, but she could not. She began to walk back towards the table, where the spell book lay. The others followed her. She glanced at the page to see the drawings had now disappeared from the page. They had been replaced with text.

"What is this I see? Words are now up on the page"
Galene began muttering them to herself.

"It just does not make sense at all. Isabella will you help me with this one. It seems to say there are *nine* to find in a *Ring 'O' Ring a roses*? At least tell me something if you know it!"

Isabella shuffled her feet on the dusty floor. She felt Jeremiah's eyes staring intensely at her.

"Ok, I am not sure if it will change the future or not... Nine refers to- nine people who are required to fulfil your destiny. I cannot say anymore Galene, please don't make me, as I think I have already said too much!" Isabella placed her hand upon the spell book to feel the new page. Her hair stood upright with static energy from the merging of the large sheet of paper. Asher laughed. He also placed his hand on the page giggling, laughing at Isabella, who removed her hand to pat his head, to smooth the hair back downwards. A bolt of static electricity hit Asher on the scalp forcing him to fall to the floor. Jeremiah began chortling now at Asher, who had smoke coming from his head.

"It's not funny Jeremiah- that hurt" Asher said with a real attitude, "Thanks a lot Isabella for doing that to me!"

Isabella held out her hand to help Asher off the floor. He eventually took a hold of it, after gently touching the finger to see if she was to release another electricity charge.

Galene read the page, over and over. She remembered most of her past or was it her future? Even she was confused. The light above the table flickered, for a moment. The room was left in complete darkness. Asher removed his sword ready for battle. Jeremiah extended the Moses Staff, just as the light came back on.

"What on earth was that all about?" Jeremiah said, resting the *Moses Staff* softly onto the floor. Galene glanced around the room to see if anything had changed. Her eye caught some movement, behind a black anthracite statue of *Goliath*.

"Darkness argi eraldatzeko , gaueko izar bat bezala! "

"Darkness transforms to light, as a star in the night!" Galene muttered, picking up some dust from the floor, she cast it from her hand towards the statue in the distance. The dust lit up, sparkling as it hovered high above in the room.

"Come out from there, where I can see you" Galene stated. Jeremiah moved slightly to the side of a bookcase, to see who it was hiding.

"Galene, its *Wepwawet*, He is free" Jeremiah shouted, viewing the *Jackals* head upon the human body.

Galene pulled up the gown to run closer to where the *Wepwawet* was hiding,

"Come out *Wepwawet*, let me see you?" Galene said quite calmly. *Wepwawet* moved out from behind the statue, his head was bowing down to Galene in a constant rhythm, "How did you get out of the cylinder?"

Wepwawet stepped forward, "But Master, you released me, but a few minutes ago. You told me that I was to guard this room against the evil one"

"Impossible, that cannot be so. I have been here all the time. The cylinder is over on the table, with the spell book" Galene began pacing rather fast to the table as she was speaking. She lifted one side of the book, to see if the cylinder was still there. "It has gone? Isabella what on this earth is happening?"

"Galene that is one of the factors I thought that you would remember. Somewhere in the future, you yourself have *time jumped* to now to alter this day" Isabella remained calm whilst saying it.

"This is so confusing! Why can I not remember any of this?" Galene enquired.

"It is because you have not done it yet, once you release the *Wepwawet* in the future that will be the time to remember… I think!" Isabella guided Galene to view *Wepwawet* face to face, "You now have the opportunity…"

Galene screwed her face up once more in puzzlement, "… Yes of course. Why did I not think of it before? *Wepwawet*, did I say anything to you when I released you from the cylinder?"

Wepwawet knelt in front of Galene,

"Yes Master. You told me that the great battle would need my help. *All* the other rooms would eventually be destroyed. I was to protect this one, as it holds the most valuable artefacts, including that which you call *PP14432 Model*"

Galene touched the *Wepwawet* on the shoulder,

"Do not kneel before me, I do not know my former self, I see you as an equal"

Isabella stroked the *Wepwawet* head, a sudden rush of images flowed through her mind.

"Such pain, maybe when all this is over. Galene will return you to your time" Galene nodded in agreement.

The single light bulb flickered once more.

"Not more surprises?" Jeremiah cried out, dropping a now compact *Moses Staff* on the floor. A thunderous roar echoed through the cavernous room. Some books fell off the shelving. Asher was sitting upon the table edge, swinging it side to side. His hand pushed the Spell book further away with his movement. A papyrus scroll had appeared at the side of him. His hand was resting upon it.

"Galene, look here… this has just materialised" he shouted, waving the scroll in the air. The table spun rapidly in a clockwise motion, throwing Asher to the floor. His sword was catapulted into the wooden bookcase, where it pierced the book of *Vladimir Drăculea,* bound in a yellow cover. The graze on his knee stung until he touched it with his glowing finger.

As Galene began to read the scroll…

Asher retrieved his sword from the book. The *Vladimir book* had a wound which was oozing blood. Asher sliced his finger with the blade edge of his sword, upon removing it. The *Vladimir blood* ran into his open wound, before he had any chance to heal himself.

The skin bound pages, stitched themselves back together, as the blade was removed…

Galene translated the scroll to Isabella, Jeremiah and now the *Wepwawet* who was standing close by waiting to hear what was written.

"It says... *The Saviour Angel ... blah, blah... blah... Upon the final passing, the Saviour Angel will find strength in others...* Wait a minute, there is a hand written message in ink at the bottom of the scroll... *message to oneself - Galene, it will not be long now before you return to the forgotten -Tic Toc for it is nearly over.* You must instruct them all in what to do! – It's my handwriting! Everybody look here... it is my handwriting!"

Isabella removed the scroll from Galene. She read the message at the bottom of the scroll to herself to confirm what Galene had said.

"It is so, it will happen as it is written on this page"

"We must continue with the mission to retrieve the pieces of the book. It is important for us all to do so!" Jeremiah said, extending the *Moses Staff* to lean upon. Galene shrank the book. She gave the *Tic Toc Ticker* to Jeremiah to keep charge of it.

Asher ran back from the bookshelf. His eyes had darkened with red blood for a brief moment.

"*Wepwawet*, give me a jug of water with a bag of soil" Galene stated. She removed a few etched stones from her pocket, throwing them across the table. They landed on the name Βαρθολομαῖος (Bartholomew).

"Interesting to see that the stones all face downwards, none of my etchings are visible to the eye. It is a sign Isabella, look at the stones. The *Tic Toc* is changing – I mean, time is changing. Why do I keep saying that?" Isabella knew why, but she just smiled.

Wepwawet waved his hand before bringing it harshly down to the floor. At the side of Galene appeared the jug along with the soil in a hessian sack. She began scooping the soil with her hand onto the floor whilst reciting the *Clear Water Spell*. The ball of water swirled before them all.

"Everybody watch closely for any clues as to where we are going! The images will be quick and fast!" Galene said, sparks flew out from the ball. A fierce cyclone wind was created; this made Galene's strawberry blonde (*gingerly red)* hair blow backwards, as if she was flying through the air.

"I see a dock with ships, it's the sea…" Jeremiah excitedly shouted, above a torrent of noise that was created by the swirling water.

"Yes, there are some small boats taking on crates" Asher shouted.

Isabella was trying to read the dock sign that was pinned to the wall of a building. An image of a red flag painted red with a white star flashed before her eyes. *Cherbourg* became visible as the image dissolved. Galene saw a newspaper front page, which was thrust to the inner surface of the water globe. She rushed forward to read the date.

"I have got it everyone. I have got the date…1912"

The *Wiz-T* translated the page from *French*.

Sparks hit Galene making her jump backwards shouting "Ouch…. I got the place and month"

Asher moved closer to the sphere. A creature with large teeth snapped at him from within the water ball. The ball exploded, covering Asher with a tidal wave of cold, salty sea water. Both Jeremiah and Isabella laughed loudly, but also shocked.

"My *Tic Toc* is running out was the message to myself! We must hurry... Jeremiah, program the *Ticker* we need to get out of here the date is clear 1912 as we have seen!" Galene shouted, patting *Wepwawet* on the arm before inputting the month and date,

"Make me proud, and protect what is *mine!*"

....

Heinz arrived firstly from the swirling dust cloud, which had been pulled through their time jump- forward to 1943. Isobel jumped off his foot onto the broken bricks of the destroyed *Dershowitz* household. Kalef glanced around to see a different world from which he had known. The German war planes that flew above him -fascinated him so. He ducked down low into the rubble, for they scared him so. Heinz opened the closet door that was hung on the wall to reveal a brick wall behind. His palm swiped across the surface to see if he could feel any power from behind it.

"Where are we? Kalef asked Isobel, "or should I say what year are we in?"

"August 1943. You are in a Germany... hisssss! The world is at war with itself. It's a constant power struggle!" Isobel began to giggle, before biting his hand. Kalef pushed her hard into the smouldering wood of some smashed furniture.

"Silence you two, There is still no sign of Frederick. He will pay dearly for his insubordination. Kalef, can you drive a car?"

Kalef seemed puzzled by the question; he translated it to Isobel,

"I can...I can... Please let me!" Isobel excitedly screamed out. Isobel jumped up and down on the spot.

"Enough of the gibberish, Kalef just inform Isobel that she can drive the car! We need to go to the ghetto. I need to contact Lieutenant Schmidt with an update"

The car was covered in a layer of dark grey ash from the fire. Isobel hopped onto the front seat, Kalef sat at the side of her holding his bitten hand. She started the engine with the key that was left in the ignition. Heinz clambered into the back seat just in the nick of time -for Isobel had sped off at such speed towards the Warsaw Ghetto. He was thrown backwards into the seat. Within minutes she reached the guard building outside the perimeter of the Ghetto. Isobel slammed the brakes on hard. It screeched, skidded, before performing a three hundred and sixty degree turn in the road. It jolted forward to a halt. Kalef's fingers bent backwards as his palms tried to restrain himself being thrown forward through the small windscreen. Heinz was bashed side to side in the rear of the car, his body thrusting forward, hitting the leather seat as she braked.

"How did I do? I drive good... Yes?" Isobel asked.

"Debatable... very terrifyingly debatable" Kalef stated, stepping out of the car -trembling. Heinz was impressed by the speed that he had arrived at the Ghetto, but not at the Isobel's driving,

"In future... you shall walk!!" "He stated, pulling his suit jacket downwards to smarten up his appearance.

The German Soldier on the gatehouse was slouching behind a wooden desk, reading a newspaper when Isobel with Kalef knocked on the window. He pulled the glass open,

"Yeah, I am busy. What do you want?" his softly spoken, German voice remarked. He noticed the superior officer in uniform - Heinz was approaching from the car.

"Heil!" he shouted, throwing his arm in the air, frightening Isobel. She hissed at him profusely.

"At ease Soldier... I need you to send a message to Lieutenant Schmidt at the Reich office in Berlin" Heinz stated.

The tracker on his arm began to flash rapidly.

"Galene... She is active again. Kalef, Isobel -do not fail me this time. We need that book"

Heinz reached into his pocket to retrieve the crystal-*Graumus*. As he opened the lid an eye appeared, staring back at him. The guard in the small office gasped at what he saw. Isobel slipped inside the small room to deal with him. She held onto his head. Kalef glanced back into the room to see the soldier rocking back and forth upon the chair. He was sucking his thumb.

"She is visible again; we need to leave now to catch her!" Heinz stated to Graumus.

"Give me the place, date, time that she is in?" Graumus asked calmly, whilst he began to compose the transportation of all three of them to the new location.

....

Galene arrived firstly at the dock, she was holding on tight to Isabella, who in turn held onto Asher.

312

Whoosh…..the broom flew off into the sky without anyone knowing!

Asher finally pulled Jeremiah through the opening that shrunk immediately as the *Ticker* was inverted upon itself. They all landed in what appeared to be a large fishing net that had been strung up to dry. Asher was hanging upside down from the net as he foot had got caught...

"Get me out of here" Asher cried out, wriggling, to try and shake his foot free.

Isabella had already clambered down the old fishing net to the cold wet stone, harbour port. She glanced upwards at the sign that she had seen in the *clear water globe*. She now could see it clearly – *Red Star Line.*

"This is the place, I remember seeing that sign" She said, pointing upwards to the wall.

It was early evening at about 06.00pm. The sun was setting behind the large clock Tower, on one of the port's highest buildings. Further along the man-made port that protruded far out into the sea, was a large group of people boarding onto two small sailing vessels. Large boxes were being wheeled up the ramps to be stored in the hull.

Asher managed to free his foot. He slid further down the net towards the ground. Jeremiah caught him.

"Now Asher will you stop that messing about" he said, placing the *Tic Toc Ticker* inside his jacket lining. Asher just grunted. Galene signalled for all them to hide behind some large wooden crates whilst she composed her thoughts.

"Okay, here is the deal. I believe we have to get on-board one of those ships... We need to find another piece of the book. I saw in the clear water. An image of a bookmark flashed against the surface. It was no ordinary bookmark"

What do you mean not ordinary?" Jeremiah asked

"It was made of skin! There was a tattoo upon the bookmark flesh"

"How grotesque, how could anybody make such a disgusting item?" Isabella blurted outwards.

Asher perked up with excitement once he heard that this piece was macabre. Jeremiah checked his pocket to make sure the *Moses Staff* was still there. He let out a sigh of relief. "What is the tattoo of? Is it significant in any way?" Jeremiah quizzed.

"Yes, it is significant. The tattoo is of a Nonagon (nine sided shape) it has flames- sparking from each of its sides" Isabella stated.

"Did you see it too?" Galene asked.

"No, But I have seen it before when I touched the *silver man*. It was fresh in his mind"

The final passenger boarded *boat one*- the horn sounded. There was a cheer from those on the deck. Asher watched as the dock staff threw the mooring ropes from the Harbour steel.

"Excuse me… everyone… Was we supposed to be on that boat?" Asher enquired, as it raised the ropes to set sail across the sea.

"It's okay Asher, there are two boats, and we still have the other one to board if we need to!" Isabella stated, focussing on the name of the boat. "That is the small one; I think it is called *Traffic*… Yes, there is the name I can see it clearly!"

Galene lifted her dark robe off the ground, pacing rather fast towards the remaining moored boat. Asher was first to follow, he threw his hands up in the air to signal that he did not know what was happening. Isabella held onto Jeremiah's shirt sleeve as they ran to catch up. At the passenger foot ramp leading up to the boat, Galene was halted by a French crew member.

"May I see your boarding pass please?"

The *Wiz-T* translated it ever so quickly, throwing up an image on her retina stating the language – *French*.

Galene tried to walk on by him and upwards onto the ramp, he tugged her robe. She stumbled backwards,

"No boarding pass. No admittance I am afraid to say my lady!"

Isabella stopped Galene going any further. She looked at the clock tower- it showed 06:25 pm. Jeremiah had hidden behind some crates that were about to be boarded via the rear board walkway.

"Pssst, over here," he shouted to get the others attention.

Galene nudged Isabella, who in turn nudged Asher. They saw Jeremiah.

"Can we get on the boat this way then?" Galene asked.

"No, but, you could use the *invisibility spell*, so we can get past that crew member you just spoke to"

Thoughts of the nursery rhyme *Three Blind Mice* went through Asher's mind as they all stood in line holding each other. Galene began muttering the spell as they walked from behind the crates. She told Asher to lead the way up the plank. The plan was working. Isabella read the name of the boat out loud to herself not realising that everybody

315

would hear it *"Nomadic"* she said, Jeremiah hushed her so by nudging forward into her. Galene reached the French man. She kicked him in the shin, before climbing upwards. He hopped around on one leg, rubbing it before falling backwards into a large waterproof cover. The cover engulfed him. Galene laughed. Asher tripped releasing his grip on Isabella. For a moment he became visible. Isabella gripped Asher's arm to become invisible again. She hoped no one had seen him…

....

Heinz with Kalef and Isobel materialised underneath the large walkway to the boat the *"Nomadic"* they heard a voice say the boat's name,

"That's Isabella" Isobel remarked, glancing upwards through the gaps in the slotted plank walkway. Heinz peered upwards also. Fading daylight shone down through each gap.

"There Master… look the boy is visible. They are using magic to hide themselves" Kalef blurted in German. Heinz hovered out from under the walkway. Asher had disappeared again.

The harbour master blew a large pea whistle, the boat horn sounded twice in preparation to set sail.

"Quickly you two, get on board the boat now. They will have no means of escape" Heinz stated, gliding up the planking. Kalef followed along with Isobel.

The horn sounded again. The walkway boarding was lowered by a pulley system to the dock area. The thick, wet rope, which moored the boat, was released from the dock.

A thick plume of smoke billowed out from a single funnel as the engine noise grew stronger. People on-board cheered loudly as it began to manoeuvre out of port towards the open sea.

Galene had led all them below deck, into the hold; they found trunks with a vast amount of clothing contained within. It was full of uniforms, cleanly pressed. Galene pulled some out of the trunk for Asher to wear as he was shivering from the coldness of the sea air. His legs had Goosebumps. Asher pulled on a small pair of trousers over his shorts, Isabella rolled up the bottom to shorten the length. She also held the small jacket open for him to wear. "You are looking pretty dapper in your new clothing" Isabella remarked,

"Look you even work for the *Red Star Line Company*. That's the logo I saw on the wall outside," she said, rubbing her finger over the stitched in white emblem of a star, within a red flag on the top outer pocket.

Heinz, Isobel and Kalef entered. They came face to face with Galene, Jeremiah, Isabella and Asher, who all gasped in shock. Heinz hovered towards Galene,

"Stop…otherwise I… I will cast a spell on all of you!" she stammered, trying to think of what to say. Asher removed his sword from his trousers ready to fight. Isabella placed the headscarf on her head to read his mind. She wanted to know his next move. Jeremiah pulled the *Moses staff* from his pocket. He pressed the crystal to extend the pole. Through the hatch, it finally arrived… Galene's broom! It was shaking its bristles violently.

"Now Galene, don't be so foolish. I want that book of yours. The German Reich needs the book. It is the only book that we shall not burn" He inched even closer to Galene, who stepped backwards. The broom moved closer to Heinz, whooshing at him!

The *Wiz-T* translated his *German* for all four of them. *"GIVE ME THAT BOOK NOW!"* Heinz growled.

"Never in all the Tic Toc's, shall you ever have my precious book" Galene suddenly remembered Graumus, The final piece fitted neatly into place within her memory,

"And neither shall you–GRAUMUS- ever see it again- until I summon you forth upon..."

"Galene, your memory... it is returning?!" Isabella excitedly remarked.

Heinz signalled to Isobel and Kalef to come closer. They stood beside him, ready to pounce upon his request. The broom hit Heinz repeatedly over the head. Heinz grabbed the broom snapping the stale in half. From the palm of his hand, he released a fireball. The broken broom tried to fly off, but the fire hit- its bristles. It fell, burning upon the polished deck floor. Asher screamed out,

"NO... Broom save yourself!" with a flood of tears running into his mouth.

It was too late.

The *Eternity Spell* had run its full course for Galene. She had remembered why she had cast the spell upon herself, all those *Tic Toc's* ago. She began to emanate a bright, pulsating light from her entire body. The final piece, recalling the past in her memory had triggered her own spell once more. Her body tattoo moved across from her shoulders to her face as a mask. Her eyes closed for just a brief moment, before opening to reveal the *Aurora Borealis* swirling in her eyes.

"I remember all... that which cannot be fulfilled!" her ghostly voice whispered.

Heinz retrieved *Graumus, the crystal* from his pocket, he flipped the lid open. Graumus stared at Galene.

"NOOOO!" he cried, "*Not again. We are so close to my release. I need her*"

Heinz moved closer, followed by Kalef and Isabella.

"*Don't get too close.... She is about to...!*" Graumus screamed in German. Graumus teeth seemed to hit the crystal facet. The crystal was engulfed by the *Aurora Borealis* lights that emanated from Galene's eyes.

He could not stop Heinz, who hovered extremely close to capture Galene. Galene's body began to spin as it rose from the polished wooden floor. An *Aura of Crystals* comprising of many vibrant colours flew outwards from her being. Asher had to bash some of the crystals away from his body with his sword, before he dived behind a large crate for cover. He watched the final moments of the burning broom as it lay dormant upon the floor.

Jeremiah ran across the polished deck to Isabella, he fell on top of her behind the clothing trunk.

Galene's body, black tattoo detached itself from her being. It began to encase her, Heinz, Kalef and Isobel. Like a spider web they were all trapped behind the lace mesh.

She was pulled upwards, crashing through the loading hatch into the night sky. She was met by a flurry of fireworks from the launch celebrations. Galene closed her eyes.

"Good Bye - Jeremiah, Isabella and Asher" she yelled,

"I have no choice. I made this spell, I cannot break it" Galene forced her eyes tightly shut.

BOOM…

She exploded into the night sky.

She became the largest firework that lit the darkness. The crowd *wowed* at the sight. She had gone, taking Heinz, Kalef and Isobel with her.

....

Jeremiah stood to peer upwards, peering through the large hatch into the night sky,

"Oh my word Isabella, Galene is gone!"

"What are we going to do now…? I am scared!" Asher cried. He kicked the remnants of what was the broom. It was now just a charcoal upon the deck.

The *Nomadic* let off two horn blasts. Isabella joined Jeremiah, who was still staring through the broken hatch. A *Red Star line Crew* member's voice shouted down at them, from above.

The *Wiz–T* translated for them standing below, *French* language

"Everybody be ready to be amazed. We are about to go aboard the biggest ship in the world. Look to the port side to witness Red Star Line's gigantic creation. Behold the wondrous sight you see before you," he shouted through a tin megaphone. *"Red Star*

Line would like to welcome you all to the all-new, unsinkable wonder. Meet the greatest ship ever built – The TITANIC"

Epilogue

Reborn

It was early September, 1941 on the outskirts of Minsk, Belarus. A most peculiar event was about to happen in earth's history...

-And so the journey begins once again, Galene was reborn into the past, the time being 1941.

It is always 1941, only the *Superior Guardians* know why! But Galene never remembers any of it! Her spell, that she had created was an eternity of repeat, from past to future, from the future to the past. *Syeira Angelica* always waits to intervene on her return to 1941 before she sends Galene to correct more errors in earth's history. The inconsistences were created by the event *Crystarlisis Aura.* Galene is nearing the final repair, from which she can then continue forward to her final task.

-Heinz and Kalef... they had also been returned to their rightful places in time, with no recollection of the events that had unfurled.

-Isobel was left floating in a dark void, between past, present and the future... trapped!

Galene was yet again *Reborn*, but after two thousand plus years, she had finally changed earth's history in the year 1943 with the *Superior Syeira's* intervention. This time she had succeeded in altering her own timeline before being *Reborn*.

The new timeline that she had created had left *three children* stranded in a different time to what they believed was their own of 1943! These three children were exactly what *Syeira Angelica* had been waiting for, as it was clear to her the final intervention was to happen soon, very soon!

History of the past was done, but the history of the future could now at last be changed. The *Guardians* had needed many *tic toc's* to prepare for this moment.

Jeremiah held onto the *Moses staff,* with no idea of what he would use it for. Asher gripped the *King Arthur's Sword* thinking it was merely just for child's play; Whilst Isabella had the *Mona Lisa headscarf.* This gave her more knowledge than she would have liked. A Knowledge - that Galene somehow in her forgetfulness… wanted her to have for the journey, which was yet to come and beyond the *Guardians* knowledge.

Isabella also knew that the *Tic Toc Ticker* had been given to her to continue with what Galene had started. Now it was merely a case of waiting once more…

……………………………..

07:37pm

All three of them were standing looking up into the starry night, through the broken hatch on board the *Nomadic*.

"What are you three doing down there? We are about to go aboard" a crew member shouted, *"Get up here and witness this most wonderful ship"*

The *Wiz-T* translated. *French* Language…

Asher gulped.

Jeremiah hesitantly spoke to Isabella,

"But... doesn't it sink?"

Isabella began to clamber upwards onto the crates, climbing out of the broken hatch above. The crew member assisted her.

"Come on you two... you want adventure and excitement don't you? Come and see this!" Isabella chirped, "It's amazing"

"It is now 7.37pm. The Ship will soon depart for Queenstown, Ireland. We need to get you all on board. Follow me" the Crew member stated, parading excitedly off towards a walkway that would be used between the boat and ship. An exuberant crowd waited to be boarded.

Jeremiah had climbed upwards followed by Asher. All three of them stood on the deck of the *Nomadic* as it approached the brightly lit *Titanic*. Asher looked upwards to the vast wall of steel as the *boat* circled around the ship from astern.

"It's amazing Jeremiah, Look at all the lights through the porthole windows" Asher breathlessly quipped, before being knocked off his feet. He lay flat upon his back, on the cold wet, deck.

"Jeremiah... Stop messing about" he wailed.

Jeremiah was stood with Isabella,

"I never touched you" Jeremiah replied, he and Isabella spun around from viewing the *Titanic*. Suddenly, Asher was pushed back up onto his feet again from behind. He felt harsh bristles, on the back of his legs. The gold locket on a chain around his neck had fallen out from his shirt.

Isabella grabbed the locket, viewing the photo inside. Her emotion and complete shock were evident on her face.

"It cannot be!' she said "Where did you get this?" Isabella asked.

There was no reply...

"Oh my word....Its Galene's broom!" he squealed, as the broom floated beside him. "But you burned... I watched you!"

"Where on earth did you come from?" Isabella enquired of the broom. The broom shot off towards the *Titanic* at great speed. Jeremiah pointed with his finger, following the broom, which catapulted straight to the steel hull plating. Before crashing into the black painted steel, it banked upwards, towards the night sky. The sea was dragged upwards with the velocity of such a sudden turn. They all watched as the broom flipped over, before it came hurtling back towards the front bow. A lonely figure was standing, leaning over the cold white painted railing.

"Is it really?" Jeremiah was shocked.

"It surely is... I just knew that it wouldn't be over just yet boys, our adventure is just beginning" Isabella said smiling.

"I...I thought that she had exploded" Asher said, revealing two large fanged teeth that glowed in the moonlight as he opened his mouth. His eyes suddenly misted over, before filling with blood. He began to lick his lips at the sight of Isabella's neck....

Backlit by the lights upon the deck of the Titanic, leaning over the white railing, dressed in a black gown, was *Galene Angelica*.